RED LIGHT

JAYNE RYLON

RED LIGHT

Copyright © 2014 Jayne Rylon

Published by Happy Endings Publishing

Edited by Mary Moran

Cover Art by Angela Waters

Formatted by IRONHORSE Formatting

www.jaynerylon.com

Facebook.com/jaynerylon

@JayneRylon on Twitter

ISBN-13: 978-1-941785-00-3

CONTENTS

Through My Window   1

Star   27

Can't Buy Love   65

Free For All   129

THROUGH MY WINDOW

JAYNE RYLON

DUSK

Through my window, a sea of strangers swirl and retreat like waves in an ocean of humanity. I brush my hair, fix my makeup and flip on the glaring red light in my booth before turning to face them on the other side of the glass.

They begin each evening like still waters. Ebbing and flowing past my window. Unaffected by buffeting winds or brewing desires. Eddying in swirls as they gather, peek around our infamous district with downcast eyes, then scatter—awkward and unsure yet inquisitive.

Curious couples setting out on tandem adventures, young men high on the moral freedom of Amsterdam and clusters of women indulging in a wild night with friends all dip their toes in the pool.

Later, much later, they will roil and crash against the glass in a typhoon of wanton excess—of food, drink, drugs and sex—that never ceases to amaze me.

Or to infect me with its primal power.

Most women shoot me glances of pity if they look at me at all. I feel sorry for them, that they don't understand. But some…some grin and nod.

Appreciation.

Respect.

Envy.

A select few go further, seeking my services so they can

share in the rush for a brief time.

Men are more likely to notice my sincere yearning to please right away. All manner of them from young to old, rich to poor, thin to fat and virile to impotent appraise me with hungry eyes.

Cynics might say my killer curves, mile-high stilettos or long mane of platinum hair are responsible for their focused attention. I don't buy that. I'm not the most attractive working girl on the block. But I'm one of the busiest.

Customers can sense I'm different than most. They recognize I'm here not because I *have* to be but because I *want* to be. I absorb their stares before returning some of my own. The authority they grant me is intoxicating and addicting.

I love enticing a kindred spirit to my lair for both our enjoyment and my profit.

The hot, red lights of my booth, along the canal slicing through the heart of De Wallen, glint off my silver-sequined costume. What little of it there is anyway. The warm air in the space caresses my bared skin each time my neighbors let someone in or show them out.

Satisfaction guaranteed.

Theirs. And mine. Ours.

Every thrilling encounter is unique. Each partner creates a new experience as their quirks mix with mine. I can't wait to see what tonight will bring. To adore what you do and be able to make others happy in the process—while earning fists full of cash. What more could a woman ask of a career?

The worldwide economy might be in the crapper, but my business is *never* slow. Hell, bad times make for peak seasons around here. And I'm glad to do my part.

Take this man, for example. I've watched him meander through the hordes, coming closer and closer to my window on every pass. He almost manages to appear casual—comfortable in a den of hedonism—and worldly.

Until I notice the way his hands are fisted in his pockets. And the outline of his monster erection, proclaiming his desire to join our forbidden display. I could hang a flag on that thing. He's no veteran to my scene.

As quick as that, I know he'll be mine. For a little while.

DARKFALL

The potential customer scans the available women. Many would like to please him. There's something undeniably attractive about guiding a novice on their first foray into sin. Most of the girls shimmy, primp or pose to capture his attention. But I simply prop one hand on the indentation of my trim waist then wait for him to make the smart selection.

No one else will sate his craving for a novel jaunt into a taboo practice as I will.

When our eyes meet, the blaze of magnetism is clear. His pupils dilate. The man glances both left and right, then left again, before sidling closer to my window. Hesitance in these situations always strikes me as adorable in its ridiculousness.

The young man lifts one finger from his pocket to signal as he approaches.

The edge of my mouth curves in a sultry smile I don't have to fake when I crack the glass for our exchange. I lean forward until my breasts press against the cool, smooth surface, anticipating how he'll begin. I wonder if he's done his research.

Maybe he took the day tour through the Prostitution Information Center. Probably asked a thousand and one questions too. Clean-shaven, button-down shirt tucked into his ironed jeans, neat wire glasses…he appears the type.

"G-good evening. How are you?" Slightly rough, his American accent beads my nipples. Definitely his first time.

"I'm great, hon." I toss in a wink and he chuckles, loosening up a little. "What can I do for you?"

"How much for a standard suck and fuck?"

Ah, he knows the lingo. A good sign.

"Do you need fifteen minutes or thirty?" I'm hoping he'll take the scenic route. Not for the money but because I'd like to make the night he loses his prostitution cherry more memorable.

"Uh… How about thirty. And I'd like to touch your breasts, with you totally nude. Two positions."

I grin. He *has* done his homework. Such a good boy.

"First time special, a hundred Euros."

"That obvious, huh?"

I smile gently. "Only to a professional. I'll take good care of you, I promise."

He nods once then passes me a crisp note through the sliver of space between the frame and my glass panel. I tuck the bill into my drop box, which is bolted to the floor, enter the transaction in my ledger then invite him through my window.

The man trips over the raised threshold but catches himself against me in the narrow opening. I would mark the hazard, since so many others do the same, but it's an easy icebreaker.

Because now he's touching me. I glance down to where he's cupping my shoulders and I smile. His hands are soft, his grip is gentle. Nice. An easy start to the evening.

"Excuse me."

"No need. Let me close up and we can get to it." I reach around his trim waist, stroking him with the side of my arm as I pull the window closed. The lock engages with a click, securing us inside. I nod in triumph at Mari, in the window on the other side of the canal, when she blows me a little kiss for my win. Then I slide the thick drape across the glass, blocking the view from the teeming masses outside.

I catch my client checking around, probably wondering what happens next.

"All the booths in this building have stairs leading to bedrooms upstairs." I approach him then slide my palm from his shoulder to his slightly sweaty hand. Our fingers link as I rub against him, gliding past him in the tight enclosure. "Follow me."

"How embarrassing." He grimaces when I smile over my shoulder.

"That you're a virgin John? Everyone is once." I explore the ridges of his knuckles with my fingertips. His hand trembles beneath mine in anticipation that I feel fortunate to share. His excitement is contagious, making my thighs damp as they slide across each other. "You're doing great."

"Thanks." He laughs, the chuckle sounding a bit surprised. "You're really sweet."

"I'm whatever you need me to be."

I begin to climb the steep rise. Old wooden planks creak beneath my feet. How many others have made this journey to satisfy an age-old yearning? I am part of history, connected to my predecessors by a shared understanding of what it's like to pay for comfort. For pleasure. For relief.

Now this man is too.

Like a psychologist or a chiropractor or a teacher, I'm pleased that my profession allows me to care for my fellow humans. And pumped that it is so exciting simultaneously.

My client groans when my ass is presented mere inches from his face. The stairs do wonders for my form as I sway from side to side as we ascend. Women of all shapes, sizes, ages and nationalities offer services in the district. There's something for everyone. I work hard to keep myself as I like best. Fit but not skinny, there's plenty to fill a man's eager hands.

I take pride in the firm swells on display. His appreciation thrills me.

At the top of the stairs, we enter a tiny room filled nearly wall-to-wall with a plush mattress. Soft lighting from a single incandescent lamp adds to the intimate ambiance. The bare bulb is obscured by a beaded lampshade Mari gave me for my birthday last year. A great inside joke. A cliché come to life. Sometimes it's best to give the tourists what they expect.

"Would you like to undress?" I turn my back to retrieve a condom from the tiny dresser along one wall. I want him to consider without pressure. In my experience, getting nude makes a man more vulnerable, but this guy doesn't seem like a clothes-on kind of lover.

"Yes, thanks." He shuffles from foot to foot.

"Let me help." I reach straight for his fly, leaving him to strip his shirt from surprisingly powerful shoulders. The clock *is* running. My nails tuck into the loop of his belt, freeing his pants from his waist before I slide them to his ankles.

He heels his shoes off then steps from the abandoned fabric. His socks stay on, but I don't pressure him in case he needs some kind of security blanket. Instead, I turn my attention to the gray briefs askew on his hips, distorted by his bold erection, which the soft cotton fabric can barely contain.

I maneuver the cloth over his cock, loving—as always—the moment the proof of a man's longing pops into view. A normal, everyday guy surrendering to his primal side gets me every time. I place my palms flat on his toned abdomen then slide them lower to cup his balls, initiating him to my touch.

"God yes." His gaze is locked on my progress, waiting for me to continue.

An overwhelming purpose consumes me, driving me to delight this man and myself in the process. I remove the condom from its wrapper and roll it over his full length. Not the biggest tool I've ever seen but far from the smallest. He'll get the job done, which is more than I can say for a portion of my customers.

I plant my knees on the pad I'm sure he didn't notice in the artificial twilight of our nest then guide his shaft to my lips. I relish the first contact of my tongue on his latex-coated cock. Some girls hate the taste of rubber. It's not my favorite, but I've come to associate it with the pure adrenaline of my intense—never casual—sexual encounters.

I concentrate on teasing the head of his cock before guiding the entire shaft deep into my mouth. He's long enough to reach my throat and I relax to allow him entry. My pussy dampens when he moans his appreciation. I take him to the base on several consecutive strokes, but his ragged shout and the sudden contraction of his balls alert me. He's straying too near the brink of orgasm.

It's only been two minutes, we can't have that.

Lesser prostitutes would allow him to spurt as soon as possible. The fee is the same, no matter what he chooses to do with his time. But I want it to be good for him. As good as it can be.

That's the only way it's good for me too.

So I wrap my fingers around the base of his erection and squeeze deep on the pressure point guaranteed to return his control. I've learned many tricks from my customers and other window dwellers over the past several years.

"Thanks." He pants as he settles his hand on my shoulders, recovering a tiny bit. He shakes his head ruefully then flexes his hips, urging me to suck him again. "I'm all right now. Sorry."

I paint my lips with the tip of his penis so he can see my genuine smile. "Never apologize to a woman because she drives you wild. It's a fantastic compliment."

The lines flanking his eyes as he considers my advice disappear, replaced by desire when I welcome him back to the warm, wet depths of my mouth. I suck him hard but steady, just below his threshold for ultimate pleasure. When his thighs begin to shake beneath my caresses, I know it's time to move on.

Besides, I'm eager to feel him inside me. The unpracticed fuck will be ambrosial—raw and a little clumsy. I don't come with each customer, but I'm sure this man will bring me gratification. Sharing his journey fires my blood.

I pull my lips from him with a slurp for effect then nudge him toward the bed. "Lie down. Get comfortable."

He complies while I whip my top off and strip out of my fringed thong. I kick away my platform heels then crawl beside his supine form. Splayed on his back, he folds his hands behind his head, as though to keep himself from touching me.

"What positions did you have in mind?" I remember how specific he was at the window.

"Woman on top." His answer is raspy, but his inhibitions are melting faster than an ice cream cone in the dead of summer. Being ultra-horny will do that to a person. Especially when I amplify his lust by cupping my breasts, molding them together in a decadent show. "A-and missionary."

"Nice combination." Sexy and sweet. Just like him.

I straddle his hips, prepared to swallow his cock with my swollen pussy. Thank God he's smart enough to let me drive first. I can blow both our minds like this before turning it over to him for the homestretch. By then he'll be mindless with need, able to hump like a dog in heat. And I'll love every second of the untamed ride.

But when I cant my hips, reaching between us to align his erection with my saturated opening, he balks.

"Wait!"

"You're not ready?" I tilt my head to study him. Painful arousal etches grooves around his mouth. It almost makes me rethink my no-kissing-on-the-lips rule.

"It's not that."

"Then what?"

"What's your name?"

"You can call me Star."

"How can I have sex with a woman if I don't know her real name?"

"It's not my name you're fucking."

His frown disturbs me so I snuggle closer then whisper into his neck. "It's not you, honey, I don't tell anyone."

"Well, at least you should know mine, Star." He grinned up at me then confessed, "I'm Jonah."

I notch the tip of his erection in the opening of my cunt then sink onto him as I say, "Nice to meet you, Jonah."

His heels drum on the slightly saggy mattress as I engulf him in my heat, working my internal muscles to massage his cock.

"Ah!" He grunts, shuddering beneath me as I begin to move, delivering what I've promised. When his fingers dig into the sheets at his side, I cover the tense digits with my hands.

"You asked permission to touch me." My mentoring penetrates his haze of ecstasy. "Go ahead, play with my breasts."

"They're beautiful," he sighs. "So huge."

"Thank you." I ride him with steady, escalating rocks of my hips. I take him to the root then lift off until the bare tip is all that remains locked inside me. I fuck him with several short strokes that tantalize his sensitive head before beginning the circuit again. When he still stares, lying limp and spellbound, I lift his hands to my chest then massage myself through his flesh.

Have the women he's been with before never showed him how to please them? This is not a matter of a man paying to be serviced so he can be selfish. Poor Jonah has no idea he's lacking.

The least I can do to help is give him some pointers. When he returns home, wherever that might be, maybe he'll keep the next girl he fucks. He seems nice enough and steady. Now he needs some carnal skills to enhance his respectable nature.

"Pinch my nipples, Jonah." I keep my rhythm steady as he gawks at me.

"B-but…" I don't blame him, I know I'm making it hard for him to speak. "Won't that hurt?"

"No, not when I'm excited." I moan when he tests my theory. Passion sizzles from my chest to my pussy. Damn, that feels good. "Every woman is different. Ask them what they like if you're not sure. Anything is better than nothing."

He averts his face and I feel his cock soften a bit inside me. I reach behind my ass to cup his balls then drop onto his shaft and grind. The motion rubs my clit in tiny circles on his pelvis, tightening my sheath around him. We both groan at the improvement.

When his gaze meets mine once more, I smile. "Nothing to get upset about. You're learning. You're improving. You're going to be great."

His nostrils flare as he absorbs my reassurance. He even begins to fuck me from the bottom, his hips arcing upward to drive deeper inside my dripping cunt.

"That's my boy." I smile as I dip forward, letting him nuzzle my breasts. A quick study, he sucks my nipple into his mouth and draws on the crinkled tip, using my escalating moans as feedback.

He surprises me—and fills me with pride—when he flips me to my back and begins to pound inside my pussy. He picks up where I left off, alternating deep thrusts with teasing dips into the mouth of my clenching channel. The variation keeps my arousal fresh and makes the full glide of his cock have more impact when he bottoms out in my contracting tissue.

"Yes, Jonah. That's right." I coo as he gets a little out of control. His stride hitches when he nears the limit of his restraint. I don't expect much for his first time out as new, improved Jonah. He'll get better with age and practice.

Knowing time is short, I reach between us. I want to share his rapture. My fingers spread around his pummeling cock then trace my slit to the engorged bundle of nerves at the top. I flutter one fingertip over my clit, loving the way Jonah's fucking presses it closer to my body with every slap of his hips.

He impresses me again when he notices, despite his mindless pursuit of ecstasy. He supports himself on his left arm then drops his right hand to mine, learning my secrets through tandem exploration. His fervent openness is too much for me to handle.

I wrap my thighs around his back and push us both over the edge with practiced undulations.

My pussy spasms around him, tempting him to bliss with wave after wave of contractions he has no hope of refusing.

"Ahhhhh—" His climactic roar is more of a moan but the sound renews my orgasm, extending both of our pleasure.

When the moment has passed, I separate our bodies with a wet sigh then remove the used condom from Jonah's limp dick. He certainly enjoyed himself. The reservoir is completely full of his thick, white cum. The aftershocks of my climax inspire a shiver that runs down my spine.

Delicious.

Beside me, my student recovers, his chest heaving. When he finally catches his breath, he cracks open his eyelids with a wince.

"Do you mind lying here? Talking?"

"You have seven minutes left, we can spend them however you like." With him I don't mind sharing pillow talk.

"I've never caused a girl to have an orgasm before. Plus, I get so worried about not making things good for her that I can't always...finish." He refuses to meet my gaze when I prop my head on my hand, observing the red stain of embarrassment climb up his neck to his cheeks. "That's one of the reasons I came here tonight. To see if there was something wrong with me. I'm so...relieved."

"You'll make a great lover, Jonah." I pat his chest, soothing his discomfort. "Once you learn to let go. Don't be afraid to ask the woman you're with what she wants. I can tell you're eager to please. That goes a long way. Trust me. And remember how you were at the end. You had it right. You're going to make some lady very happy."

"Can I ask you something...personal?"

The irony of that question strikes us both at the same time and we break into a fit of giggles, crashing on our sides, facing each other in the mountain of perfumed pillows I've supplied.

"Sorry. Dumb question. So…how big does a guy's…"

"Cock?"

"Yeah. How big does it have to be for you to really enjoy sex?"

"You've got more than enough to be effective. Or didn't you notice?"

I adore the self-satisfied smile spreading across his handsome face. I realize now, his good looks deceived me. He's younger than I first estimated. Early twenties—younger than me. Though not by that much in years, he's decades behind in experience.

"It felt amazing when you came around me. Your pussy clenched so tight, I thought you'd squeeze me in half. I couldn't stop coming and coming. I'm surprised I didn't have a heart attack on the spot."

I laugh, thrilled to see him like this—carefree, light and relaxed. I love knowing I had a hand in helping him find this new place. "I'm glad you enjoyed yourself."

"Thank you." He's so serious as he nods. "For everything."

"You're welcome."

"Well, I guess I better go. My friends think I've gone out to buy postcards to send home."

"You don't really think they believe that, do you?" I shake my head as we both dress.

"Would you look at me and assume I'm the kind of guy to buy a fuck with a stranger and enjoy it?"

He heads down the stairs, but I catch him at the bottom of the steep run, laying my hand on his shoulder before he can escape on that note.

"I did. The moment I laid eyes on you I knew you'd be a terrific client. I saw a hell of a lot more than your bland exterior. If they don't notice what's inside, then forget them. I hope you don't hide for anyone. Never again." Usually I keep my opinions to myself, but Jonah brought something different out in me too.

Each customer builds their own relationship.

Every encounter is unique.

With Jonah, I feel comfortable sharing this. More, I feel as if

I would do him a disservice not to. "You seem like a terrific guy. Be yourself and stop worrying about everyone else. The rest will fall into place."

"This might turn out to be the most important thirty minutes of my life. I'll never forget what you've done." He kisses my knuckles before spinning away, drawing the curtain aside and marching through the window.

The frame closes with a snick. I lay my hand on the glass and stare as Jonah strides, confident and determined, into the night.

When I lose sight of him in the crowd, now more rowdy and scantily clad, I sink to my stool and smile.

I have the best job in the world.

MIDNIGHT

Three standard blowjobs and one whipping session—him, not me—later, I'm still thinking about my more meaningful interaction. I wish I could watch Jonah with his next woman. I'm sure he'd impress me.

A staccato rap startles me from my reverie.

"I'm on break." A familiar face grins in at me through my window. "Just have time for a fuck. No nonsense. Fifteen minutes."

I open the window. Rick, a frequent customer, hops inside and passes me a fifty. No stumbling over the step for him. He locks the door and draws the curtain himself. I hear the *shwwp* of his zipper while my back is turned. By the time I finish putting away his cash, his cock is out, framed in his black uniform pants.

"A hot show tonight?" I cover his impressive hard-on with brisk efficiency so different than the deliberate care I took with Jonah earlier. The other girls despise me for being Rick's favorite. They try to lure him away with healthy competition. And though he goes for variety on occasion, he always comes back to me.

Jealous stares will lance me when I opened the curtain after he leaves.

Nothing new there.

"Yeah, I should get a fucking allowance. Being a bouncer at a live sex show ends up costing me more than I make some nights."

I chuckle. "But it's cheaper than paying to see the show on your own before you head to the district. You know you would anyway, you perv."

"Yeah, yeah." Rick grins as he spins me around then bends me over the stool I use to sit on when my feet get tired of my shoes at the end of the evening. He yanks the thin strip of cloth covering my pussy to the side. "You're probably right."

I watch over my shoulder as he strangles his cock with a meaty fist then slams inside me with one thrust. Fuck that feels good. Full. Possessed.

He starts fucking me hard, fast and deep. From zero to sixty in no time at all.

"Shit, your pussy is soaked tonight, Star." He growls as he pummels me, tipping the stool forward with each thrust. He's right. Loud slurps and wet slaps accompany his fucking as my pussy overflows. "You must have had a lively one before me."

"A newbie." I moan when Rick grinds deeper. Damn, he's huge. His cock connects with a particularly sensitive spot inside me when he forces himself to the max. There's no controlling him, no topping from the bottom. And I adore surrendering to his desires.

"Oh, you do love to corrupt them don't you, baby?"

"Mmm."

"I bet he didn't drill you like this though, did he?"

"Hell no." I know Rick well enough that I don't worry when he wraps his fingers with my hair. With a reputation for protecting the women at his job, and those he frequents in the district, he'd never really hurt me. In fact, the mild sting in my scalp starts to turn me on again.

Too bad he won't last that long.

On break or not, he's never needed more than the basic. I probably won't have time to come again. Oh well, I can always take care of myself before the next customer...or wait and unleash my passion with a lucky guest.

But damn, his driving lunges feel good. They sway my breasts beneath me, brushing my nipples over the fabric of the seat.

"Fuck me, Rick. Give it to me hard." He loves it when I talk dirty because he knows I mean it, unlike some. A grunt accompanies each of his drives inside me. His balls slap my clit on each pass. Damn, maybe it won't take long for me either. "Give me your cock please."

"Yeah, Star." Air bellows in and out of his lungs in giant pants as he works harder and harder to fuck me. My pussy clutches him tighter, forcing him to slam into my willing body. "You're so dirty, baby. Getting off on my Euro. I love it."

He groans then clutches my hips for leverage.

Better hurry. He won't maintain this pace for long. Too bad because it feels divine. I arch my back, angling my hips to maximize the impact of his scrotum on my clit. He plunges into me hard enough that my ass jiggles between each reentry.

When he begins to grunt behind me, the earthy sound pushes me over the edge. I scream as I shatter around his impaling cock. My passion drags Rick under. He fucks me with short, animalistic jabs as he fills his condom with jet after jet of hot semen.

He withdraws as soon as he's finished, stripping the latex from his purple flesh and tying it off with one practiced motion. I stand up quick, my orgasm still lingering. The rush of blood to my brain has me reaching out to steady myself with one palm on the red brocade wallpaper.

"Hey, you okay?" Rick tucks himself back into his uniform then plops onto the stairs. He drags me to his lap, holding me against his still-heaving chest for a moment. His concern touches me. "I didn't hurt you, did I?"

"Nah, stood up too fast. You know I like it rough with you." That's the truth.

"Thank God 'cause you destroyed me. But what does that mean, you like it with me?" He scrunches his eyebrows, studying my flushed face with an intensity and nearness that makes me a little uncomfortable despite all we've done together. "You're like a sexual chameleon, you know that? Taking on patterns to blend with whatever you're near. But...unlike the other ladies I spend time with, you really enjoy it."

"I didn't know you were a poet," I smile. The relationship between me and my clients can be many things, he's right about that. But this is one of my favorites. Relaxed friendship, no-strings erotic interludes with someone I've come to trust over a series of meetings.

"Me either but there's something about you, Star." He grins. "Maybe someday you'll tell me your *real* name, huh?"

"Not even after a fuck like that." I pat his cheek as I get to my feet, rearranging my costume to cover my pussy. "Besides, you're going to be late if you don't hurry."

"Shit, you're right." He kisses my shoulder on the way out. "See you soon."

I wave through the window as he backs away with a smile.

Tonight is going to be a good night.

EARLY MORNING

I've long ago made enough to cover the rent on my window and the nightly take required to maintain my standard of living. Some girls work nonstop to guarantee their future. I stay each night until morning because I want more.

Not a bigger house.

Not a cushy retirement fund.

Not jewelry, or a car, or fancy clothes.

Though I've ended up with those things for myself, I want more of this feeling.

The crowds have begun to thin a little, only the hardcore and the determined left out and about. So I'm surprised to catch sight of the older couple, conservatively dressed, who make their way—hand in hand—toward my window.

About twenty feet out, the somewhat overweight man turns to his partner and asks her something. I can't hear from this distance but I see her nod. He strokes her hair from her face then kisses her with enough love to generate a shockwave of affection that reaches my post.

They turn toward me once more, the woman smiling when she catches me witnessing their exchange. She's a lucky lady and she knows it. Still, they continue toward my window and shock me again by nodding discretely.

I open the glass and wait to hear what they'll request.

"Do you enjoy being with other women?" The gentleman

makes a polite inquiry. Nothing crude here.

"I do service them, yes." I nod.

"But do you enjoy it?" He stands firm on his inquiry.

"Yes, depending on the woman." I shift my gaze from him to the lady beside him. "I would like to entertain you and your…"

"My wife." He can't help the involuntary smile the proclamation brings, even after what I would guess is some time spent in marriage. They're a perfect couple.

"I'd be honored to join you in seeking pleasure together." I open the door before we've negotiated specifics or rates, something I seldom do, but standing in the open with them violates my sense of intimacy. Another rare occurrence.

I close the curtain then perch on the stairs since the space in the booth is limited for two, never mind three.

"How can I help you?" I study the pair as they take stock of their surroundings. For some, coming inside is like Alice falling down the rabbit hole. Through my window is another world. I get the feeling they've done this before, but never quite like this.

"I—I'm having trouble performing lately." The man glares at the floor, but his wife doesn't allow him to feel shame. She rubs his back then wraps her arms around his waist. He grips her wrists, squeezes then takes a deep breath. "I'd like you to make love to my wife. Using a strap-on. I want to watch."

I look between them and nod. Not a request I'd take on for just anyone. I consider situations like these on a case-by-case basis. I never want to fulfill a man's fantasy at the expense of his wife. Or entangle myself in a highly emotional situation if I can't justify the end result to myself.

"Are you attracted to me?" I ask his wife.

"I thought you were gorgeous in the window, but after speaking with you, I'm sure." She nods then sighs, rubbing her breasts against her husband as though she can't help herself. "It's been so long. I'd love for you to fuck me. Make me come. We agreed another man will never be inside me. It doesn't feel right. But with you it does. Please help us?"

"I recommend an hour session so we're not rushed." I turn to the husband in time to see his relief and joy mingle.

"Will two hundred Euro cover the cost?" He pulls the bills from his wallet.

I would take this job for free, though most prostitutes would wring an exorbitant price knowing how badly they want the experience.

"Yes, that will do fine. Please put the cash in the drop box." There's no room for me to maneuver between them.

The man hands his wife the bills then adds a third at the last instant. A lovely gesture.

"Follow me." I head up the stairs, stripping my costume as we ascend. By the time we reach the top, I'm naked. I pause to collect supplies—a few condoms, some lubrication and the strap-on I keep in the top drawer—before climbing onto the bed to make room for my guests.

The husband's glance flicks to my bared breasts as I lounge on the bed.

"She's beautiful, isn't she?" His wife grins at the sheepish look on his face. "It's okay to look."

"Undress your wife," I suggest from my vantage point.

He does as instructed. I love watching them function as a team. She raises her arms for him to lift her shirt. She turns so he can unhook her bra. They operate without discussion. No instructions are necessary between them.

When she turns back, they kiss. A quick, perfunctory peck before he moves on to her skirt. He slides the fabric down her hips, revealing her nude beneath. No panties cover her pussy and no hair decorates her mound.

"Nice." I recline against the wall and spread my legs. I don't realize I've moved one hand to massage my breasts and the other to tease my swollen pussy until they turn their attention to me. "Join me."

I hold out my hand to steady the wife as she settles onto the mattress. Her position must grant her husband a world-class view of her ass and glistening core. I hear him whisper, "Jesus."

His wife and I share a mischievous grin and a chuckle. She knows the power of taunting a man before granting him what he wants most. How would it feel to be incapable of bestowing ultimate pleasure on my customers?

Suddenly it is her I empathize with, not him. He has lost something to be sure, but she has lost more. I welcome her into my embrace, enjoying the way our bodies fit together, softness to softness. She looks into my eyes and sees my empathy, recognizes our bond.

Before I realize what's happened I've broken one of my cardinal rules. Her mouth descends, covering mine with supple lips that massage and tease rather than plunder. I reach out my tongue to lick the taste of mint from her lips. I lose myself in the exchange, pressing her to her back on the bed while I settle between her now-spread thighs.

Our breasts press against each other. Our hard nipples dent the soft flesh of each other's form. A ragged groan breaks into our serenity. We turn to look at the agonized face of her husband.

"It's always been a fantasy of mine." He grimaces. "How ironic that when it finally happens, I can't enjoy it."

His wife stiffens beneath me, some of her enjoyment lost.

"Being unable orgasm, or get totally hard, doesn't mean you can't enjoy this." His wife nods at my words. She squeezes my hand, encouraging me to continue. "Why don't you take off your clothes? Lie down next to us. Relax. Kiss your wife. Hold her. Share the moment. Just because you can't experience sex as you've always known it doesn't mean these things are no longer pleasurable. Yes?"

"Yes." The single word cracks as he utters it. Moisture lends his eyes a touching sheen in the indirect light of my loft.

"If something more happens, then fine. Don't put so much pressure on yourself. Enjoy what's there and see what happens, okay?"

It must be okay because he begins to remove his shoes. His socks, shirt and pants follow. He's not the most attractive man I've ever laid eyes on, but something about him makes him far sexier than the body he was born with. His wife agrees. She shifts below me, stroking our skin across each other, ready for the next stage of our adventure.

I can smell the musk of her arousal and it turns me on.

The bed shifts as her husband joins us, gathering her close to his solid trunk. She turns her face from me to greet him with a searing kiss. One hand lands on his haired chest, seeking connection with the man she loves. Watching their interaction up close is one of the most arousing things I can remember seeing.

I adjust my position so our legs interlock. My thigh presses her steaming center, drawing a moan from deep in her throat. At the same time, I straddle her wider leg and begin to move, grinding on her in a pattern guaranteed to stoke the embers in her core.

Only, I can't pleasure her without doing the same to myself.

Their kiss breaks when she gasps, writhing beneath me now.

"She needs more," her husband knows as well as I do when it's time to move on. I bet he was a phenomenal lover in his prime. I want him to be part of this. Want him to give his wife as much as he can. Otherwise, he will never obtain satisfaction.

"Help me get ready?" His pupils dilate and he growls. A sound that thrills me. He reaches across his wife's torso, pausing to caress her breasts, and collects the harness I'd set out. His curiosity drives him to inspect the device.

Attached to the leather strapping, a dildo faces outward. A shorter, curved, insertable plug rides high on the interior, intended to pleasure the woman wearing the contraption. I rise onto my knees so he can fit the tip of my end to the opening of my pussy.

He works the blunt instrument into my channel bit by bit, making my head fall back as I welcome the thick intrusion as deep as it will go. His wife moans then shifts beneath me, urging us to hurry. He buckles the flat, black leather around my waist, tightening the straps until the bullet vibrator embedded in the center tucks against my clit.

A heavy rubber cock juts from between my legs. The weight of the appendage tugs on the segment buried inside me. I want to fuck as never before, but I hand a condom and the lube to the husband first.

He groans as he rips open the package with his teeth as though he's done it a million times before. The rubber is rolled down the artificial length of my cock within seconds. I wait for him to drizzle lubrication on the shaft, but he dips his fingers between my hips and his wife's instead.

He brings the glistening digits to his mouth and cleans her arousal from them. "She doesn't need this."

The tube is dropped to the floor, forgotten.

The man grabs hold of the strap-on more roughly than I

would have. Guys have a way of knowing their limits when it comes to the hard flesh between their legs. Even I am not as bold as a fully aroused man when he touches his own cock.

He guides me to his wife, fitting the broad, plum-shaped head to her saturated folds. The resistance of her clenched muscles drives the portion of the device inside me deeper, making me shudder and moan.

I can't help but push again and again until I work the strap-on inside her even as I grind myself on the solid intrusion. Soon we are both moaning and wriggling together. Her husband alternates seductive kisses at her mouth with love bites on her neck and breasts.

When I am lodged as far as I can be in her pussy, our slick tissue is separated only by the thin panel of leather our toys are riveted to and the metal sphere it also holds. Oh God. The vibrator! This experience has me so carried away I almost forgot.

I grab the remote from my pile of supplies and hand it to the husband. He grins when he sees what I've given him. The ability to control our ecstasy now lies in his grasp.

I begin to fuck with steady strokes—slower, deeper and more gently than any man has made love to me. The motion highlights every nerve ending, caresses every pleasure point and arouses with every decadent glide. Focused on assuring our pleasure, I lose track of the husband.

Moans and sighs fill the air. I can't say if they're mine or the wife's or both. Just when I think I have to move faster or kill us both with unfulfilled longing, her stare flies to mine. I cry out with the intense rapture assaulting my clit. But as quick as it appeared, it vanishes.

My mouth hangs open as I turn to face the husband. He now reclines with a grin worthy of the Cheshire cat, his hand idly stroking his half-hard cock. With no pressure to perform, it seems he's able to regain some ground. His wife's hand has meandered up his thigh. Her fingertips manipulate his shriveled scrotum, making his balls roll between her fingers.

I'll have to remember that trick.

It sure as hell seems to drive her husband wild.

When he catches us staring, he blasts us with pulses from the vibrator. The riot of sensation washes over me, shocking me back into action. I buck my hips, glad to see his wife doing the same. We fuck each other, grinding into the vibrator between us when we need more stimulation or away if it becomes too much.

Between us, the balance is perfect.

With the control in hand, her devious husband keeps us suspended on the brink of orgasm for longer than I can keep track. Time slips away in a haze of pleasure, surpassing anything I have known tonight. Maybe ever.

We continue our dance, one of us leading while the other follows before our roles reverse again until—finally—the wife cries for mercy beneath me.

"Please, please." She cries, her body shaking. "Make me come. Fuck me harder."

Her gaze leaves mine, focusing only on her husband. "Make us come."

The buzz between us reaches a fevered pitch and neither one of us can resist his control. The soft flesh beneath me, cradling me, convulses. It jiggles and cushions my tense muscles. My hardened nipples leave an impression in her warmth and my pussy smothers the object within it as I explode.

The husband places a hand on my back, rubbing soothing circles when I begin to come down from the peak. He kisses his wife as he drinks in her fulfillment.

I lay shivering and spent, completely wrecked, over the beautiful, limp woman beneath me. Together we snuggle, getting comfortable as we turn our attention to the man who made our experience possible.

I'm surprised when he kneels over us, tall and confident, a full erection in his grip.

I start to get to my knees, already reaching for the last condom behind me, but it's too late.

He bellows as his orgasm slams into him. His wife and I watch as cum arcs from the slit in head of his penis. She sighs when he paints her breasts with the pearly liquid. Line after line splatter across the mounds of her chest, decorating her in a decent imitation of a Jackson Pollock painting.

His orgasm is impressive, unleashing months—if not years—of unsatisfied lust. And when it is complete, his wife reaches for his hip then draws him near. She laps the last drop dangling from his shrinking organ and savors the taste. The moment.

I feel like a trespasser violating their intimate success. I avert my eyes and stir, but the wife redoubles the embrace of her arms around my shoulders. Her husband joins us in a pile of boneless limbs, soft words and lingering caresses that outlast our prescribed hour.

When we finally rise, gather our clothes and head downstairs, I'm exhausted.

The husband kisses my cheek then exits the tight space, waiting for his wife on the cobblestone street outside.

"Thank you for saying what I couldn't find words for. I think that made all the difference." The wife leans forward to kiss me—soft, slow and sincere—before parting with a smile. "I'll always remember you."

"Same here. Good luck."

I am many things—whore, lover, teacher, psychologist, nurse—but, above all, a woman like any other. Watching the couple depart, their bond strengthened, cemented, does my heart good. Knowing that I had a tiny part in their happiness warms my soul as much as it clenched my pussy.

Sharing their joy is a benefit of my position I could never quantify or adequately explain to someone who has never experienced it before.

I smile to myself as I realize they never asked my name. And that, had they wondered, I would have told them.

To them, I am not important. Not me specifically.

The anonymity makes the encounter perfect and my night complete.

DAYBREAK

Through my window, the dawn is approaching.

I don't see the trampled fliers advertising women who fuck dogs on stage, the empty drug baggies or the condom wrappers littering the streets—flotsam and jetsam of another stormy night in Amsterdam—as I lock my window behind me. I choose to watch the halo building over the row houses and the elegant swans gliding along the canal in the reflection on the pane instead.

I stretch my tired muscles as I turn toward home, prepared to crawl into bed—alone—and dream of the next time I'll be so connected to the heartbeat of life.

I smile at the promise of another night to come, another series of adventures.

From the outside, looking in, I know there are more lessons to be learned about myself and the world surrounding me.

Though my window is my destiny.

STAR
JAYNE RYLON

OVERTURE

Through my window, snow is falling. Unique flakes dazzle me as they swarm and crash then disperse, earthbound, in the glow from my red light. Gorgeous and yet a pain in the ass—like so many things in life.

Let me count the ways.

Customers stay indoors to avoid the chill or romp through the rare weather, making for slow nights in Amsterdam's infamous district. Unless you factor in the men who seek alternative methods to keep toasty and stranded passengers from Schipol taking advantage their airline delays.

Slut shoes plus treacherous icy cobblestones equal a terrifying combination. I'm not the sort of woman who wears rubbers to work—at least not the kind that protect my investment in my Louboutins—only to slip on sumptuous six-inch stilettos at the last instant. My pride rebels. The mystique generated by my stacked heels is part of who I am.

Which is why I cringe when Rick, a frequent customer, fills me in on the news.

"Damn it, Star." He pants as his orgasm weakens him. My liquefied bones leave me unable to protest as he withdraws his softening cock from my pussy and crashes to the mattress in my booth's loft. The hint of frustration in his tone has me squinting.

"You're not satisfied?" A complaint would be a first for me. Not that whores have the equivalent to a corporate comment box system, but my popularity and the abundance of my repeat clients reassure me of my skill.

I sit up, crossing my legs, lifting his head to rest on my thigh as I play with his hair. Dozens of shared sessions with him have taught me I don't have to hesitate to explore in the aftermath of our pleasure. I figure he craves the interaction. After all, he purchased a full hour tonight when he never requires more than a quarter of that to reach satisfaction in my body, usually dragging me along with him.

Something about his honest craving for *me*—not just an easy lay—affects me. The chemistry between us makes serving him a pleasure. Sure, he hires other girls in the district from time to time. Then again, I sometimes try a new ice cream flavor before indulging in Rocky Road for my standard Saturday night treat.

"No. I mean, yes. I'm satisfied. More than."

I massage Rick's scalp until he rewards me with his content relaxation. Before I can gloat to myself, he shakes his head, caressing me with his thick mane. When he tilts his face to meet my curious stare, his nostrils flare in response to the scent of the arousal he's inspired.

He laughs. "I can't think straight when I'm near you. What I meant is, I didn't come here for this."

"You didn't?" What else would he seek from me? I'm providing his essentials.

Rapture.

Friendship.

Intimacy without responsibility.

"Not tonight." He levers upright, granting me the opportunity to admire his toned torso as he rests his shoulders on the wall beside me.

A far cry from baby's-butt smooth or steroid-strong. A natural ideal. Nice.

"Star, I have a proposition." He links our fingers as though he misses our contact as much as I do.

"I thought I already resolved your proposition."

He rolls his eyes, soliciting a giggle. A reaction not every customer can inspire.

"Not a request for myself. For Chloe." He sighs as he rubs the five o'clock shadow darkening his jaw, his scruffiness multiplying his handsomeness.

I cup my breast with my free hand, remembering how his whiskers applied the precise amount of roughness I prefer to my skin. So different than the touch of a woman. "Chloe? The principal at Triple X?"

Rick works as a bouncer for a live sex show near my window. When he nods, I wince. I hate to disappoint.

"Sorry, Rick. I'm not attracted to her. If you hire me so you can watch me with another woman, or arrange a threesome, I could suggest—"

"Holy shit. Stop. Right there." He gulps in breaths until he resembles my goldfish Goldy. "Or I'll need another fuck before I can finish our business."

"It could be fun to ride you and chat at the same time." Why do I hunger to please him—and myself in the process—again so soon? The night is young. There will be plenty of other customers to share with. "Now, oral sex and conversation, that's trickier. But I *am* a professional, you know. I could probably handle it."

"Maybe you should put some clothes on." Rick grumbles then tugs my satin sheet over his better-than-average form.

Disappointment suffuses me. It's quickly replaced with concern. I usually have no trouble becoming exactly what my customer needs, whatever they may desire. He's certainly never turned away from me before.

What am I missing?

"Am I annoying you?" I can't quite catch my balance tonight.

"No, Star." He gathers me to his side, the damn fabric separating us even as the barrier heats with our joint radiance. Somehow the temperature seems to spike when we're near. "You could never do that. I'm trying to tell you Chloe had an accident."

"Oh shit. Is she all right? Are you?" I raise my head to weigh his reaction. His compassion for his charges is legendary— something I've always admired.

"I'm fine. She will be too, but she fractured her hip. Damn boots with gargantuan heels were not made for these conditions." He grunted. "She was running late, as usual. Rushing."

"Wearing her thigh-highs? Red leather? Buckles up the

sides?"

He nods.

"They were designed to make her legs look ten miles long. And they do." Chloe may not have my heart racing. Her boots...they're another matter. The sleek material oozes sexuality no human can ignore.

Mmm. I rub my pussy against Rick's sheathed hip.

He grips my waist, refraining from acting on the arousal stiffening his cock once more. I force my fingers to stay where they've landed on his taut abdomen instead of drifting lower to stroke the bulge tenting the silky material.

At least for the moment.

Rick's powers of concentration degrade at an alarming rate. I'd love to indulge in another round of mattress gymnastics, except he's incited my curiosity. I sense he wouldn't appreciate my intervention, so I nudge him back on track.

After all, I'm here to serve. Whatever he needs.

"Wasn't Chloe the lead in the Kinkmas pageant?" Dozens of fliers for the adult spectacular have decorated windows, littered the ground and been passed from tourist to tourist in the past month.

Hell, if I didn't have to work, I might have checked it out myself. Christmas Eve—all holidays for that matter—are popular nights for average Joes to slake their loneliness. Like a waiter at a fancy restaurant hosting company parties or a harried department store clerk, I capitalize on the season.

No rest for the wicked.

"Yeah. Not possible now. She can't even spread her legs, never mind take all they had scripted."

"Who's her understudy?"

"This isn't Broadway, Star!" Rick tousles my hair as he cracks up, goading me to smack his impressive biceps. "Sorry, sweetheart. Just picturing the playbill for Kinkmas. Priceless. Maybe I should suggest it to Tommy as a souvenir."

Triple X's owner has earned a reputation for ruthless pursuit of profit, though never at the expense of his performers. I settle against Rick once more, enjoying the warmth he lends me. "He won't go for it. Too many of the performers are incognito. No pictures. No proof."

"You're right. Still, the Kinkmas pageant is why I came to you tonight." He draws a breath deep enough to raise me several inches as I ride his inflating chest. "Tommy's looking for someone to step in. Tomorrow night. Someone who can live up to all the hype he's set in motion. Someone breathtaking."

I can't help myself. I peer into his glittering blue eyes. I think I discern respect, tenderness and admiration swirling in them. Maybe I'm imagining it.

"And you thought of *me*?" In a city full of prostitutes and women willing to use their assets to the fullest advantage, it wouldn't take five minutes for Tommy to assemble a line a mile long—brimming with women who'd claw each other's eyes out—to audition for a gig with that kind of exposure. That kind of incentive.

"Yeah."

I'd be lying if I said the opportunity didn't intrigue me. Not for the glory. Not for the money, but for the chance to experiment. "I've never fucked onstage before."

"Only you would make the perfect Star of Kinkmas. Will you come with me? Talk to him?"

Well, shit, how can I say no when something in my gut is doing flip-flops at the compliment. "Yes. But on one condition…"

"What's that?" He cups my cheek in his hand as he smiles. I think he might grant me all sorts of favors to earn my compliance.

"Let me thank you right."

ACT ONE

Tommy's huge grin reveals a bleached-white grill too perfect to be anything but artificial. His straight, even chompers cause me to imagine the mogul eating me alive when Rick leads me into his boss's office with one hand on the small of my back. I justify the protective gesture by reminding myself it's his job. Triple X can't afford to lose another performer.

If that's what I'm to become tonight.

I'm still in shock. I snuffed my red light with plenty of hours remaining before sunrise. One first in a night full of firsts. Most notable so far, Rick departing my window with a boner he refused to permit me to attend to. He'd declined my service, saying it made him uncomfortable. Though he'd paid for the full hour, he didn't want a gratitude fuck—didn't want to imply he'd had an ulterior motive for his gesture.

Damn him and his bizarre, misguided sense of honor! Doesn't he realize our abstinence punishes us both?

"Star!" Tommy steeples his fingers as he leans over his obsidian and chrome desk. I ignore him staring at my breasts while I take a seat in the modern chair Rick presents for me. "I didn't think our boy had it in him to convince you."

"Clearly you underestimate him." I begin to wonder if I've made a mistake by coming here. "You should give him a raise."

"Ah, you'd like that, wouldn't you? He'd visit you twice a night then."

Glare from the glass tabletops, the one-way mirror opening to the stage below and even Tommy's over-gelled ebony hair offend my eyes, which are much more accustomed to the soft glow of my loft. I peer at the framed stills of gluttonous debauchery, which have occurred under the blinding lights below, and wince.

This is a mass-market sex production. I'm a craftsman who delights in personal touches. I miss the ultimate control I have over the universe through my window.

"In that case, yes, I would. Pleasing Rick pleases me. Do you object?"

"Not at all, honey." Tommy chuckles. "In fact, I assumed an enterprising young lady of your caliber to be too far above the illusion of glamour I manufacture. Most of my girls will never know the success you've achieved. They dress up in naughty lingerie. Sensuality is part of your soul. No gimmicks needed."

"High praise from someone who's never visited my window."

Do I imagine Rick's sigh of relief?

I think not. Interesting.

He's never been the jealous type before. A half-dozen of his friends at least have stopped by—informing me he supplied glowing recommendations for my services—becoming somewhat-regular customers themselves.

"A benefit of being the boss." Tommy smiles, not unkindly. "Women flock to me, not the other way around. But Rick is hard to impress, and there aren't any who hold his attention as you do."

To each his own. I've seen enough in my career to destroy any judgmental tendencies I might have once possessed. If the casting couch works for Tommy and his girls—or guys—so be it.

"So, what exactly is it you're looking for?" I hate playing games. Honest passion excites me, not the pretense of desire. So far, Triple X seems propped on a foundation of smoke and mirrors. The thrill of a novel chance may not be enough to lure me into their domain.

"The Star of Kinkmas." Tommy laughs, not one to take himself too serious. "Ironic and somehow fitting, don't you think?"

"I suppose." I check in with Rick, who smiles, patting my thigh before withdrawing almost sheepishly—opposite entirely from the man who usually rides me hard, fast and without apology. How odd, neither of us understand the rules outside our standard playing field.

"The show is slated to run with a handful of escalating acts." Tommy ticks them off on his fingers. "Santa spanking a naughty girl. A couple sixty-nining under the mistletoe. Some straight fucking after a party scene. A woman who gives her husband anal sex for Christmas. And a little people orgy. You know, it's all about the elves."

I can't help but laugh at the absurdity.

"The highlight of the season is always the Christmas tree lighting and the star on top," he continues with a self-satisfied smirk.

"I'll have to take your word for it." I try not to wince when Rick's clenched fingers on my knee make me realize I've revealed too much. I resort to humor to cover my gaff. It's almost as effective a distraction as sex. "I would have thought nothing could top the elf orgy."

"Electrophilia can." I pretend I see giant, gold Euro signs flash in Tommy's eyes, like Uncle Scrooge before he meets up with the infamous Christmas ghosts. "It's a fetish we don't showcase very often. Mostly because there aren't many performers willing to demonstrate."

The shallow breaths sawing from Rick's lungs beneath the force of his genuine arousal motivate me a thousand times more than Tommy's greed. Rick groans as he hijacks Tommy's explanation. "For the grand finale, Jeremy planned to turn Chloe into the tree, decorating her then lighting her up."

I can't deny the shiver racing up my spine stems from excitement since the temperature in the theater is set high with the nude actors in mind. Damn. A fetish I enjoy but rarely indulge in calls my name. Sure, I administer electric play on occasion. Yet I've only received the jolt of pleasure it can deliver once, at the hands of the man who trained me in the use of my apparatus.

Anton had been interested in selling equipment. This man, Jeremy, would take things far beyond a clinical demonstration. I tap my manicured nails on the arm of the chair.

Jeremy… No, I can't place him. Don't think I know him at all.

"So what do you say? You up to it, Star?"

"Honestly, Tommy, I'm not sure." I close my eyes for a second. "I'm not used to this presentation. With me, everything is real. Lust isn't scripted. Dictating how I might feel or what I might do before I'm in the moment leaves me a little cold. I'm not the kind of woman to play up the fake moans to please the crowd."

"Exactly why they'll love you, honey." Tommy seemed to grow more excited by the second. "People come here to watch. To sit in the shadows and pretend they're peeking in on someone's private life. The best acts are the ones that aren't a show at all. They're a gift. The performers share their genuine experiences with the rest of the crowd, who'd kill to be so lucky."

I nod as the secret to his success is revealed. "Still…"

"You'll love working with Jeremy. He's new here, but he held positions as a Dom for ten years in London's best clubs. He's skilled. Been driving Chloe wild for weeks as they trained."

Instead of reassuring me, the news solidifies my objections.

"I don't do electro-play with clients I've just met. I can't say I feel different about one of your studs, no matter how adept. I appreciate your time. Unfortunately, I don't think I'm the right woman for the job. I'll spread the word. I'm sure one of the other ladies will jump at the chance. Thank you."

I aim my gratitude at Rick, who nods, accepting my decision gracefully.

"Wait!"

I jerk my head toward Tommy, his emphatic plea sharp enough to alarm me.

"What if I find another dude? One you trust? Pick whoever you like. You're made for this, Star."

"I'm sorry, Tommy."

"Look, I didn't build the best show in the district without an eye for talent. Just this once. Trust me. You wouldn't have stepped through your window tonight if the idea didn't interest you. Are you going to walk away from the fantasy that easy?"

"Tommy." Rick enfolds my elbow in a steady hold, supporting me as I rise to leave. "That's enough. Let me walk her back then we'll figure something out."

"You!" Tommy jumps to his feet, his thumbs and forefingers aimed at Rick like twin pistols.

"What?" Rick stops short, my arm still in his firm yet gentle grasp. "What about me?"

"The two of you have fucked a million times."

"Not quite a million."

I arch an eyebrow. The corner of my mouth kicks up at Rick's hesitation. As if people in the district don't talk.

"If you don't trust me or Jeremy, trust him. Trust Rick." Tommy scratches his jaw. "He's been in all the practice sessions. Watched the training. Yeah, yeah, this'll work."

No wonder Rick has visited me frequently in the past couple of weeks, his lust overwhelming and more insistent than usual.

"*What* will work?" Rick swings his gaze from me to his boss. I would laugh at the disbelief etched in his strong brow but I fear I might offend him.

Tommy beams when I nod from behind Rick's shoulder.

"Merry Christmas, kid. This one's on me. Hell, I'll even pay you double what I paid Jeremy. Suit up. You're going onstage with Star."

"I'm a fucking bodyguard. Not a performer!"

"You're a horny bastard, and I love you for it." Tommy slaps Rick on the shoulder as he rounds his desk, ushering us both along the hall toward the dressing rooms. "Star's a hooker. I'm desperate. We're all being flexible."

Rick faces me with his mouth hanging open. "You'd let me do this?"

"I won't *let* you."

The sparkle in his blue eyes dims.

"I'll ask you." Familiar arousal dampens my thighs for the first time since I entered Triple X. I can't restrain myself from laying my palms on Rick's chest as I look up and ask, "Would you share this with me? I'd like to give it a try."

"Jesus." He adjusts his polo shirt, which hugs his toned upper body. The discreet shift can't obscure his solid erection. "I guess. It's weird though, I never pictured myself up there. Talk about stage fright."

"A definite job hazard." Tommy winks before chuckling. "I can't have a limp dick for the big event tomorrow night. How about an audition? An *undressed* rehearsal in ten minutes. Take Giovanna and Anthony's slot tonight. If you two can pull it off— if the crowd approves—you're hired."

"You want us to do the whole act? Right now?" Rick's innocence somehow comforts me, reassuring me I've made the right decision.

"Nah. Save the good shit." Tommy's smile spreads. "Go on, have a good time—a straight fuck. However you like. Tomorrow afternoon I'll have Jeremy work with you on the advanced stuff."

"My rate is thirty percent of the admission take both nights." I prop my hand on my hip, refusing to budge.

"Show me you're worth it and I'll include the bar profits."

We shake on the deal. Tommy strolls to the theater entrance, whistling *Let it Snow*.

"You realize I'd do this for free, right?" Rick speaks directly to me now.

"I would have too." I reach up to kiss his cheek with a loud smack. "But it looks like you'll be treating your family and friends to fantastic Christmas presents."

"I know, right?" He squeezes me in a giant hug. *Mmm.* "Jeremy has the highest rate of all the dudes in the show."

"And I'm cutting you in on my share." As in porn, women command prices tenfold higher than the men who perform in live sex shows.

"What?" He gawks at me as if I'm crazy. "No. No way. You're out the money you would have raked in tonight and tomorrow. Hell, I practically had to make an appointment to see you before."

I'd apologized to the huddle of men leaning against the canal railing when I left them hanging, referring them to Mari—whose window faces mine. Their disappointment guaranteed future sales.

"Through my window, I'm the boss." I shuffle him toward the dressing room. "This is your world. I'm visiting. Here, we're equals."

"Does that mean you'll finally tell me your name?" he whispers in my ear as he holds open the door to the darkened space brimming with leather furniture and lush velvet curtains.

I shake my head in instinctive denial as Tommy's assistants drag us to opposite corners of the prep area. Their urgent instructions lead me to believe there's not much time until we have to go on. Better that way, I think. No time to balk—for me or Rick.

They strip off our clothes, breaking my line of sight. I hear a familiar grunt soon after. The fluffer must be performing her duties, priming Rick's cock with her hand or mouth. Now it's my turn to battle the twinge of jealousy surprising the hell out of me.

Well, I'd hoped for something new. Something different.

"The last two acts were warm-ups, giving the early crowd some time to down a couple of drinks and unwind. They're primed. Horny. Waiting for a big finish. That means you two fuck until Rick comes. Tommy's trying to close the set. The guests should leave, satisfied they got their money's worth, and make room for the second wave of customers piling up outside." The friendly attendant coaches me as she fixes my makeup. "There's lube stashed in the pillowcase all the way on the bottom of the pile."

"Not necessary." We laugh as I fidget, restless, attempting to ease the ache building between my thighs at the thought of so many eyes witnessing me bring Rick fulfillment.

"No kidding." She sighs as she finishes applying a thick layer of lip gloss to my blossoming smile. "I've tried for almost a year to tempt him into fucking me. No dice. Rick is the only guy who works for Tommy who doesn't sample the merchandise. Figures, the hottest one of the bunch has to have *morals*. I told Delilah I'm fluffing tomorrow night. No way is she lucky enough to touch him twice. That bitch."

I'm thankful for the twilight of the backstage area, which obscures my smirk. If she knew how many times her crush had sought me out in the middle of the night, I'm sure she wouldn't have done such a kick-ass job on my styling.

"It's time." A man I swear I've serviced once or twice before appears at my side. Another bouncer, I assume. He leads me around cables, props and stagehands—who manage the lights and soundtrack—to the far side of the platform where a circular bed waits. He gestures for me to climb on, so I comply. "I'd tell you to break a leg but it seems like poor taste. You're going to destroy them out there."

"Thanks." I hear the retreat of his footsteps. "Where's Rick?"

"He'll be out soon. He needs another minute. Tommy doesn't like to lose momentum. Kick the act off solo. If our boy's watching from the sideline, he'll be ready in a flash. I know I would be."

Up to the challenge, I debate how best to tempt Rick to join me in the limelight. I recall our sessions, the uninhibited passion we've shared. I'm determined to goad him into hurrying.

"Do what comes natural, Star."

I position myself on the bed with my legs curled beneath me, my hands propped backward on the fuzzy sheet to thrust my breasts forward. I refuse to hide or shy away. The bed lurches a little then slides, rolling out toward the center of the stage, driven by a small motor I hear working underneath.

Fun.

A low murmur sweeps through the crowd as I am revealed inch by inch to their hungry stares. The intense spotlight singes my skin. It melts away my chill. I tip my head back and shake out my hair, basking in the glow and the heat on my bare chest. The motion shimmies my breasts, topped with hardened nipples.

Cheers and whistles float above the low music, which sets the tone for my debut with heavy, bass reverberations. I lower my lids, peeking through the haze toward the vague figures lurking in mock obscurity. The thrill of their existence—distant yet undeniable—propels one of my hands to glide from the luxurious bedding to my moisturized calf.

I stroke the smooth skin, attempting to mute the outrageous desire materializing in every pore of my being at the thought of becoming their erotic centerpiece. I only succeed in torturing myself. My fingers meander across the landscape of my figure, enjoying the familiar dips and curves along the path, past my hip and across my quivering belly.

"Lower!" someone shouts.

The crowd shushes the impatient attendee, though I am glad

to oblige. I nibble my bottom lip as my fingers flutter over my nude mound to stroke the damp slit below.

Power races through my veins. I sense every stare locked on my most minute motions and I can't stop myself from testing the boundaries. I fall onto the mountain of pillows, my arms flung wide as I savor the decadent plushness. Careful to keep my knees pressed tight together, I prop my feet flat on the mattress. My legs bend in front of me, slightly below chest height.

I tease the gathering of voyeurs by parting my thighs until a tiny sliver of my pussy is visible. When the air becomes still and quiet enough I imagine I can hear men rustling below their waistbands to cup their cocks. I snap my legs closed once more. Anticipation sizzles through the auditorium, punctuated by a smattering of grudging laughter, frustrated groans and longing sighs.

Absolute influence is addictive.

I lick my lips then insert my index finger into my mouth, dampening the tip with my saliva and traces of shiny pink gloss. I swirl the mixture around one nipple while peeking down at my chest to ensure the rosy tip glistens as I intend. Pretty.

It's effortless to surrender to instinct, though performing violates the code of conduct I'm accustomed to. Usually I take requests, enact fantasies, embody my clients' wishes and transform them into reality while divining my own enjoyment from satisfying a patron.

I move on to the other nipple, treating it to the same attentions.

When I want.

For as long as I want.

As hard as I want. Or not.

Here, now, I'm free to do as I please, secure in the knowledge my viewers feed off *my* ecstasy. Their rapture will follow mine tonight.

I kick my feet, raising them high, flashing my ass and the compressed folds of my pussy. The freedom of my display rushes to my brain. Delirious with indulgence, I giggle like a naughty child.

Lost in my own delight, the unbreakable hold of strong fingers, which easily surround my ankles, catches me off guard.

Rick! My heart races as my legs are yanked in opposite directions, my feet pinned near my shoulders, spread wide before the fascinated crowd.

Good thing I practice yoga.

A round of applause—and my earnest moans—encourages Rick to continue. From my perch on the round bed, I cant my head backward to study his form. His erect cock proclaims his lack of performance anxiety. I reach up, my hands locking behind his thick thighs, then tug.

He doesn't resist.

Rick climbs onto the bed, kneeling with one leg on either side of my head. His furred shins trap my arms to the mattress, heightening my surrender. I wouldn't have imagined relinquishing control would thrill me. It does.

My muscles liquefy in his hold, waiting for him to signal where he intends to lead us next. He sinks lower. I part my lips to admit his swollen hard-on when it brushes my lips, not all that surprised by his selection.

I mean, he *is* a man.

What shocks me is the earthy tang of his shaft and the salty fluid coating the tip like rich icing. I've never touched him without a layer of latex between us—certainly have never tasted him.

When I freeze, he caresses the inside of my knees. His pets escalate to kneading on my thighs. Still, he doesn't thrust farther into my willing mouth. Ever the gentleman, he provides time and space for me to object.

To hell with that. I lunge upward, sucking him so deep my lips bump his sac. Holding him in my throat, I wiggle my tongue along the topside of his shaft until I can lip his balls. His flavor bursts along my taste buds, more refreshing than an after-dinner mint.

Rick growls.

He strokes the rippling muscles of my throat before he gathers one of my legs close to his chest, supporting the back of my knee in the crook of his elbow. With a stern tap on my inner thigh, he communicates his orders. I'm to hold the other in a similar fashion, spreading myself for our guests.

The angle parts the lips of my pussy, leaving my nectarous

center exposed.

Vulnerable.

Ragged grunts and groans explode from the crowd on random occasion. They remind me of making popcorn. The first premature eruptions occur few and far between, warning of the impending epidemic of ecstasy.

I can't wait.

"I've never seen so many guys lose it before the fucking begins." Rick whispers his encouragement for my ears alone. "You're gorgeous. One of a kind, Star."

He walks the fingertips of his free hand across my tensed abdomen. My hips flex, using the leg in his grasp for leverage. He avoids touching my steaming core.

Two can play this game.

I allow my lips to uncurl from my teeth, exposing his veined shaft to the sharp edges of my incisors. His cock makes mini-thrusts into my mouth as he chuckles. "No biting, bad girl."

He delivers a series of light slaps to my pussy, detonating an explosion. A shockwave of pleasure zips up my spine. I moan around Rick's substantial girth. In the darkness, another patron comes, bringing their night to an early end.

"I'll give you what you need. Let me torture them first. I want them to see what I'm about to have. I'm the luckiest bastard in this room, Star." He runs his index and middle fingers through the furrow of my sex, one on each side of my pussy. I try to hump his hand. Straining to grind my clit on the apex of his digits, I can't quite place him where I like.

"Soon, love," he whispers as he splays his hand, opening me wider. The spotlight illuminates every detail of my anatomy for the crowd of onlookers. Rick rims the mouth of my pussy with the tip of one broad finger, driving me insane.

By degrees, he tests the softness of my engorged tissue—sinking in until my cunt swallows his knuckles—then withdraws completely, slower than I would have believed possible. The steady penetration awakens nerve-endings along my channel I swear I've never activated before.

His thumb strums light and quick over my clit, making my eyes roll in my skull. I shudder in his hold.

This time when I hear someone's shout of completion, it

startles me. The crowd is disappearing from my awareness as Rick consumes my field of vision. He's becoming my universe. It's a place where the pursuit of pleasure is my single objective.

I fight back, lavishing his cock and balls with generous attention until he trembles in my grasp. My smile spreads across his wrinkled flesh when he admits defeat.

"One more second and I'll shoot." Rick pants. "To hell with Tommy and his show."

I release his shaft, unwilling to forsake the chance to have him stretching me, pounding me. He's a master of raw, untamed fucking. Exactly what I crave tonight.

With a groan, he settles onto his haunches. He abandons my leg to raise my shoulders, avoiding sitting on me, which I appreciate. No sooner am I propped in front of him, he shifts again. This time, he reclines on the mountain of pillows, drawing me into his lap, my back pressed to his chest.

We're beyond flirting now. Beyond control or tact. He levers me into place with one arm while he aims his cock at my dripping pussy. He leans forward to whisper into my hair, "There are condoms in the pillowcase if you'd like me to wear one."

I squirm in his restraining hold until his bare tip prods my entrance. I can't smother the cry escaping my lungs when I settle onto his shaft, his cock drilling deep.

Sexuality whips around the room. Mine. Rick's. It oozes from the faceless men and women in the audience.

Ours.

Rick puts me on display. He supports my hips, raising and lowering me on his full erection while he slips his knees beneath mine and spreads us both. White noise generated by audience members shedding clothing fills the auditorium. My moans and whimpers layer on top.

I undulate my pelvis to stroke Rick as fully as possible. In this position, he has far more authority to set our pace. He presents me to the crowd, allowing the ambiguous people to worship my form and the desire we magnify in each other.

A light sheen of perspiration coats my skin from the fever he lights inside me. I have to have more. Something harder, faster and deeper than this showcase fuck.

"More!" I scream in frustration.

Rick obliges by tipping forward, sending me scrambling to my hands and knees. Before I recover my balance, he slams to the hilt in my pussy. He hunches over my ass, which sticks into the air, and bites my neck hard enough to leave a mark.

"Yes." I rock backward to meet his second lunge, dislodging his mouth in the process. "Again. Make me yours. Show them I belong to you alone."

I don't bother to pitch my demands low. I don't care who hears. In fact, all I can focus on—all that matters—is Rick and our joint satisfaction.

With a feral snarl, he releases my hips, exchanging them for my shoulders. When he cups them in his large palms, he rears up, taking me with him. I hang, my torso suspended in his grasp, my chest perpendicular to his, my knees planted on the mattress. He impales me with violent plows of his trim hips.

He bottoms out in my pussy time after time.

He fucks me with abandon. Rings of muscle respond, clenching him tighter on each pass. One strong thrust knocks me from his grip. I slip to the mattress, my shoulder turned.

Rick keeps fucking, driving into me from behind. We improvise. I lay on my side. He straddles my bottom thigh, which is straight along the mattress. His arms wrap around my top leg, trapping it tight to his huffing chest. My calf dangles over his shoulder.

Holy Christmas!

I don't recognize the mewling pouring from between my parted lips as he screws farther inside me the lower he drops his hips. We grind together in sinuous spiral as he continues to plunge to the extremity of my pussy. He hammers inside me, stimulating the walls of my channel as he shuttles in and out.

Over and over.

When I think we've maximized the sensual potential of the experience, the motor on the bed kicks in again. The circular mattress begins to rotate, exhibiting our coupling from all angles. My breasts jiggle as he fucks me. My pussy becomes the central attraction as we spin. Then, from the backside, his thick cock must appear to tunnel between my ass cheeks.

Curses, pants and cheers echo around us.

Rick rides me like a wild man, proving to every dude

watching he's the only one who can rule my fierce sexuality. No one has inspired the titanic pressure escalating in my belly before him. Before tonight.

I look over my shoulder, hoping to see the same confused surrender on his handsome face. The instant our gazes lock, we both quake, our epic orgasms inevitable.

We hang on for a few more synchronized thrusts, accompanied by a twist of our hips, then disintegrate together. A dull roar from the stands, which I'd completely forgotten, forms a wave of lust, ambushing me with its force.

My hand flies out to the side, finding Rick's white-knuckled fingers at my hip without hesitation. I grip him tight as I shatter, strangling his cock as I come harder than ever before in my life.

Desire, passion, ecstasy…affection?

A massive ball of swirling emotions augments the physical gift he's bestowed.

The simultaneous riot of all the muscles in my body leave me seizing. Rick yanks his cock from my still-clenching pussy and strangles the base. He roars, tendons straining in his neck as he pumps his thick, white come all over my flushed torso. Jet after jet burst from the plum head of his erection to splatter on my ribs, my breast and my lips.

The warm splash triggers another round of contractions, extending my pleasure.

Somewhere in the distance, several men grunt their shared satisfaction.

Then all is eerily quiet.

The curtain drops. Thick fabric can't dampen the rumble of cheers or the thunderous clapping that barrages it from the other side. Similar hoots and high-fives sprinkle across the crew's stations behind the stage.

Rick climbs to his feet, wavering a little as he regains his equilibrium. He extends his hand to me, a secret smile curving his lips.

I accept, allowing him tug me into his strong arms for a tender embrace. He dips his head as though to kiss me, but my reflexes kick in and I avert my face. I never kiss on the lips at work.

Well, there was one time…

Rick doesn't pressure me. He nuzzles my cheek instead.

"Third set opening in five minutes!" A stagehand resets the props and checks the supplies near our spot.

"Let's get out of here."

I nod.

Hand in hand, we dart from the stage.

We accept the lavish compliments of the staff as they clean us up. We help each other into our street clothes. Rick seems as eager as I am to escape prying eyes and figure out what the hell kind of bond just materialized between us.

He has a grip on the long metal-bar handle of the black-painted door when Tommy hollers from across the room. "You're hired! Take this contract. Read it. Sign it."

He hands me a stack of papers.

"Rick, show up early to practice with Jeremy. The two of you are going to make us all rich."

INTERMISSION

"Son of a bitch!"

"What's wrong? Are you sore? Tired? I can slow down." Rick grimaces. We stride through the alley toward the main canal, impatient and eager to minimize our exposure to the cold. "I got a little carried away in there."

"No, you were perfect." I smile and pat his cheek. "It's just that I loathe paperwork. One of the perks of being a prostitute is avoiding the mountains of bureaucracy most desk jockeys have to endure."

Rick turned a disbelieving stare on me. "You're always a surprise, Star. Candid. Direct. Honest. You're kind of my idol."

I can't look away from the admiration mingling with the remnants of lust in his sapphire eyes. Distracted, I slip on a frozen puddle. I could catch my balance on my own, but I'm not about to shove off his strong arms, which bundle me to his cozy side.

"Careful." His cinnamon-flavored breath washes over my cheek. When we reach the street, we both hesitate. Where do we go from here?

"May I walk you home?"

"Ah, that's probably not a good idea, Rick." Already I'm wondering how I'll separate this experience from our routine the next time he appears at my window. And he will. Of that, I'm certain.

Still, I don't relish the thought of my empty apartment right now either. Adrenaline lingers, rushing through my veins, distributed by my pounding heart. I could return to work. Every other customer would pale by comparison and I don't believe in providing half-assed service.

"Would you like to grab some breakfast?" The tightening in my gut must be from hunger. Right?

"Yeah. Sure. I worked up one hell of an appetite. We can sort through this contract together. How about Seven Swans?"

The cafe stays open twenty-four hours. "My favorite. I wonder if they'll have the chicken *satay* tonight."

"Mmm. That *does* sound good."

He keeps hold of my hand as we wind through the canyons created by the crooked townhouses lining the canals. I allow myself to believe my safety is his primary concern.

The smell of peanut sauce greets us when we duck through the weathered entrance to take a seat behind the massive bar constructed from timbers ripped from the galley of an old trading vessel. I imagine all the things the polished boards have seen.

I'm almost positive none of them have been odder than a hooker and a bodyguard devouring platters of gooey skewers while deciphering legalese intended to put guardrails around an extreme, for-profit sexual encounter.

I tug the sheaf to my side of the table and shelter it with my hand while I sign on the dotted line, right below Rick's autograph. It strikes me that I never knew his last name, Brouwer. I admire the way our signatures fit together before folding the document, tucking it into my purse.

"I'll take care of this." It has my real name on it. Immediately below his. Something about the juxtaposition feels intimate. Surreal.

"Star."

"Hmm?"

"What happens after the show?"

"I suppose things return to normal. I'll work my window and you'll be a bodyguard. Unless…" I try to erase my frown, though I doubt I'm entirely successful. "Do you want to be a performer now? You could talk to Tommy—"

"No!"

His emphatic denial thrills me. And shames me. How could I think less of him for aspiring to share his passion when I sell mine every day?

"I didn't mean that, Star."

"What did you mean?"

"I meant this." He stares pointedly at my beaded nipples. Yearning turns his eyes smoky.

"'This'?" I can't force anything else past the lump in my throat.

"Us. I want you more than ever—need more than what I take through your window. I don't mind seeing you like that if I have to, but I'd like to give *you* more. Do you date? Have boyfriends socially? Can I ask you out?"

I can't help it. I burst into a raucous fit of laughter.

His pinched mouth and balled fist—crumpling his napkin— cut me off.

"Shit. Sorry. I—"

"No, I understand. I should have realized I didn't have a chance with you."

"Huh? Are you nuts? It's hysterical because… Well, I can't imagine a man interested in dating a hooker unless he's looking to be her pimp or score a freebie."

"Jesus. Star, that's not at all what I had in mind." He tosses his fork onto his plate with a clatter then starts to rise as though I've destroyed his appetite. "You must think I'm a complete asshole."

"No!" Now it's my turn to shout. I panic, afraid I've caused him more damage than a bruised ego. When I lay my fingers on his forearm, the power in his bunched muscles thrills me. He allows me to guide him into his chair once more. "I think you're…gallant. Fun. Sexy. And I don't understand why you'd care to give *me* the honor of being yours when any number of women would be thrilled to have you. You can fuck me any time you like. You know where to find me. Why would you want a girlfriend who has sex with other men?"

"Do you plan to be a whore for the rest of your life?" It sounds far more harsh than his delivery indicates. He speaks softly, not a fleck of recrimination tinting his interest.

"I—I don't know." I bite my lip. The truth will surely destroy our rapport.

"Don't start lying now. I'm not judging. I'm asking."

I nod then take a deep breath. "Yes. This is what I want to do until I retire. I care about you, Rick. I enjoy sex with you. It's easy to talk to you and you always make me laugh. But—"

"Not the 'but'." He shakes his head. One corner of his mouth curves up in a sardonic grin.

"See, like that." I can't help but chuckle. "*But*… I love my job. It thrills me to share myself. I know it sounds ridiculous, but I feel like a public servant. Sure, there's lots of meaningless sex. Yet sometimes it's more. I help people. I guess what I'm saying is, I don't think I can give it up. And what man would accept me as I am? Who could love a woman who does what I do? Who would want *me* as a girlfriend?"

For one crazy second, I think he might destroy all my assumptions. His lips part and I pretend I can see arguments and denials about to fly free.

Then he sighs.

"It's a lot to ask of a man. It turns me on to imagine you with other clients. It'd be easy to deny the complications and say that's all that matters. *But* how does that work long term? Would you get married? Have a family? I can't picture it, Star."

A tiny piece of my heart breaks. "I can't either."

I've sacrificed something fantastic for something soul-deep— a calling interwoven in the fabric of my being. So I try to assuage his conscience. After all, I forced him to admit my irreparable faults. I don't blame him for making the only sane choice.

"It's not as if you could take a hooker home and introduce her to your parents during a traditional holiday dinner, right? What a disaster."

He chuckles with me at the idea, but his hand blankets my fingers, squeezing lightly. "At least we have the window."

"I'll always be glad to see you there, Rick."

"Same here, Star. Same here."

Act Two

I can hardly believe this is the same place Rick stretched our boundaries. Triple X has been transformed into a wicked winter wonderland. I stand beside my guide into this unusual territory, our fingers linked. When had that happened?

An ice-blue silk robe wraps around my nude form, more to limit distractions than to protect my vacant sense of modesty.

"Who knew Santa's Workshop could party like that?" I tilt my head to puzzle out what's what in the tangle of limbs on top of a toy workbench.

"No shit."

"Are you nervous, Rick?" His palm is sweating in my grasp.

"Terrified." He angles his body toward me until we're standing face-to-face. "I've never seen this kind of crowd. I'm positive we're violating the fire marshal's limit. Tommy told me this morning a flood of calls hit the ticket booth asking for admission at any cost after our performance last night."

The knowledge warms me. I would pay an awful lot to be there again, in his arms, exploring our raw passion.

"Don't be nervous. Ignore them. All that matters is what we share. The scene and the sparks between us."

"Nice one." He shakes off some of his gloom and laughs.

Except I hadn't intended my statement to be funny. The inadvertent pun does strike a chord though. "How did the session with Jeremy go this morning?"

"Umm. It was enlightening." He won't meet my stare. "I've watched him training Chloe for this show. Dozens of sessions. It's different when you're the one administering the electrostimulation. Or receiving it."

Holy shit.

"You let Jeremy touch you?" Why hadn't I come to observe? The thought has me panting.

"Yeah. I wasn't comfortable doing something to you unless I understood what it felt like firsthand." I swear his cheeks are turning brighter by the minute. "He drained me dry. I hope you enjoy yourself as much as I did."

"At your hands, I'm sure I will."

"Star, I know Tommy gave us a safe word, but you have other options. If you change your mind or can't go through with it, we can act it out. No one has to know. No pressure." He cups my shoulders in his capable hands. "I'll take you out of here so fast no one will figure out what happened until it's too late."

"You'd lose your job."

"There are other places to work." He rubs his thumb over my cheek. It thrills me enough I don't remind him of my stage makeup. "You're more important. I don't care what papers we signed."

"And that's why I can't wait for the orgy to finish." I lean into his caressing fingers. "I want this. With you."

"Is there anything I can do to make it better for you?"

His generosity elates me. How many guys give a shit about my pleasure?

"You know, I never permit men to tie me up. Ever. I've never played with someone I felt comfortable enough with to try."

"I promise not to hold you down in any way."

"No, Rick. I *want* you to. Please?" I suck his thumb into my mouth, hoping the frenzy of groans means we're about to go on. I can't wait much longer. "I trust you completely. Show me what you've learned."

"Star." His moan disappears beneath the commotion as no less than a dozen performers exit the stage, sweating, exhausted and dripping come.

We're bustled into position. Someone strips off my robe. As I step onto the contraption that holds my mark, I see a new fire in

Rick's gorgeous eyes. A determination and dominance I never suspected him capable of transforms his easygoing nature into something dangerous, something alluring.

I can't tear my gaze away. We stare, unblinking, until my platform rotates, turning my back to him, stealing him from my sight.

Fake snow drifts onto my upturned face from the rafters above as the curtain is raised on the Kinkmas pageant grand finale. The crowd settles into a reverent hush. A narrator bridges the gap between scenes with some clever monologue about the spirit of the season, unqualified altruism shared by lovers and the importance of non-material gifts.

The deep voice exalts the significance of the tree and the lighting of the star while making lewd comparisons I choose to ignore. All I can think of is the seductive confidence I glimpsed in Rick's eyes before this damn set tore me from him.

I can't grab him and bolt for my window because the vertical triangle separating us turns again. What appeared to be a cut-out of a pine tree to the audience is revealed as the nucleus of the act. My legs are spread wide as I stand with my shoulders pressed tight against the slightly reclined board. Each of my wrists lays a foot or so away from my hips until my body mimics the form of the tree-shaped platform.

I hold on to the loops of leather stitched to the surface to keep myself in the perfect position.

The set looks disarmingly like a common living room, something each man or woman in attendance might find welcoming them home in the early morning hours of this Christmas. It makes it easy for me to imagine I'm alone with Rick, in his home. When I detect him approaching in my peripheral vision, I wish it were true.

"What a beautiful tree I have this year." He stalks near and inspects his bounty. He pokes and prods me as he bestows a flurry of compliments the audience agrees with, if their claps and whistles are anything to gauge by.

Rick pauses his speech, deviating from the script before we've been onstage two minutes. I grin, encouraging his spontaneity.

"I believe I should begin the decoration by adding some

lights." He crosses to the edge of the stage and yanks on a dangling strand of tiny white bulbs. They unclip from their outlet with a snap, coiling onto the floor at his feet. "And perhaps some garland."

I barely contain a laugh at Rick's mischievous smirk and Tommy waving his arms in an attempt to attract his bouncer's attention. The serious arousal creating a bulge at the crotch of Rick's jeans keeps me in line. Not to mention the tinsel rope gathered in his fist, which draws my eye to his gleaming, oiled chest.

He pets me again when he nears, as though he can't help but touch me a little. I arch toward his hand without abandoning my perch or shifting my limbs from their predetermined positions. I am the tree. I trust him to metamorphose me from something ordinary into something brilliant.

Rick ties the garland to my handhold then wraps it snugly around my wrist. He loops the shimmering silver across my arms then behind the surface supporting me. The process is repeated on my other side. Soon, the tinsel forms an X before me, locking my upper body to the form.

When the soft, shiny rope runs out, I strain, testing my limits. I start with subtle wiggles that escalate to full-out yanks when I confirm I'm well and truly held. Whispers race through the shadowy seats when a moment of fear widens my eyes.

Rick is there in an instant. "Shush, Star. Let me give you what you need."

There's no hesitation in his baritone. Only sweet comfort and steely reassurance.

"Yes," I moan.

He grins, feral and full of anticipation as he retrieves the strand of lights. Soon my ankles and legs receive the same treatment as my arms and torso. Bound, captured, trussed in a flash of silver and white. The lingering heat from the extinguished bulbs singes my flesh. The bite fades before I can complain.

I whimper.

"You like that, don't you? A little sting." Rick strokes his fingers from my ankles to my waist as he verifies my bindings are comfortable yet inescapable. Exactly what I've requested.

A surge of moisture floods my pussy, dampening the aching center of my body.

"You need more?"

He knows that I do. Still, his hands hover a hairsbreadth from my chest until I tender my admission. "Yes please. Something stronger."

"Like this?" He stands to the side so our witnesses don't miss a single detail when he teases my breasts with gentle pinches, firm slaps and finally the nip of his teeth.

"Yes!" Heat races through me, centered around the contact of his consuming lips.

"Mmm." He steps back to admire his handiwork with a critical eye. "You do look lovely. I think it's time to illuminate you for our guests."

He monitors my reaction carefully. His gaze flicks to the pulse hammering along the side of my neck and the juice spreading onto the tops of my thighs from my saturated pussy.

When I don't object, he crosses with two strides to the pedestal nearby. He bunches the cheery red-and-gold tablecloth covering it in his fist then whips it to the side, revealing the digital power box beneath.

I shiver as the crowd surrenders a collective gasp.

The industrial unit looks far more powerful and imposing than the moderate Transcutaneous Electrical Nerve Stimulator I've employed for some of my specialty customers. The TENS works wonders by supplying a variety of sensations from a mild oscillation to a substantial muscle spasm used in BDSM edge play.

Grown men have fallen apart, begging me for more at the first pulse of its power. They keep groveling when I extend their orgasms, tumbling and crashing them through wave after wave of contractions in the grip of nature's greatest force.

This equipment can take things to a whole new level. I've heard of the programs available to modulate the current, mutating common electricity into an invisible hand that strokes muscles and nerves beneath the skin. Almost like an internal vibrator.

Each person reacts differently to the stimulus. How will it feel on me?

Rick senses my trepidation. It underlies the arousal causing my thighs to quiver. He selects two pad electrodes, the most basic and gentle, then stretches the leads toward me. "We'll start from the bottom and work our way up. I'll light up the Star only when you're ready."

Plus, we both know current above the waist requires advanced skill and a degree of risk unmitigated by any amount of training. Passing current through the chest cavity can turn deadly—quick. E-stimming above the shoulders is strictly forbidden. I don't think for one second he would put me in danger. I trust they've arranged some alternate method of sustaining the illusion.

To be frank, I don't give a damn. All I care about is Rick, our pleasure and indulging in sinful delights. I'm willing to share that with the hoard of customers who are not fortunate enough to be me—the object of Rick's desire.

As though he can read my mind, he smiles before kneeling at my feet. He kisses each of my ankles with brushes of his full lips. I squirm in the efficient restraints he improvised. From his pocket, he removes a tube of electoconductive gel and slathers it on the rubber housing of the electrodes.

He adheres one to the skin on the inside of each of my ankles. A new trick to me. I can't imagine they'd do a lot of good in this position. Refusing to question, I relax, allowing myself to float in the wake of his superior control. He'll take me where he wants me to go.

With him, I know I'll enjoy following.

Rick stands from his crouch, adjusting the lay of his cramped hard-on.

"May I see you?" I whisper as he passes in front of me to take his place at the controls.

"Not yet, Star. You're too much temptation."

"Fuck her!" A man hollers from the audience, reminding me of their presence.

"In due time." Rick's sensual promise reverberates in the wide-open space.

"I need you." My plea triggers several moans yet meets with firm denial from the only man who matters.

"My way. Let me give you this." He stands strong, not

afflicted by my sudden weakness. I would argue more. He terminates my ability by flipping the switch on the power box. All thoughts flee my mind.

A pleasant tingling begins in my toes, curling and uncurling them involuntarily. I can't say I feel the effects directly in my pussy, but all my internal muscles clench at the idea of what's to come. Rick returns to me, kissing, licking and stroking my breasts as I acclimate to the subtle vibrations awakening my nerves.

"These are monopolar pads." He informs me along with the spectators between slurps on my distended nipples. "Electricity is arcing through your body, the current whisking from one diode to the other. Up your legs. Straight through your pussy."

"I don't feel anything there." At least I don't think I do. The clenching of my empty channel has everything to do with impatience.

"Then why are your hips twitching in time to the pulse I've selected?"

I focus on the motion, awed to see it matches the flashing red light on the power box. E-stim taps into the most fundamental systems of my body, making me feel as if everything I experience is caused by subconscious, internal stimuli. The result is natural. Awesome.

"For that matter…" He spreads the soaked lips of my pussy. "Look at how you clasp and throb to the rhythm. Your clit is swollen. Beautiful."

Grunts and soft curses drift from the artificial dusk beyond the stage as my center is exposed for the customers' approval.

Rick beams at me then pets my flank. "You're doing great. I can show you more. Take you farther."

I nod. "Just get there quick."

He laughs. "Bad girls find coal in their stockings, not endless orgasms. My way, Star."

"Bastard." I groan when he flicks a setting on the generator. The subtle buzz turns into a flutter, making my pussy dance to the rhythm of his will.

He leaves me suspended for several minutes as he permits the crowd to admire his handiwork and the devastating effect it has on me. When he returns, more diodes overflow his large palm.

"I'm going to fill you with this, Star." He holds up a long silver dildo for my inspection. "There are copper wires embedded on both sides. The bipolar insert will blow your mind. On a separate channel from the pads at your ankles, I can direct the current independently. It can instigate some exceptionally unique and satisfying reflexive muscle contractions. Or so I'm told…"

Liar! The truth is plain in his eyes. He took it up the ass this afternoon. Knowing he allowed Jeremy to insert the unit and rule his pleasure poises me on the brink of orgasm.

Rick shuts off the current from the power box for both our safety. It'd be easy to create an unintentional circuit if he handled the diodes live. He plugs the latest addition into the generator then slides the blunt tip between my legs. He feeds it to me an inch at a time until the entire length of the smooth device is buried in my pussy.

I hug the invader with well-developed muscles. Mmm. It's so nice to be full.

Two wires, one black and one red, protrude from the base of the diode. A spreader bar at the top holds the lips of my pussy open and a final diode—this one a tiny cup—settles over my clit like a thimble. A set of clips on the bar allow Rick to pin the folds of my pussy open for an ideal view that won't vanish when I begin to writhe.

Two ribbons are tied to grommets on either side of the base. He uses them to fasten the device around my waist, locking it in place. The cool material on my swollen genitals incites waves of anticipation.

It takes a few minutes for the passion clouding my vision to clear. When it does, I realize Rick has unleashed his cock and stands—stroking himself—as he observes his creation.

"There you go, Star." He encourages me to meet his gaze. His dilated pupils turn his eyes stormy with longing. "Tell me you need it."

"I do." I yell as I thrash in my bonds, eager to experience energy bringing me to life for him—for all the men observing him mold me into his plaything.

He flips the switch with a flick of his wrist. I'm thankful for the restraints keeping me from dislodging the probes. They impart sumptuous floods of stimulation to all the important pathways of my pleasure system. Networks of nerves light up like a switchboard. Every cell in my body strains for the release promised by the pulsating waves arcing through my pussy.

Another button pressed engages the shield over my clit. I can see my thighs tensing and relaxing in response to the digital commands Rick issues. Whether he intended it or not, it's impossible to endure more than a few seconds of this bliss without flying apart.

"Rick." I gasp as my orgasm cartwheels through my pussy, radiating outward to every part of my body. Even my fingertips clench and release in time to the signal. He directs my pleasure, adding a short fizzle that maintains my climax. He laughs out loud as he oscillates the current, building my rapture then expanding it until I crash through pinnacle after pinnacle.

He allows me to rest a minute before triggering another round of ecstasy. I've never imagined anything so sweet. He makes me orgasm at will. Repeatedly.

"I could watch you come all night long, Star." Rick groans as another series of spasms rack my body. He licks a silver ring then holds it in front of my slitted eyes. "One last offering, love. Will you accept it?"

A bipolar diode, intended for my right breast to avoid completing a pathway across my chest cavity, too near my heart. Still a risk. A calculated one. I've come this far, I must live the full experience.

"Yes!" Another cycle of the everlasting orgasm batters my senses but I'm clear on the choice I've made. Only now do I realize the board I'm strapped to is lighting up. Hidden LEDs—unrelated to the real circuitry pumping amperage into my willing form—dazzle the crowd. The glow expands past my ankles, past my waist, to my chest.

Rick times his actions to the sparkling glow. When it reaches the same level as my breasts, he affixes the nipple diode and activates the proper channel.

I'm lost.

My entire body twitches in compulsory seizures focused to deliver unparalleled ecstasy—a whole body orgasm. If not for the restraints he provided, I'd flop around the floor like a fish out of water.

The crowd goes wild, moaning, cheering and shouting.

At the same time, the hot splash of Rick's come paints me with proof of his appreciation for my total supplication.

We're linked in a cycle of pleasure.

Me.

Rick.

Our audience.

As shouts join ours from all across the room, the balcony and even the stage behind us, the star on top of the tree-shaped backing board I'm strapped to glows bright.

Lights blossom into rainbows through the prisms of my tears. I close my eyes, one betraying droplet escaping from beneath my lids, as I wish it were real. Why can't this be Rick's living room? Why can't we share something genuine and exciting on the eve of a new era?

This experience could fundamentally alter who we are and the path we'll walk together from here forward with the elemental power of our passion.

We exchange a present beyond value.

The gift of a lifetime.

As suddenly as it began, the arc of electricity abandons me, ending my continuous climax. I hang limp and exhausted in my bonds.

"Thank you," Rick whispers an instant before the stillness explodes into applause and an impossible chant.

Encore. Encore. Encore.

We have nothing left to share. We've left it all onstage beneath the harsh beams and the scrutiny of a few hundred of Tommy's new best friends.

Stagehands rescue me, freeing me from electrodes, wires and restraints I would have worn forever if offered a choice. They sweep us to the dressing room as two of the club's regulars appear for one last quickie to appease any stranglers or those who were inspired to a second or third round of arousal by our offering.

ENCORE

I shouldn't be here, but I couldn't resist.

When Rick offered to share his home with me, to spend the rest of the night by my side, I caved to his earnest invitation. We tumbled into his bed and slept the night away, locked in each other's arms. Now, in the harsh light of midmorning, I try not to count the cost.

The price will be steep because resting here, in his sanctuary, in his arms, guarantees I'll miss him when I return to reality.

We're only delaying the inevitable.

"Star."

"Yes?" I whisper, afraid to shatter the perfect peace surrounding us.

"Remember yesterday, when you joked about Christmas dinner?"

"Uh-huh." I sigh. He pets my hair.

"I have to leave soon. Why can't you come with me?" He tucks his chin to study my reaction as I burrow deeper against his chest. "My family is open-minded. Like me. I'd like to believe they'd welcome whomever I choose to spend my time with. Share my life with."

"It's too much, Rick. You can't spring it on them like that. No warning, no notice." I shake my head. For him, I have to choose the right thing despite my selfish craving to indulge. Like an addict, it'd be too easy to treat myself to a little more then a little more until things spiraled out of control. "It's not right. I won't ruin your holiday. Or your relationship with your family. It's too precious..."

I cut off before he can ask questions I don't feel like thinking about, never mind answering.

"You're not going to change your mind, are you?"

"No. I'm so sorry."

"Then I'd like to give you your present now." He slips his finger beneath my chin and lifts my mouth to his for a lingering kiss. I so rarely indulge in this intimacy. It steals my breath. Though I suspect the glide of his tongue would have more impact than all the rest of the kisses in the world. His lips brush across mine, affectionate and gentle enough to bring tears to my eyes.

The soft exchange of affection is a worthy offering. I'm surprised when he rolls me to my back and nibbles a trail along my torso.

"Rick?"

"I want to pleasure you for once." He pauses to draw on my breasts with tender sips then meanders below the covers. "Relax, Star. I'll do the work. Let *me* take care of *you*."

He takes ages exploring every facet of my pussy with his fingers, lips and tongue. He ingests the arousal he draws from my body, a testament to his skill and the emotion ricocheting between us. After the monumental release I experienced last night, this should be impossible.

It seems so odd to lie still and allow him to work on me for a change. Yet, I relish every second. He laves the flesh between my thighs, soothing and enflaming all at once. When I whimper, he presses a single digit into my aching channel, giving me something to hold on to.

I bury my fingers in his hair, keeping him pressed close to me.

Rick swirls his tongue over my clit then encloses the swollen bundle of nerves with his lips. He caresses it with tiny sucks intermixed with the brush of his tongue until a gentle wave of relief washes over me.

He cleans the juice pouring from me with tiny laps that soothe my tired, replete pussy then rubs my belly, my thighs and my ass until I drift off into a satisfied daze, halfway to slumber.

I indulge in ten or fifteen minutes of snuggling, a glorious treat, before he climbs from the bed, heading toward the shower with a reluctant sigh. I'm a coward. I keep my eyes closed, my breathing shallow until the door shuts and the splash of water ensures his preoccupation.

If I don't escape now I won't have the strength to do what I know is necessary. I dress as quickly as my slack muscles can manage then draw a scrap paper from my purse. A flier for the Kinkmas pageant. Fitting.

I scribble my note inside then fold it in half, taking time to write his name as elegantly as possible on the outside of the red, tented paper. At the last second, impulse spurs me to enfold the cursive in a bold heart, as though I were still in junior high school.

I drop my pen into my bag not a moment too soon. The water shuts off. I slip on my heels, fluff my hair then withdraw from his house.

When I cross the sidewalk in front of his living room, I can't prevent myself from pausing to admire the lit tree in the window. Rick appears beside it, a towel slung low on his hips, my note in his hand. The disappointment etched between his drawn brows eases as he glances at the single line I jotted for him. The best present I could think of.

His sad smile expands when he raises his gaze to mine.

"Merry Christmas, *Sarah*." Rick mouths then blows me a kiss.

I hold my palm up, pressing it to the glass. He aligns his hand with mine.

We touch, through the window.

I smile and walk away.

CAN'T BUY LOVE

JAYNE RYLON

Bleeding Love

I scour the bobbing faces that comprise the current of humanity streaming past my window. None of the unfamiliar features belong to the man I crave. Rick. Where is he? He should stride by my booth in Amsterdam's red light district, or maybe hop inside for quick relief—his and mine—and end up being a few minutes late to his post as a bouncer for the live sex show debauching the other end of the block.

Should.

If he maintains his clockwork schedule. Sometime in the past three years since I'd opened my window to negotiate the first of a million not-so-standard suck and fucks with him, I'd noted his rock-solid patterns in the recess of my mind. Worse, I'd become accustomed to his routine. Until he let me down by withholding my glimpse of him.

For two weeks straight.

My cell phone's simple bell tone startles me, jarring me from my obsessive inspection. I don't have to leave my perch on my stool to reach the tiny stand holding my ledger, a lockbox, a clock and my phone. I tilt the screen toward myself, hoping the glowing readout proclaims Rick is attempting to contact me despite never having given him my unlisted number.

Oh crap. Not only is it not him, but it also seems I've been busted.

I hit the receive button, bracing myself for a typhoon of well-intended scolding.

"Perk it up over there, sister!"

I can't help it. I laugh when Mari shouts so I can hear while I bring the device to my ear. She's not psychic. She works the booth across the street from mine. I glance up to witness her blowing me a kiss. Instead of catching it, I bat it back with my middle finger.

A couple stares at me as though I'm crass simply because of my profession. Well, if the gesture fits…

"Don't you have anybody else to harass? Your regular Tuesday-at-nine customer likes it when you spank him. Save it for someone who will reward your effort."

Mari sticks her tongue out at me, catching the interest of a young man in ripped jeans who probably couldn't afford a fifteen-minute session with the high-end workers in this section of the district. Too bad, he seems cute and frisky. Exactly the type Mari prefers and attracts with her lighthearted, playful offering.

"Seriously, Star." Mari pauses her habitual swaying to meet my gaze across the canal and the river of people passing us by. "Are you all right? I've never seen you so solemn. No dancing, no flirting, no smiles for the shy guys…"

"I'm fine."

"Just lovesick."

"How the hell did this happen?" I massage the ache at the base of my neck.

"Well, you met this smoking-hot guy who doesn't seem to mind that you service other men for a living. Then somehow you left him hanging."

"Mari—"

"Sorry, Star, I'm just joking. Not the right time. I know." She's seldom serious and I can't fault her for it now. Men adore banging her silly. Perky and intelligent don't often pair up. And it's not as though she's entirely wrong. "I hate that you're hurting. It's like the time that drunk bastard hit me when I wouldn't agree to anal and you flew off the handle. I don't know what I would have done if you hadn't chased him off with your wicked heels. I just… Let me be here for you?"

"I appreciate the thought. But there's no bad guy this time.

No one to hunt and destroy."

"More like someone to hold hostage and perform all your tricks for until he sees what a mistake he's making. Look, maybe Rick's spending an extended time with his family. You said he's close to them, right? He headed home for the holidays. I'm sure…"

"I convinced myself that was the case for the first week. The holiday season is peak time around here, sex shows included. Tommy can't be down his best bouncer for that long. Rick has to be back by now."

"Do you want me to ask around? I can take a break later tonight and run over there quick. I can be stealthy."

"What part of daisy dukes and two sunflowers on fishing line covering your ginormous tits will camouflage you in the middle of winter?" I glare at her from my post. "Don't you dare. No way. I won't be *that* girl. Come on, how attractive is it when one of our clients turns clingy? Takes things too far. Rick and I fucked. Onstage. For a ton of cash. And celebrated afterward in private. It might not have meant anything more to him."

"And you?"

"It doesn't matter if he never shows up at my window again. He's allowed to change his mind."

"Shit, and he was a loyal customer too. Maybe your best."

"No kidding. I'll miss…" I can't bring myself to admit it. "The income."

"Liar."

"Bitch." I smile as I deliver the lighthearted curse. "Pay attention. The younger, blond-haired guy approaching from the north looks interested. He's done a not-so-subtle browse twice already, debating. Seems like he could be a fun one. Nice body under that soft gray fleece."

"Damn, you're right. I gotta go. I'll check in later. Maybe we can grab some breakfast?"

"Sure." If my appetite for nourishment in forms other than a hunky bouncer reappears anytime soon.

Why did Mari have to plant her wild ideas in my brain—in my heart? She couldn't have known Rick's boss Tommy had arranged to drop off my check from the Kinkmas pageant in less than a half an hour. How hard would it be to ask, casually, if

Rick had made it home yet?

Damn it, no. If my costar—my client, my friend and the only true lover I've ever had—cares for me to know where the hell he's vanished to, he'll impart the news himself. Did my decision to walk away after a night of public thrills and private sharing kill any chance we had to sustain even our casual relationship? Had he realized dating a sex worker couldn't lead to anything but disaster?

Truth is, I'm afraid to ask. I've nurtured the fuzzy tingles in my belly, hoping for another chance to stretch our boundaries or at least return to the intimate exchange of pleasure we've perfected over numerous sessions in my window.

The answer could fracture the delicate spark glowing in my core. It's too new, too brilliant for me to take the chance.

So, I stand here, wearing the platform-heeled boots that make me the perfect height for Rick to fuck while I'm standing, bent over on my loft stairs. I wait—not so patiently. I dream—of what might have been with one special partner while hundreds of others consider purchasing the goods I would freely give my absent lover. A fraction of what I'd gift him with really since our trust ensures I'd journey deeper into kinky sexuality in his arms than I would with the average patron.

Our electrifying Christmas show had proved the extremes we were willing to indulge in onstage before the admiring gazes of a thousand or so strangers. Could Rick abandon what they'd all applauded, the chemistry arcing between us as bright as the sparks he'd harnessed to thrill me? My hand slips over my ribs to cup my breast, rubbing my straining nipple.

A man crashes into the bicycle rack in front of my window.

Not the first time that's happened. Mari and I have joked about strapping a pillow to the weathered metal or covering the flaking paint with a coat of florescent orange to avoid a negligence lawsuit.

Even the unintended compliment can't inspire my smile for long. I miss the radiance of Rick's eyes, the imperfection of his twice-broken nose and the well-muscled frame he fills out so damn well. Almost as much as I mourn the loss of his open-minded acceptance, genuine attentiveness and the natural attraction that billows between us like a mushroom cloud whenever we enter the same space.

A gnawing ache twists my stomach. Hunger has built inside me since I rejected the feast Rick offered on Christmas day. Despite my ironclad belief it had been the right decision for Rick and his family, fifteen days have oozed by with the bizarre unnaturalness of ultra-slow-motion video. By running out on Christmas day, I sacrificed my chance to go back for seconds, thirds or five hundred and seventy-sixths of the passion he inspires in me, sweeter than any dessert. Like a woman on a restrictive fad diet, the longing for a taste of him—even just a quick blowjob—is driving me insane.

When did I become the sort of woman who reconsiders her outfit in case a particular male happens to catch a glimpse of it? Or one who fusses with arranging herself at the best possible angle for viewing from his usual direction of approach?

I can't pinpoint the exact moment he altered me.

Still, that doesn't stop me from scrutinizing each tall tourist with close-cut yet messy hair or wilting a tiny bit more with each near miss.

I glance at the clock beside my ledger. Quarter after nine. His shift has already begun. He's never late—too dependable for tardiness. A do-gooder bad boy, if such a thing is possible. He's not coming. Again.

My sigh buffets the soft, natural waves of my hair, which hides my eyes as I study the ancient hardwood flooring. Until a familiar triple knock rattles the glass.

Snapping to attention, I lift my face. The neon lights outside blind me for a moment as my pupils dilate. I can't mistake the distinctive rap of one of my key customers.

Oh thank you, thank you.

Despite three hundred and sixty-three hours of imagining this instant, I'm stuck drifting like a sailboat with no wind when it finally arrives.

Frozen, I stare into his usually welcoming face. Tonight it suits the blustery weather better than the radiance of my satin sheets after his skin has infused them with his heat. Enthralled by his odd grin, tinged with more than a dash of grimace, I don't notice his gesture immediately.

This time it's *his* palm pressed to *my* window. I lift my hand toward it, prepared to meet him halfway, before I realize there's a light blue piece of rectangular paper trapped between his broad fingers and the chilled glass.

Not a social call.

And not the kind of business transaction I'd have settled for, attempting to hide my disappointment over. This is why every hooker knows better than to allow attachment.

Every one but me.

I should have refused to service him the moment affection developed between us. But if I'm honest, I often rely on empathy to mold myself into the perfect partner for my guests. Wise or not, I'm connected to almost all the people who request my services whether they seek physical relief, companionship or something more complex. It's one of the reasons I command top prices in the district and have so many repeat clients.

Like the one I spot approaching behind Rick.

No, no, no. Not now! I never refuse a prospective client I have a positive history with. Reputation precedes me.

There's a handy weathered wooden bench right beside the infamous bike rack. Men have oftentimes sat and waited for an availability, occasionally meeting a fellow flesh connoisseur who they share their session with or join afterward at the bar for a beer and a fond recounting of the services they selected.

I try to focus on Rick. Still, he must notice my gaze flicker to the man settling in for the long haul. The guy on deck withdraws a fancy phone from his pocket and tinkers with the screen. Reading, checking the stock market or surfing porn, I have no idea. Not likely to bore quickly and give up in any case.

Rick angles his muscular chest to block the guy's view of the document he slips through a crack in the glass. I attempt to open the door. He pins it closed.

"Take it." His low speech is muffled by the window. Good thing I'm used to translating.

"Tommy sent you to do his bidding?" I can't help it. I wallow in my disappointment and frustration for one moment of snarkiness.

"I think he's trying to play matchmaker." Rick frowns. "Put that away before anyone notices."

I glance at the five figures handwritten on the check.

I blink.

Then I raise my wide eyes.

"I know." He laughs. A real laugh. The deep rumble I've dreamt of for two long weeks. "I think I almost crapped my pants when Tommy handed me mine."

"I told you, I'm giving you half my cut."

"I would refuse except..." He winces. "Tommy already paid me fifty percent of your take. That *is* your portion, as we defined it."

"Holy shit."

"Yeah. He says you're welcome to guest star anytime you like."

"Only with you." I would drop to my knees and beg him for an encore presentation if I thought it would persuade him. Disgust at my weakness follows quickly, spinning my carousel of emotions faster and faster until I'm dizzy and can't tell which direction to turn.

"My acting days are over, Star."

"So now it was all for show? Bullshit. The magic between us had nothing to do with pretense."

"That's not what I meant."

"Then what did you mean, Rick? Why won't you come inside?"

"Because I can't fuck you and pretend it doesn't mean anything anymore. I stayed away because I knew if I saw you, I'd have to have you," he whispers. I can hear every phrase as though he etches it onto the wreckage of my heart.

I press on the window frame. He leans against it with equal and opposite force. "I'm not asking you to hide from what's evolving between us."

"Then why did you leave my house?"

"You know why. It wasn't the right time. I had to think. So did you, Rick."

"And now I have."

"What did you decide?" A lump the size of the knot that had blocked my windpipe the first time I climbed the narrow staircase to the infamous bookcase in the Anne Frank house nearby lodges in my throat as I wait for him to enlighten me.

"Nothing. I'm not sure that what I want and what I should do are the same thing." He sinks forward, resting his forehead on the glass of my booth. "No matter how long or hard I consider the situation…us…I can't decide what's right."

"Can we talk? Figure this out together?"

"If I step over this threshold, I'll be buried inside you in two seconds flat. I won't even bother to shut the curtain. Mari and the rest of the world will watch as I show them how badly I need you." He growls. "Don't tell me it's any different for you. I swear I can smell your pussy from here."

"I've ached for you since the moment I crawled from your bed." I slip my hand between my legs, pressing on the bare, puffy lips of my cunt through my skimpy bikini bottoms.

"Excuse me."

Rick's head swivels sharply. For a man always aware of his surroundings, he'd been as oblivious as I was to the approach of my waiting guest.

"I was wondering…"

The would-be customer stalls when he catches an up-close-and-personal glimpse of the raw need raging in Rick's eyes. Impressive, I agree.

"Oh sorry. It seemed like you weren't intending to… I mean, I sort of have an appointment elsewhere later and I'll have to… I'll stop by another time, Star. Sorry to interrupt."

"Wait." Rick's command startles us both, if my client's flinch is any indication. "Go ahead. I'm finished with her."

"Rick—"

"I can come back another day, really." The gentleman pivots as though to leave.

"No. You're fine. Have a good time." It's hard to tell if Rick is speaking to me or my customer. When I would object again, he shakes his head. "Drop that in the lockbox."

I finger the parchment, reluctant to relinquish my grasp when he'd held it so recently. He keeps his hand on the window closure until I fold the check and deposit it. It'd be crazy not to cash the instrument, which could pay my rent for a year with some to spare for the battered women's shelter I volunteer at, simply to have a relic of our liaison nearby. I'm still tempted to do exactly that.

Rick walks backward, nodding. He allows my client to step in front of him then mouths, "Later, Sarah."

A weak smile curves my trembling lips as I open the glass separating me from the man Rick has left me with—instructed me to care for. The unassuming client could be just what *I* need tonight.

LOVE HAS NO PRIDE

"Good evening, Star."

"Hello, Dane. What can I do for you?"

We negotiate before I allow him to enter, as is customary. Not because I don't trust him or wish to haggle, but because I've found it enhances his excitement to engage in the ritual despite our mutual understanding of exactly what he requires.

"A half-hour session, missionary, with you fully naked. I want to suck on your tits—"

I tune out his requests, which we both know I won't deny.

"Star?" Dane, one of my more mature, less-aggressive customers, shifts from scuffed shoe to scuffed shoe, tossing uneasy glances over his shoulder. "Is…is that okay?"

"I'm sorry for your wait." I reach out and enfold his chilled hand in mine. "That's fine. Come inside so I can warm you up."

"Never a problem there." He pats my fingers as he slips through my window.

I lock the door behind him and slide the curtain across the pane, obscuring us from the world outside, blocking the teeming reality beyond my sanctuary. Inside, there's only us and the encounter we build together.

Companioned by my lingering disappointment.

"Are you sure you're all right?" Dane pauses with substantial bills folded, poised above the slot on top of my lockbox. "I can come back another time."

"It's not that." My bond with my customers allows emotion to flow between us, generally in one direction. I absorb their need, feed off it. They vent. I accept the burden.

Occasionally it goes the other way. I offer comfort, healing and no-questions-asked acceptance of their desire. Tonight, I wish I could be the one to unload. Maybe I'll do some window shopping of my own in the last hour before dawn.

Or maybe… "Would you mind—"

What am I thinking? People employ sex workers for the privilege of a strings-free relationship. Despite our friendly rapport, Dane doesn't give a shit about my issues.

"This isn't like you, Star." He brushes his thumb over the spot I bit on my lip. "Are you in trouble? Is it the man outside? Is that tall guy bothering you? I'll call the authorities. I'll vouch for you."

He's already digging in his jacket pocket for his cell.

"No!"

"You don't have to be afraid."

I still him with light pressure on his wrist. "The only thing Rick makes me fear is a broken heart."

"Your boyfriend?" He tilts his head, an adorable wrinkle appearing in his brow.

"Maybe. I'm not sure. Is that even possible? Who would date a working girl?"

"Jesus." He laughs. "I see your point. No offense, Star. Relationships are brutal. Heck, I've been married three times. Took awhile to figure out I'm not intended for that lifestyle. I'll say this, only you can determine what works for you. Don't be trapped by what society believes your affair should look like. The rules that count are the ones you both agree are important. It would take a man more secure than I could ever hope to be to know you were in here, servicing customers. If anyone can make it work, though, it will be you."

I can't help myself. I strip off his jacket. The cash he held flutters to the floor beneath the crumpled garment. He doesn't resist when I lead him upstairs to my loft, barely big enough to accommodate the moderate mattress and ancient dresser, which holds my supplies.

I reach in a drawer for a condom before facing Dane. Unlike

some of my clients, who are satisfied to yank my thong to the side and dive in, his cock is always hardest when there's skin-to-skin contact between us. Even more, he seems to enjoy undressing me himself, so I grant him the privilege.

I raise my arms so he can peel the skin-tight, sequined tank from my torso.

His cheeks flush when my breasts are revealed. The lingering chill beads my nipples, presenting the perfect treat for my guest. He glances at me and I nod. "Go ahead."

"You have great tits, Star." He buries his face between the natural mounds and inhales deep enough to draw a breeze across my cleavage. Between my extreme heels and his slighter stature, he doesn't have to lean very far.

His appreciative groan has my stomach fluttering. I'm looking forward to inviting him inside my body to seek his relief. When the time is right.

I blanket Dane's hands with mine and guide them from my ribs to my hips and lower. He pauses his lavish attention at my chest long enough to tuck his thumbs beneath the waistband of my panties and caress the soft flesh between my bellybutton and my mound.

Like almost all of my customer interactions, the touch is for his benefit, not mine. The bulge of his small-end-of-normal erection bunches the fabric of his neat slacks. Still, something about becoming what he needs turns me on beyond belief. Knowing I can grant him what he seeks is an honor I don't think I'll ever tire of earning.

I wiggle my ass to facilitate his progress as he nudges the super-stretchy satin and lace from the curviest section of my figure.

"Damn, that's sexy." He stares as I continue to gyrate in time to the soundtrack thumping in my brain. Or is that the beat of my heart? The thrill of this moment never dulls. The anticipation is new, dangerous, wicked and oh so sweet. Every time.

What would Rick do if I danced for him? In no circumstance can I picture him waiting for me to encourage him to play. He'd probably drag me to his lap and put my energy to good use.

A tiny moan slips from my lips as I cup my breasts to ease the ache in them.

"What's that for?" Dane is more observant than most of my customers. Hearing he's failed at his attempted relationships disturbs me. If someone like him can't succeed, who can? "Thinking of the tall guy in the street?"

Should I lie? Deception violates so many of my principles.

"Yes." I wince.

"Don't worry. I don't mind." Dane loosens his tie then whips it over his head. "It's kind of hot actually."

"We're both a mess, aren't we?" I return his grin as he unbuttons his plain white, starched shirt.

"I'll be better in—" He glances at his watch, which he never bothers to remove. "Twenty minutes or so."

"Me too. I hope." I don't bother to unlace my boots before crawling onto the mattress, treating him to a world-class view of my ass and nearly bald pussy before flopping onto my back. My fingers roam my torso while he strips off his basic black pants. "I keep trying to snuff this flame, but the more I try to suppress my arousal, the worse it becomes."

"I can't say I'm sorry for that." Dane winks as he joins me on the mattress. He crouches between my spread knees, allowing me to roll a condom over his cock. "Your man could be good for business. You're always a fantastic fuck, Star. Worth every cent. Tonight there's something raw layered over your sensual calm. I'm glad I came."

"Me too." I wrap my fingers easily around his girth and guide him toward his target. I admit I might have found my mind wandering to my grocery list or my outstanding chores if he'd been one of the men who settles for any worker in the district so long as she performs a proficient suck and fuck.

My focus never strays from the link pulsing between Dane and me.

This is the kind of interaction that defines my world. *This* is the reason I choose to stay open for business when I've amassed a nest egg large enough to retire and live a conservative life on. No amount of money could replace this symbiotic exchange.

I clench my muscles, making Dane work to penetrate. He grits his teeth against the initial shock of his sheathed cock entering my pussy. The blunt cap nudges inside by degrees.

A sigh puffs from between my parted lips when he's cradled

fully at the juncture of my thighs, his pudgy yet adorable stomach brushing my mound.

"You've got it bad, don't you?" He pants as he traces the trimmed patch of hair above my clit with the tip of one finger. The heart pattern brings his hand close to the top of my slit with every circuit.

I groan then arch, attempting to rub myself on his hand or his cock. Either will do.

My writhing baits him into plunging inside my drenched channel. "Damn it. Would love to tease you. Can't."

His grimace disturbs me. "This is your time, Dane. No worries."

"Guess I'd like to pretend for a minute that it matters." He pumps harder between my legs. "That you're mine. Not like a stalker. Like—"

"I understand what you mean." I slide my palm from his heaving chest to tangle my fingers in his too-long hair. I draw him down and cup the back of his head as I guide his lips to my chest. Accommodating his request is my job.

It's also my pleasure.

His tongue swirls around my puckered flesh. He nibbles as he fucks me with uneven twitches of his hips. The irregular rhythm leaves me suspended, waiting for the next contact with bated breath. Periodically he finds a sweet spot inside me, but there are more misses than hits. It's not enough to tip me over the edge.

I reach between us without disrupting his lavish partaking. He wasn't kidding when he said he wanted to suck my tits tonight. My fingers wedge between us, fluttering over the engorged knot of my clit.

He tilts his face to the side, murmuring against my breasts. "Imagine I'm him. That you're with the tall guy."

My eyes drift closed when his strokes add pressure, tapping the regular swirls of my rubbing into an unpredictable pattern. Tease!

If he were really Rick, the timid grasp on my hips would be fierce, the cock inside me longer and thicker, the rhythm of his fucking harder, stronger. And somehow twice as sweet.

"Can feel you. Tighter." He scrunches his eyes closed as he humps faster, grunting with every re-entry. "Too good."

His raspy communication turns into a rising shriek. I cradle his head against my bosom. "It's okay to surrender, Dane. I'm with you."

"Star!"

Something about hearing my name on his lips, even if it's not my real one, infuses me with pleasure. He needs me. Tonight I needed him too.

My orgasm washes through my system, light and sparkling, resetting some of my elevated drives, which transforms me into a bolder version of myself.

If that's even possible.

Dane's fingers ball into fists in the light cotton of my sheets. He shudders between my thighs, emptying his longing into the condom he wears, the latex calling shenanigans on the illusion we'd attempted to cast.

Because nothing is as satisfying as the real thing. Sex with Rick wrings me out, leaves me wasted. The thought alone reignites a flame in my belly. Small and manageable for now. Present nonetheless.

"Did that help?" Dane tucks a lock of hair behind my ear then rests on his heels, reminding me of my fish Goldy while he gulps for breath, so I can dispose of his condom.

"A little." Not nearly enough. If anything, it made me crave Rick more—the relief only he can grant.

"I know exactly what you mean." Dane shrugs with a smile that lifts one corner of his lips. I stretch then swing my legs over the edge of the mattress, gathering my thoughts and my balance as he replaces his dress clothes. They're a little wrinkled and worse for wear. Disarray is cute on him.

"What's that look for?" He cups my cheek in his palm then hands me my tiny scraps of lace and glitter. I'm dressed in two-point-six seconds flat.

"Thinking I'm glad our paths crossed. The first time, every time. Especially this time."

"Same here. So, is your guy going to try to kick my ass when I leave?" The twinkle in his eye draws another chuckle from me. "I may not be much to look at but I'm still pretty quick for an old man."

"Well, he is a bouncer."

Dane winces.

"Rick isn't that kind of guy. He relies on nasty glares to convince drunk kids on vacation they shouldn't mess with him or his charges over at Tommy's live sex show. You know, Triple X."

"Ah. I thought he seemed familiar. Wait, is he the man from the Kinkmas pageant?"

"You were there?" The idea of Dane watching Rick top me sends shivers along my spine.

He nods then groans. "Can't think about it now or I'll need a repeat and I really do have to be somewhere. Damn, the two of you were spectacular."

"Thank you."

"Well, I hope he's the kind of guy who figures out how lucky he is before it's too late."

The wistful note in his whisper makes me wonder. "If you enjoy this lifestyle, why did you get married? Three times."

"Simple. You can't buy love. Despite the fact that I'm likely to fuck it up sooner or later, I'll probably attempt it again. Fourth time's the charm, right?"

"Only if you come at it different. Maybe you should be open about your desires instead of forcing yourself into an arrangement that doesn't fit. Just like some of the other ladies who jam themselves into corsets they have to change out of after an hour or two once they realize they can't breathe."

"Or like a whore who dreams of a boyfriend who doesn't mind her profession?" We trundle down the stairs together, both gripping the railing to offset our wobbly legs.

"Yes. Like that."

"I don't think I'm as brave as you, Star." Dane draws on his coat and collects the cash we'd abandoned on the floor of my booth earlier. In the small space, he reaches my lockbox before I can step in front of him.

"No, don't."

He frowns.

"Tonight's on the house."

"That isn't how the world works. Good luck, Star." Dane drops the bills into container, half-full after a busy start to the evening. He cuddles me against his chest then brushes his lips over my temple before slipping through my window.

A puff of freezing air erodes the warmth we'd generated together, sending shivers down my spine.

Crazy Little Thing Called Love

My thoughts stray as I kneel on the pillow I keep handy for customers with straightforward requests. Some are comfortable venturing barely over the edge into my window, and others find their experience enhanced by staying downstairs, relishing the thought of the crowd within reach, on the other side of the flimsy curtain and glass while they indulge their wild cravings.

"Jordaan, move over."

"As far as I can go, Alfons."

The two punked-out ravers before me barely fit shoulder to shoulder in the confines of my booth, despite stacking my stool on top of the tiny table holding the essentials for my business. They open their euro-electronica-inspired coats, revealing tight, florescent T-shirts. One of them grunts as he takes an elbow to the ribs in their rush to unbuckle their spiked belts and unzip their slashed and chained jeans.

The familiar scent of rich Belgian beer isn't heavy enough to have forced me to decline the pair. It makes me eager to finish my shift and grab a pint with Mari over eggs. A traditional sex worker breakfast.

I hand them each a glow-in-the-dark condom that matches the fast, digitized melodies I imagine them bouncing to in a packed club then monitor their hasty precision in donning them. Experienced yet a little nervous. A potent combination.

"I'll take good care of you boys." I can't help but smile at the grateful lust that rages in their charcoal-lined eyes and deepens the color the weather has placed in their cheeks. "Who's first? Or would you rather do this together?"

"Uh…" Jordaan balks as Alfons shoots him a bewildered glance.

I slather my palms with lube while they work it out between them. The tension rolling off the pair lifts my brows. Maybe they're unwilling to admit the truth, to themselves or each other. I have no trouble recognizing latent desire when I see it.

Interesting.

"Not *together* together, but if you can do us simultaneously, then we should probably stick with that. Fifteen minutes isn't a hell of a lot of time."

"I bet you only last five, Jordie."

"Asshole. I'll hang on longer than your ten seconds."

Men never cease to amuse me. There's not a chance in hell either of them will require the full allocation they've paid for. I'm much better than that. "All right, boys. I can handle it if you can. May the best man win."

I waste no time grasping their stiff cocks.

Instead of heading straight for the hardcore pumping they might expect, I toy with them, brushing the pads of my thumbs over the long bump decorating the bottom of each of their shafts. Their respectable lengths are an even match, like most everything else about the duo.

I circle the ridge beneath their mushroomed heads. Jordaan gasps. He uses his tongue to toy with the silver hoop in his lip. The echo of Alfons' chuckle vibrates through the side of my palm when it connects with his heavily tattooed torso. "Like I said…"

I ripple my fingers at the base of his erection, morphing his tease into a gurgle.

Each man inches closer, as though trying to bury himself deeper in my grasp. The only possibility dictates they turn inward, angling toward each other to accomplish their goal. Jordaan's cock jerks in my hold when he peeks toward his friend, noting the unbridled lust on Alfons' face as I massage them identically.

I sprinkle in a few of the wiles I've mastered over the past several years until their hips meet every stroke of my hand with an urgent thrust. The jingle of metal zippers, buckles, chains and piercings acts as a lascivious metronome, setting the hurried tempo of our dance. Wild lunges edge them forward until my knuckles nearly bang together. The slippery combination of my lubed hand on latex ensures one of them will break my hold as their motion escalates.

I tip my head back to assess the situation. Jordaan has forgotten I exist, focusing on Alfons' rapturous expression as he savors the pleasure they've purchased. I can't suppress my grin as I loosen my hold a fraction on Alfons' insistent cock.

Alfons groans with a hint of desperation when he escapes my fingers and his cock deflects off my other hand, gliding his rubber-encased shaft across the tip of his friend's cock. The contours of his notable veins caress Jordaan, who shudders in my hold.

I squeeze on the base of Jordaan's cock, hard, preventing him from instant explosion, which would end the firework display about to begin in my booth. He sighs and brushes my arm with a light touch from his black-tipped fingers. I toss him a wink.

Instead of recoiling or pausing for me to re-grip, Alfons repeats the motion, impressing me with his open-minded pursuit of rapture. I start slowly—cautious, monitoring them for any sign of objection—by placing my palm on the top side of Alfons' cock, pressing it tighter to Jordaan's. The position allows Alfons to aid me in adding weight to my now shortened strokes on the head of Jordaan's cock.

"Oh fuck. Yes." Jordaan scrunches his eyes closed for an instant before forcing them open as though he can't bear to miss a single second of our encounter. I'm guessing he's dreamed of this for a while.

What other career allows you to share in people's most secret desires—help bring them to life? I love my job.

I adjust my fingers to grant Alfons greater access. His shaft slides along the full length of Jordaan's cock. It requires hardly any alteration to envelop them both in my hand, bundling their hard-ons in my half-closed grasp. They overflow my palm. I add my other hand, cupping their cocks together as they begin to fuck my joined fists.

"Christ." Alfons mutters as he strains to penetrate the tightening ring of my hands in decadent counterpoint to his friend. Their exaggerated motion ensures they fuck along the entire length of each other with every re-entry.

I allow them to wring ecstasy from the arcs of their trim hips for a couple of minutes before I notice the novelty of the position begins to dim. I monitor the arousal I've raised to a fever pitch between them. Both men alternate between staring at the juncture of our bodies and stealing glimpses of the lust evident on the other man's face. Smoky eyes, corded tendons in their necks and flushed cheeks paint an unmistakable picture.

They're ready. I can escort them a little farther into the realm of shadowed desires.

I grasp them separately, ignoring their grunts and groans of protest. I'm sure of what's best. "Trust me."

Giant breaths bellow their chests as they teeter away from the cliff they were rushing too fast toward. Suddenly, neither one seems to be in a hurry to conclude our business. They still have a solid five minutes remaining and I'm determined to make it the best three-hundred seconds of their lives.

I tilt Alfons' cock until the head is pressed to the center seam of Jordaan's sac.

"Fuck."

I'm not sure which one of them whispers the curse but I nod. "Push gently."

Jordaan rises to tip-toes as best he's able in his midnight eyelet knee-high combat boots, aligning the men more perfectly so Alfons can do a proper job of caressing his friend's tight balls with shallow, careful strokes. The motion destroys the eager brutality of their earlier fierce fucking through my hands.

It modifies the moment—re-plots the course of their relationship.

Alfons' gentle delivery of rapture makes my eyes sting. I nuzzle their thighs, light enough to avoid nudging them off balance, to ease the pressure. The subtle slide of crinkled skin over Alfons' ultrasensitive cock head must feel divine. He imparts a sensual kiss with the tip of his erection to Jordaan's genitals.

When Jordaan shivers, moaning, Alfons grins.

Oh no, I won't allow him to lord over Jordaan.

They're both even in my booth.

Alfons protests when I release the pressure keeping him in position. His cock smacks his taut belly. It stands at attention between the open flaps of designer denim as I grant Jordaan a chance to return the favor.

"Yes. God yes." He practically whimpers as he rubs himself over Alfons' balls. I count on the subtle pleasure to evolve the frenzy of delight they could have achieved minutes ago to something deeper, soul-wrenching, impossible to deny once they abandon the surreal cocoon of my window.

Jordaan's hands ball into fists at his side. Alfons grows impatient, bending his knees to increase the pressure of his friend's timid explorations. I can only do so much to impede the overwhelming passion bearing down on them both like a freight train.

I gather their cocks together once more, allowing them to fuck—in synch this time—unaided for a dozen or so powerful thrusts.

Then I go for the kill.

I lean forward and wrap my lips over the top of my fist, welcoming the protruding tips of their cocks into the moist heat of my mouth at the apex of every plunge. When I swirl my tongue over their heads, dark purple even through the thin, luminous barrier, Jordaan stumbles.

Alfons leans forward until their chests meet. They support each other like the poles of a teepee. So close they can't possibly ignore the revelation of their evening together. I wish I could watch the moist exchange of lips and tongues I can hear occurring above me, though their bodies obscure my view.

Somehow it seems fitting for their mating mouths to remain private.

Their heated kiss involves more than sex, more than an indulgence of base need. My heart cheers as I seal the deal by hollowing my cheeks and sucking them hard. They fuck my hands and mouth in unison.

They don't need to warn me. Or each other. Their cocks swell then pulse in my gasp. I pull off for a moment to study the spray of come spurting from their bodies, filling the reservoirs of their condoms. They surrender as one to the enchanted moment we created together.

I'm privileged to witness their lust pour into the rubber sheathing them. I crouch—grateful for my heels, which facilitate the position—and continue to manipulate them with gentle strokes, bringing them down safely from an impossible high.

I could be invisible.

They continue to make out. Alfons sucks Jordaan's sassy silver hoop into his mouth and nips the man's lip. Supportive arms loop around one another's backs.

I strip the used condoms from their softening flesh and clean them with a microfiber towel I keep a stash of in the back corner of my booth, not surprised by the urge to tend to them. When they've calmed, Jordaan breaks their kiss with a tender smile that melts both me and its recipient.

"How long have you hoped for that?"

"Forever, Alfons."

"Why didn't you ask?"

"I was afraid you'd say no."

Alfons frowns as he confesses in a whisper that floats through the dim interior of my booth, "If only I could rewind life. I should have reached for what I wanted no matter how impossible it seemed. I won the lottery today. I suppose sometimes people do take home the jackpot."

"Sometimes more than one person gets lucky." Jordaan can't seem to help himself. He steals another taste of his lover.

A rare emotion snakes through my system, attempting to sabotage my empathetic bliss. Jealousy scorches my intestines until I smother the poisonous attack.

Could lightning strike twice in one night? How many people played only to lose? It doesn't matter to me anymore. I'm willing to risk the odds. For the first time in two weeks, the path I need to take is clear.

I'm not the kind of woman to relinquish my goals without a fight.

Some might call me stubborn. Maybe even stupid, clueless or idealistic.

I prefer persistent, determined or optimistic.

I tuck the men's cocks carefully inside their jeans and

refasten the myriad clasps it had taken to restrain their lust for each other. This time temporarily. As though they're a living mirror image, they each enfold one of my elbows in a supporting grasp and lever me to my feet, hanging on until I'm steady.

"Sometimes my clients are students. Tonight you've been the teachers." I smooth damp strands of neon green and orange hair from their brows with a lingering touch they don't seem to mind.

"Can I ask how we helped?" Jordaan leans into my caress. "I think it'd make me feel as though our interaction was a bit more…balanced."

"You reminded me of two fundamental tenants of my personal philosophy."

"A metaphysical ass-peddler?" Alfons grins. "Is this is a window or a rabbit hole?"

"Alfons!" Jordaan smacks his lover's abdomen. "I'm glad we could return even a fraction of the gift you've given us."

We both glare at Alfons when he digs in his pocket for his wallet. He grimaces and replaces the vinyl pouch when he realizes I'm likely to shove a tip up his ass and make him like it.

"I'm not a fan of pleading, but I will if I have to." Jordaan stares at the floor until Alfons lifts his chin.

"No one will force you to beg for anything."

They don't need me to tell them what they've already figured out. I speak to reinforce the learning for myself.

"Stay true to your dreams, no matter the odds." I smile as I watch them link hands before sharing my other cardinal belief. "Love is unconditional."

"You're pure genius, you know?"

"Not lately." I frown as I recall how I've hunkered in this booth instead of charging toward Rick and his open arms.

Like a person momentarily blinded by the brilliance of the sun after an epic winter, I stumbled and almost wiped out. Until a brief cloud shaded the rays, allowing my vision to adjust to brighter prospects.

I'm ready to bathe naked in the light of Rick's affection, despite the risks. I pray I don't end up with a massive yet temporary burn from a quick burst of heat or a more deadly cancer caused by extended exposure to toxic radiance that appears glorious on the surface.

For the first time in my career, I glance at the clock on the stand despite the overwhelming success of my case. As though Jordaan and Alfons can sense my eagerness to usher them—no longer requiring my assistance—through my window, the pair turn to depart.

"Thanks." Alfons nods as Jordaan wraps me in a brief hug. "We'll never forget you…"

He blushes when he realizes I haven't shared my name.

I grin. "Star."

LOVE IS A BATTLEFIELD

For the second time since I've worked this booth, I prepare to close up shop before dawn paints the sky with iridescent pastels. Rick won't expect me to seek him out.

I never have before.

Not him or any other man.

I grab my long faux-fur coat and keys from the antique crystal dish in a drawer in the table, prepared to lock up behind me and my guests as we leave wonderland behind. Alfons and Jordaan have to split up, like a stream running over a boulder, to avoid slamming into the unmovable figure before them.

"Oh! What are you doing here, Rick?" I ignore the appraising stares my prior clients launch in my direction.

"Hoping I'd stay away?"

"Are you blitzed? I'm pretty sure she was about to hunt you down." Alfons gawks at Rick.

Rick turns his bouncer face on Alfons. Jordaan decides it's safer to worry about their own relationship and tugs his new lover toward the tram line. With a small wave and a brief pause to ensure I don't object, they leave me alone with my…well, whatever it is Rick's become.

A friend at least. I hope.

"Is that true?" Tiny lines crease the corners of his eyes when he squints.

"Yes." I extend my hand to him. "Will you come inside?"

"I'm on break." He shakes his head. "Not a lot of time."

"Tommy won't fire you for stepping out this once."

"This was a bad idea." He retreats a pace.

"Just to talk. I'm freezing out here." With three people in my booth, I hadn't been able to slip into my coat inside. Not all of the chill raising goose bumps on my arms has to do with the weather. I refuse to retract my fingers empty. "Please?"

"Impossible. If I cross through that window, I'm not about to stop until I'm inside *you*." He mutters as he stuffs his fists in the pockets of his leather jacket. "Although you probably won't even notice after those guys. Did you take them both at once? Did you get off on them stretching you? Did it cost them extra for a double or do you offer a price break?"

"If you intend to shame me, you'll have to try a lot harder than that." I storm into my small booth, dump my coat on the stool, wishing there were more floor to pace. Had I really been about to sacrifice my world for a chance with that asshole?

Damn it. Yes.

He knocks on the auto-locking window, which closed behind me none gently.

"I didn't mean that, Sarah." He winces. "Open the window. Please."

I shake my head and gnash my teeth. Anything is better than allowing myself to cry in front of him, the one person I thought understood me. "Go away."

His forehead bangs on the glass. "I'm an idiot."

"A hypocritical moron. Don't come back here."

"I— Shit." Rick looks over his shoulder then lowers his voice a few decibels. "I'm sorry. I'm all fucked up. It turned me on to think of them both with you. What kind of loser does that make me? To want a woman so much it hurts, even more when I think of her with other guys? I was mad at myself, not you. I promise. I didn't mean it."

I release the latch so I can snarl in his face. "If you ever insult my profession again, we're done."

"It won't happen. I promise you, I have nothing but respect for you. It's me I can't figure out." He staggers through my window and stands toe-to-toe with me. "You're screwing with my head."

"Not on purpose."

"I know. I just… I've wondered." He scrubs his hand over his jaw. The light scruff there makes me suspect he's been as distracted as I have. Could he have forgotten to shave?

"Genuine curiosity won't offend me. Judgment will."

He nods then tugs me toward him, chaffing my bare arms. "What's it like with other customers. Could I ever be enough? Or the right thing? What could I give you that you don't get from them?"

How can I stay angry when we're both navigating through the dark?

I wrap my arms around his middle beneath the open sides of his coat, inhaling the scent of the laundry detergent on his thermal shirt and the leather protecting his broad chest.

"It's two different things. Entirely." I can't figure out how else to make him understand. How can I show him the vast disparity in the experiences? "Would you want to watch me with other men? See for yourself?"

I search for any sign of tension in his long back muscles and find none. Or hardly any.

"I must be even more fucked up than I thought." He buries his face in my hair. "I like the idea."

"I can tell." I grind against his pelvis until a whistle from outside reminds me I haven't drawn the curtain.

I spin to grab the fabric and catch Mari cheering from her window. When I turn around, hoping for more of Rick's embrace, he's about to shatter my dreams again.

Not one to be beaten twice in one night, I lunge for the table and block his goal.

"If you don't remove your hand from that lockbox right now, I'm leaving."

"Rick, I'd rather you walk away than pay me for sex so you can feel righteous about a carefree aftermath."

"*What*? That's not what this is about. Look, I'm not trying to score freebies because of what happened on Christmas. When I take your time here, you'll be compensated for it or I'll do without. No big deal."

His cock must not have been copied on that memo. It's hard as ever, forming a sizable lump in his black cargo pants.

He sighs when I don't budge.

Our standoff comes to a peaceful conclusion when he lays the bills on the table. "Let's see how it feels after…"

"Fair enough." I'll never accept his cash again.

I entwine our fingers and lead him upstairs. Somehow the trek up the steep incline seems longer than all the times before. Nerves steal my certainty, distorting my unique but steadfast moral compass like an abnormal magnetic field. Is this the right direction to go?

I unravel the laces of my boots faster than I'd have thought possible before kicking them off. They bang into the dresser an instant before I drop six inches to my unenhanced height. My stare lands somewhere around Rick's diaphragm.

"Sometimes I forget how little you are." He strokes my hair. "How delicate."

"Don't kid yourself." I grab his package in one hand before he can flinch. "I can take care of myself when necessary."

"Jesus." He peels one finger at a time from his crotch. "If you want to molest me, let me ditch these first."

Rick shucks his pants and boxer briefs with one swipe of his deft fingers. He shrugs out of his coat then crosses his arms over his head to whip his form-fitting shirt from his buff chest.

I desperately try not to study his ass as he bends to remove his boots and socks. No luck. I swallow hard. He's gorgeous. An everyday, average guy…except not. To me, he's the most attractive man to ever grace this loft. Or the entire European Union.

"Less staring, more stripping." He groans as I shed my clothing. "Two weeks of pure hell, I swear. I haven't gone that long without a fuck since I was eighteen."

"You could have visited another prostitute. They all adore you."

"Could have."

"But you didn't?"

"No." He surrounds me in a bear hug and nibbles a path from behind my ear to my collarbone. "Wouldn't it have ruined my chances with you?"

"I'm not sure how I could hold it against you when I've probably screwed a hundred guys and a handful of girls since I saw you last."

His bites escalate to something a little fiercer. I wouldn't be surprised if he's left a light mark for my future customers to wonder about.

"Did any of them make you feel like this?" He pauses to appraise the sincerity in my eyes.

"No. Not even close." I shove his chest, knocking him backward.

His knee hits the corner of the mattress and he allows himself to fall. His feet rest on the floor, his knees bent, the majority of his body crashed sideways on the bed. Strong hands encircle my waist, drawing me over his supine form.

I straddle his hips, more eager than him to join our bodies. "I hoped you'd come. Every day. I needed this."

"I'm sorry." His head dips and he groans as my pussy glides over the length of his shaft. "Right now it's hard to conjure any reason for staying away. I'm a moron."

I tip forward, blanketing his trembling body with mine. His fingers splay across the skin of my ass, guiding my short, quick passes over him. My breath catches when the tip of his cock prods my clit.

"Condom." He growls as I lick and nip his rugged throat, the underside of his prominent jaw. I'm not the only one who will bear evidence of our encounter.

I rise up on straight-locked arms, my head canted. What is he saying?

"Star, grab a condom. Quick. Or I'll fuck you bare."

How could I have forgotten? I never have before.

I lash out with one hand, irritated at myself and the world that necessitates the barrier between us, however thin. My fingers strike the stash of latex beneath a pillow. I bite my lip as Rick toys with my breasts while I dress him for the main event.

My fingers hold him upright, perpendicular to his torso, as I roll the condom over his proud length. No sooner is he encased in the protective sheath then I follow with my own steaming, moist enclosure.

Despite his earlier fears, I am well aware of every inch of his cock my pussy swallows. I cry out as a blast of pleasure stabs my belly when I'm seated on his upper thighs, his hard-on embedded fully inside me.

He's moaning, urging me to move, but I'm afraid I'll come on the spot.

When I don't respond, he slaps my ass. The sting propels me forward, stroking my clit on the pad of muscle above his pelvic bone. Now that I've had a taste of the scrumptious friction, I have to have more. I tuck the tops of my pointed feet on the insides of his knees for leverage and begin to ride him, using his body to rub me in all the right places, inside and out.

I plant my hands on his chest and swivel my hips in a figure eight that delivers the most sensation to my clit. He attempts to pinch my nipples, aborting the mission when I destroy his coordination and his ability to do anything other than accept my passion. I have plenty for us both.

"Beautiful." He grunts between the heavy impacts of my full weight bouncing vigorously over him. I should slow down, tease him, drag the rapture out until it hurts.

Except it already does.

I throw my head from side to side, trying to deny the inevitable.

"Don't." He slaps my ass again, only worsening my dilemma. "Don't resist. Take what you need."

I bite my lip, squeeze my muscles around his bulging erection and grind on his body. Completely out of control. Terrifying. Wondrous. Unstoppable.

Without considering his satisfaction, another first in my loft, I concentrate on the ache in my core, expanding its effects. Intense euphoria washes over me, starting with my pointed toes. It travels up my legs like mercury in a thermometer on the hottest day of the year.

When it hits the apex of my thighs, I scream and shatter.

My eyes fly open in time to watch Rick come apart as he witnesses my abandon. His cock thickens inside me and he fucks upward, his hips arching off the bed to pound every last bit of his shaft into my spasming pussy. I visualize the bursts of his come filling the condom buried in my pussy a moment before I collapse onto his heaving chest.

He wraps one arm around my waist and flips us. We come to rest with my head on the pillows, fully sprawled on the mattress.

He peers into the rubble of my loose smile. Finally relief. Where nothing else has helped, finally, finally, I'm free of the burning arousal that's haunted me for two weeks. Until he withdraws to dispose of his rubber. The exit of his persistent, semi-hard cock triggers a rebirth of fresh awareness.

I miss his presence deep inside me.

"Damn it." The fire in my gut hasn't been extinguished by the flood of rapture Rick instigated. Merely appeased for a brief moment. I long for the ultimate satisfaction that had melted my bones on Christmas Eve. "What the hell is wrong with me? It must be hormones."

"If that's what you want to call it." He tugs on his cock, which still refuses to turn completely flaccid. Another first. Can he sense the lingering sparks arcing between us?

"Did you just roll your eyes at me, Rick?"

"Fuck yes."

"How old are you?" I can't help the nervous giggle that escapes. My head crashes onto his shoulder when he settles beside me. It's not all amusement though. What is he feeling? Was it fantastic for him? Good enough to crave seconds or did my rough ride leave him unsatisfied too?

He destroys my insight and instinct. Disorienting.

"Twenty-eight." His serious tone sobers me pretty damn quick. "How old are you, *Sarah*?"

A shudder runs down my spine when he breaks out my legal name. A gift I've given only to him in all my time as a sex worker. "Twenty-five."

"So young." His cock stirs against my inner thigh. Could he be as unfulfilled by our quick fuck as I am? The hundreds of other times we've indulged have done just fine for us both. Something has changed. It's the end of an era.

Could it be the beginning of another?

I bite my lip as I raise my head to gaze into his eyes, a million questions stirring in my mind.

"I don't know the answers," he whispers. "All I know is I need more. Of you. More than a fifteen-minute budget quickie."

He sucks my lip into his mouth, soothing the spot I'd chewed.

This time his assault is borne of tenderness. The difference terrifies me.

I try to break from his hold, but he fuses his lips to mine, stealing a full-mouth kiss. A delicacy I never indulge in with customers.

I whimper, attempting to turn my head to avoid the overwhelming desire for more than his body, which threatens to leave me vulnerable, exposed. He doesn't supply an opportunity to indulge my instinctive reaction.

Rick pursues my lips no matter how I angle my face, slipping his tongue into my mouth when I open my jaw to protest. I fight harder, trying to buck him from on top of me, but he's too large. He adjusts his bulk to secure my position beneath him while he plunders my mouth.

All I have to do is scream and it'll be over. Prostitutes are well protected here. My neighbors will hit their panic buttons and the police stationed in the small district outside will arrive within half a minute.

But I can't make a single peep.

Don't want to. Not really.

I force myself to go lax in his hold, every muscle turning limp and loose as they usually are after we fuck.

The change has him backing off, searching my eyes with a beam of hope and longing.

I'm desperate to be the woman he seeks. Without discussing it first, making sure we're on the same page, I'm afraid to hand over my entire being. Does he realize the power he has over all of me, not just my physical form?

"Stop, Rick. You're asking for more than I can give."

"Can or will?" His raspy panting buffets my face, washing me with the scent of his favorite wintergreen gum. "You're running, love. I thought you were tougher than this."

He captures my mouth once again, tempting me to cave, seducing me with gentle licks and caresses that are a lot more likely to injure me than the brute force I'm used to on occasion. This is something entirely new. Petrifying. His thumbs caress my skittering pulse in my wrists. My resistance melts, allowing me to indulge in the surrender of my will to his. For a moment.

Then I bite his lip hard enough to ensure he jerks with a curse.

"Are you really planning to force yourself on me when I've

said no?" My dreams begin to shrivel and die.

"I've paid for this goddamn half-hour. I intend to get my money's worth."

I flinch as though he smacked me. A bitch slap would have been kinder.

"Exactly what I feared." Who is this man and what has he done with my sunshine? The dangerous game we've been playing backfires, sending shrapnel through my chest. My heart turns brittle and cracks beneath the blow.

A single tear leaks from the corner of my eye.

The droplet acts like a magic elixir, instantly transforming the demanding monster on top of me into my softhearted bad boy.

"Oh Christ." He crashes to his side on the mattress, his ribs expanding beneath the force of labored breaths. "What the fuck am I doing? You're driving me insane, I swear. I can't erase you from my mind. I smell you in my bed, on my sheets, my pillow. I can't settle for less than everything. I've turned into some obsessed stalker."

His muscles bunch as though he prepares to leap from my loft. I lay my palm on his cheek, preventing him from fleeing.

"I'm *so* fucking sorry. I would never hurt you, Sarah." He reaches for me but stops halfway, as though he doesn't trust himself. "Except I already have. At least twice tonight."

Fuck that. I burrow against his chest, wrapping my arm around his waist to stroke his trembling shoulders. "It's not in your nature to harm another human being, especially not a woman. You're a protector. Not a raider."

"I almost… You have no idea how badly I want you."

"Believe me." I install enough distance between us to allow him a glimpse of the desperation in my gaze. "I do."

He rolls, swinging to his feet, slapping a hand on the dresser when his balance suffers from our dizzying exchange. "So we're right back to where we were."

"I don't think so." I scoot off the mattress and step into my clothes. Where the hell are my boots? I have to examine his eyes up close.

He trundles down the stairs and lingers by the door, staring at the cash on the table.

"You're right. Things are *worse* than before. Because it didn't help. Fucking. Like this. It will never suffice." He closes his eyes as he shrugs on his jacket. I tuck the money from the table into his pocket. The first refund I've ever given.

Dane's advice floats into my mind. "You can buy sex, Rick. But you can't buy love."

"No shit. You prove that every day. Hell, we confirmed it tonight, didn't we?"

"We did." I grimace.

"So now what?" His skull clunks on the glass of my window. "I knew I wouldn't be able to talk to you here. For once, I wish I'd been wrong."

He takes my hand in his and lifts it to his mouth, kissing my knuckles as we scramble for an easy answer where none exists.

"I…" I clear my throat. "I agree, this isn't the place. Would you still be open to seeing me outside of work?"

I hold my breath.

Fortunately it doesn't take him more than a millionth of a second to agree. "Fuck yes. Would you do that? Would you…go out with me?"

"Yes." My heart flutters in my chest. I've never been on an official date.

"Where would you like me to take you? Somewhere we can talk." His fingertips trace the edge of my cheek. "Somewhere special."

"I've been to your apartment. Would it be okay if I had you over to my home? I'll cook dinner. For you." I scribble my address on a corner of my ledger then rip it out. At the last second I add my phone number below it.

Rick tucks the information close to his heart in the inside breast pocket of his jacket, checking to make sure the zip is securely fastened before returning his full attention.

"Thank you." He cups my face between his palms and delivers a kiss that guarantees he understands. I've never allowed a customer to know where I live. Certainly have never permitted them inside.

"We're both off on Mondays. How about then?" I whisper when his gesture trails to butterfly brushes of his lips over mine. I need a few days to beg Mari to teach me how to prepare a meal worthy of the most important night of my life. Besides, neither of us can afford to lose hours during the booming weekend in Amsterdam.

"This is going to be the longest week in the history of the universe." Rick glides his cheek against mine.

"No, that was a tie between last week and the one before." I hug him tight. We sigh together when we have to part. "I'm so glad you came back."

"Me too, Sarah. See you Monday."

Love Me Tender

A buzzer riots, scaring me half to death.

I've never used my houseboat apartment's kitchen before. At least it was one less room I'd had to declutter to prepare for my guest. I glance around, quadruple checking all my arrangements. Another blast of the insistent timer jolts me into action.

I wrench open the oven then stand there, head tilted, staring. What the heck is pork satay supposed to look like when it's done? I've only ever beheld the finished product, meat and sauce mingled together in a mass of gooey scrumptiousness on a restaurant's plate. Hints of rich Indonesian culture are sprinkled across Amsterdam, a relic of colonial conquests. The exotic influences are some of my favorites.

I suppose the bubbling liquid in the pot and the chunk of pork emitting juicy steam could be correct. At the last second, I remember to check Mari's note.

Use the thermometer. When it hits 70°C take the tenderloin out and cover it with aluminum foil until you're ready to eat.

Right. I rummage in the sack of supplies she gave me as a late Christmas present until I put my hand on something that looks more like an oil gauge on a stick than my idea of a thermometer. A few degrees over, good enough.

Two hand towels from my bathroom serve as makeshift potholders. I slide the roasting pan onto the cooktop then grab the pot handle, intending to slather my sauce over the meat until

I read the next line of her instructions.

Do NOT combine the dishes until you serve them.

Damn. Can it truly matter? Better play it safe. I stop the thick concoction just before it spills over the lip. My overcorrection slops some out the side, onto my hand.

My shriek and curses come at the same instant as the ringing doorbell, followed by a louder version of the knock I adore.

"Sarah?" Rick shouts from the deck of the vessel I rent.

I bite my lip and try to tone down my swearing.

I lick the cooled glop from the crook between my thumb and forefinger. Not bad! Then I hurry across the hardwood to admit my visitor. I don't even have time to check out the long curls Mari dressed in my hair before flipping open the door.

"Hi." *Really? Brilliant, Sarah.*

"Hi." Rick peers around me toward the kitchen. "Everything all right?"

"Uh-huh." I hide my hand behind my back and step aside so he can enter.

He bends down to kiss me. We both freeze, unsure of how to proceed. I refuse to make the only date of my life awkward. Denying our physical attraction now would be ridiculous. I savor his lips, loving the thrill such a simple treasure can inspire.

"Mmm." He doesn't pursue more than a brief yet thorough welcome. "These are for you."

He offers me a giant bouquet from Amsterdam's famous flower market. No boring roses here. I recognize the green chrysanthemums, a few orchids and sprigs of verbena—making me wonder if Rick could possible enjoy Faulkner as much as I— between the tiny twisted twigs and unusual samples of beauty.

Unique, gorgeous and vital, they call to me instantly.

I extend my hand to accept.

"What the—" He inspects the red splotch darkening my tender skin.

"Little mishap. Nothing major." I try to hide the damage, but it's too late.

"Like hell. Come on." He steers me toward the galley, easily visible in the open layout of my efficient apartment. "Run it under cold water."

I sigh, reclining against his chest as the warm circle of his embrace shelters me and the cool stream from the tap soothes my stinging flesh. If only I could chill the rest of my rioting nerves.

"It smells great in here." His compliment wafts tendrils of hair from my face.

"I hope dinner is edible. I'm not much of a cook." I wince when I consider how Rick devoured his meal the last time we ate out together. Eating is clearly a highlight of his day.

"I would have done the honors if you'd asked." He kisses my temple then folds the edge of the foil off my masterpiece. "Doesn't seem like you needed my help though."

"I wanted to try it. For you." I slip my fingers from his then shut off the water. "For us."

"Better?" He picks up my hand and presses a featherlight kiss to the wound.

"Much, thank you."

"I'd love a tour. Houseboats this near the skinny bridge are hard to come by, but…" His stomach growls. "I'm starved. Can we eat first?"

"Sure." A ridiculous thrill tingles my insides as Rick makes himself at home, carving the pork and serving us both. While he's occupied, I pour the rich Spanish priorat I'd aerated in the crystal carafe I bought myself for Christmas.

"I thought maybe you'd given me a fake address." He picks up the conversation when we settle in around the hardwood table bolted to the dining room floor. Though the water in Amsterdam's canals is usually smooth as glass, I suspect my houseboat has as many stories to tell as I do, if only someone could listen. "I've seen you leave the district heading the opposite direction about a million times. I thought you lived over near Dam Square."

"I'm careful. Never know when a customer will decide to follow me home for more."

He blinks at me, his fork frozen halfway to his parted lips.

I wince. "Not like this. Never like this before. Sorry, it's all so new. I guess my habits are old-fashioned paranoia."

"You're not unreasonable, Sarah. Smart." He twirls a piece of meat through the sauce on his plate then pops it in his mouth. "I've had to warn a slew of cretins from bugging Tommy's girls. I'm glad you take precautions."

"Always. I adore my job. Truly." I swallow my first bite of the meal I've prepared, pleasantly surprised with the tang spreading across my tongue. "Still, I never allow myself to romanticize the situation."

"I've noticed." Rick groans. "Damn. This is fantastic."

"Thank Mari." I grin.

"Don't worry, I will." We both pause as the overtones hang in the air. Is it okay to acknowledge Rick's visits to the other women in the district?

"If you're not comfortable…" He winces.

"No, no. Please. We both know the score."

He nods then dedicates himself to worshipping the meal before him.

When I finish my portion, I lean back and twirl the stem of the glass holding my respectable wine. I study Rick's flexing throat, wondering how something as simple as a man eating can turn me on. Damn him and his sexy ways.

He groans as he rubs his tight abs, slightly bowed from his indulgence.

I rise to clean the plates and he attempts to follow. I still him with light pressure on his brawny shoulder. "Let me."

"Don't assume you have to wait on me here."

"I realize you don't expect me to serve you outside the window. Good thing too." His concern warms my heart. "I'm choosing to do this. This time. Next time you're on kitchen duty, big guy."

"Deal." He smiles then wanders the main living area while I settle our plates and silverware in the dishwasher. "This place is fantastic, Sarah."

I glance over my shoulder to spot him running a fingertip over the intricate woodwork in the living room as he admires the view through the lace curtains shielding my window. Outside, an enclosed glass patio filled with greenery makes the ideal spot for sunbathing or tourist watching on warm afternoons. The details of the houseboat apartment have captivated me often. "I knew the moment I stepped inside this was my home. I've been talking to the landlord about buying him out. He's hesitant to sell. I'm hoping some of the Kinkmas pageant paycheck will finally change his mind."

Rick nods, appraising the luxurious appointments in the cozy space. "A solid investment."

I towel my hands dry then wave him toward the private end of the boat. "The bedrooms are over here."

I take him through the efficiently concealed and stowed laundry space, the glistening tile of the main bathroom, the soft amber hues of the guest suite and finally to my haven. White silk floats over the canopy—and a mountain of decadent pillows—stirred by heat rising from vents in the base of the paneled walls.

"I'm in a love goddess's lair. Will you have to kill me now that I'm privy to the location of your secret hideout?" One corner of his mouth kicks up in a sultry smile. "Or maybe you'll keep me chained to your bed for eternity. If I can't escape, I can't spill your secrets."

"I kind of like that option." I grin. "Except, I think I'd like to try being the person tied up one of these days. You piqued my curiosity when you bound me with the Christmas lights onstage during the Kinkmas pageant. I loved being at your mercy."

"Shit." He braces his broad palm on my dresser, shaking it with the contact. It never seemed dainty before. "I'm trying to behave."

"Why?"

"Because, despite the fantasy-come-true it would be to lay you down on that cloud of fluff and make love to you so slowly neither of us can stand it, I won't risk missing the chance to show you how much more there could be to this." He waves his hand in the shrinking space between us.

"The least you can do is hold me while we talk." I reach for his fingers, entwining our shaking hands and lead him to my bed. I slip off my heels then crawl onto the center of the mattress, relishing the glide of my luxurious stockings and modest black dress against the rich, clean bedding. "I missed you."

Rick groans as he toes off his shoes and joins me. He bundles me in his arms, squeezing tight. My nest has never seemed as comfortable as it does with him beside me.

"Me too, love." He rubs his chin over my head. "I'm sorry both of us suffered. I had some serious thinking to do."

"What did all that brain power come up with?"

"I decided I have to try this, try...something." He's never

looked so serious before. "One of the reasons I'm so attracted to you is your uninhibited acceptance of nature. Of arousal. Of sexuality."

"You understand. I can tell you share my values."

"So, I hope you won't freak out when I admit I don't really believe people were intended to be monogamous. Too many relationships crash and burn in spectacular failures because of sex. Either one person loses the spark or they find it with someone else and hide the exhilaration of that discovery from their partner, who may or may not experience the rush for their mate any longer."

I don't realize my grip pinches his arm until he flinches. Could he be saying what I think? "No kidding, Rick. Do you have any idea how many men, or women, I service because they need something they can't find at home and are riddled with guilt over seeking it elsewhere?"

"Because they still love their spouse, right?"

"Yes. They just aren't attracted anymore." I sigh.

"Or there's so much tension built up over their different desires they can't enjoy themselves with all that drama sleeping in bed with them."

"I suppose that's true."

"I'm sure it is, Sarah. Story of my life really. My parents divorced before I finished elementary school. Both remarried a handful of times. They still love each other. It's insane. They stay apart because of archaic social values they probably don't even believe in. They're not happy apart. They can't stay together."

I burrow beneath his heavy biceps, nudging him until he rolls to his back and invites me close to his heart. I curl up against his chest, laying my cheek on the toasty sweater covering his pecs.

"I always swore I'd never tie myself to one person, guaranteeing I'd continue the cycle of misery. I never understood why someone would believe any single woman could be enough."

"And now you're going to tell me some Christmas miracle changed your mind?" As much as I wish it were true, my experiences make it hard for me accept monogamy as a viable long-term arrangement. Rick's understanding has been one of the things I've always admired.

"No. Sorry." He strokes my hair absently, naturally.

"Thank God." I peek up at him and can't resist stealing a taste of his taut lips. A tiny sip, a caress more intimate than the most crude fucks I've had through my window.

"I guess I started to hope I'd finally found the one woman who could understand my viewpoint without trying to change me or convince me I need counseling. My mom said—"

"Wait. You told your mom about me?"

"Yeah." His eyes turn warm and his smile reminds me of the time I bought him a half-smashed cupcake from the automatiek at Febo for his birthday.

"Well, how the heck did that go?"

"She smacked me upside the head for not inviting you to Christmas. Thanks a lot, by the way."

A chuckle escapes as I imagine his surprised offence. "Sorry. Still think I made the right call there. It's one thing to break the news you're crazy enough to date a prostitute in a quiet kitchen moment and another entirely to show up with her to Christmas dinner."

"I wish I didn't agree..." He grimaced. "You were right. Anyway, my mom said we each have to craft our own form of happiness and that she hasn't seen me look this excited since her and my dad caved to my constant begging for a puppy when I was five."

"Glad to know I rank up there with Fido." Damn. I didn't mean to cloud his gorgeous eyes.

"Carver."

"Excuse me?"

"My dog's name was Carver." He cups my chin and tilts it up until I can't deny the honesty in his gaze. Rick never lies to me. He never attempts to mask the gritty realities of our adventure together with sentimental smoke and mirrors. "I value this, whatever this is between us, and you far more than that mutt, and he was my best friend for close to fifteen years. No matter what happens here or if we can really pull off something this ludicrous, I'll always have you on a pedestal."

Tears sting my eyes.

"Hey, crap." He pats my shoulder with an awkward jerk of

his hand. "What'd I say?"

"I guess that's one of the few things that freak me out about my job." I haven't admitted this to anyone, even myself, so plainly before. "When men assume I'm less than human, some animated object they can rent for a handful of minutes because I chose this profession. I refuse to service clients like that for repeat performances."

"I've heard."

"You have?"

"Sure. And bonus points to Mari for keeping my secrets like she promised she would." Rick doesn't continue.

My lids sink until his wry smile turns hazy in my narrowed stare.

"Don't take it out on her. I made her promise not to blab about the guy I wiped the floor with." His fingers flex on my ribs as though he can still feel the ache resulting from his legendary right hook. "Heard him bitching to his loser friend in the alley outside her window while I paced, waiting for you to finish up with someone else one night. I guess he'd had his pride stung when you refused to service him. He'd gone for a few brews then came back full of distorted perspective and unwise bravado, bragging about how he'd show you what you'd missed out on."

"Oh."

Rick traces the ring of my pursed lips with the tip of one finger.

"The only thing that terrifies me about your job is the thought of someone hurting you. I'm not going to lie… I saw red when he described all he had planned, even though he probably couldn't have gotten it up as drunk as he was. He took one step toward your window and next thing I knew I'd laid him out on the cobblestones. Mari tugged me off him before I went too far. She hustled me inside."

"Calmed you right down, did she?" I snort as I imagine how thrilled she must have been.

"She's pretty good at her job."

I laugh out loud, pressing my palms to his flaming cheeks. "So how odd does it make me that I'm glad you had someone there for you when you needed comfort?"

"I'm confident you're more rare than a 1926 Ducati SpA."

I arch a brow.

"And despite the fact you have no idea what one of the coolest motorcycles of all time is, I still adore you."

The lavish kiss he bestows curls my toes and melts my insides.

"Besides, I'm *positive* I'm a freak. Not only am I okay with you being with other guys, it sort of turns me on." The enormous erection tenting his dress slacks declares his confession the understatement of the century.

"It's not the same, Rick." I can't help myself. I glide my thigh over the evidence of his approval. "With other customers. They're all unique and none of them make me ache like you do."

"I wish I could see the difference." His whisper turns rough. "I spent a hell of a lot of time fantasizing about what you asked the other day. I'd love to watch you with a client."

"I'm sure it can be arranged." I moan when he tenses his hips, pressing closer to the juncture of my thighs. "The idea makes me hotter than you can guess."

"I can smell you, love." He growls. "I didn't plan to do this tonight, I swear I didn't, but I think I'll starve if you don't let me have some of your sweetness for dessert."

"I might have to hurt you if you leave me like this." I stroke my hard nipples across his abs. "Tonight, no one except you will satisfy my craving."

"Same here, Sarah." He rolls over, pressing my shoulders into the down pillow-top. "You're incredible, you know that, right?"

"Many men have said so." I shiver when he traces the delicate chain of my choker. "Their opinions never seemed as important as yours though."

Rick inches the loose, flowing fabric of my dress up my legs from my knees to my thighs. His fingers caress every centimeter of stocking he exposes with tiny swirls. I squirm beneath the tantalizing desire making my heart race and my insides heavy.

"Son of a bitch. So sexy," he mutters when he encounters the lace tops of my thigh-highs. Before I can beg for more, he dips between my spread legs, nudging them wide enough to accommodate his broad chest. Then he licks along the junction of the frilly fabric and my pale skin. "So sweet."

Rick's hands glide upward, lifting my skirt to expose my

matching panties. Stretchy lace highlights the toned curve and dip of my hips. He nuzzles the thin covering over my pussy, inhaling deep and strong until the scent of my arousal overflows his lungs. He releases his breath on a groan that rumbles across my clit.

I whimper, spearing my fingers into the spikes of his hair.

"Not yet."

I can't tell who he's reminding—himself or me.

"Don't have to rush tonight," he murmurs as he nibbles my belly above the waistband of my panties. He licks, nips and kisses a path up my torso, removing my dress as he progresses slower than a dollop of ketchup leaving a freshly opened bottle.

I hold my breath when he uncovers my push-up bra, which showcases my cleavage for his inspection. He surprises me by avoiding temptation a little bit longer. He slips his hands beneath me, his fingers practically encircling my ribs, then lifts.

"Arms up, Sarah." His command sends shivers racing from the base of my spine upward. I smile when the motion draws his gaze to my shimmying breasts. He's not as impervious as he would like to pretend.

Rick peels the dress from my torso, leaving my wrists tangled in the bunched fabric above my head. The angle prevents me from extracting them despite several experimental tugs. "I don't suppose you'd like to free me?"

"Is that what you really want?"

"No."

"I didn't think so. Stay still." He takes my bottom lip between his and drags his teeth over the swollen tissue. My brain ceases to function as he seduces my mouth with endless barrages of coercion from his tongue, lips and teeth.

Rick feeds me his affection, staring deep into my eyes as he savors our intimate interaction. For longer than I can keep track of, we're content to indulge in the not-so-innocent exchange. I learn the contours of his mouth, every ridge and cranny guaranteed to make him moan or raid my open offering more completely.

The luxury of enjoying the journey more than the destination is not lost on either of us. I could gladly kiss him for a year or twenty while he massages my scalp, lulling me into a trance filled with simmering heat and sexual energy so strong it has the potential to destroy us or send us to the moon.

As long as we're together, I don't care which.

The fuzz of his sweater rubs over my body. It's soft and warm with the heat radiating from his powerful muscles, carefully restrained. I long to connect with him skin on skin. I reach for the hem of his sweater. My dress prevents me from obtaining my goal. I whimper when a rush of pleasure swamps my senses. Arousal spills from my pussy, dampening the thin barrier between my legs.

Rick waits patiently yet expectantly. I can't bear to disappoint him. Don't wish to escape his clutches in any case. I stop struggling and melt beneath his fully clothed frame.

"That's right." He purrs against my neck. "Tell me what you're after. I'll give you anything you like. Whatever you need."

"Have to feel you against me. Bare." I would never have thought I'd beg a man for anything, but a plea escapes my parted lips before I can prevent it. "Please. Let me feel you."

Rick sits on his haunches between my knees, keeping one hand low on my belly until he's sure I don't intend to pursue him. He bathes in my adoring stare, deliberately displaying his magnificent physique for my hungry eyes when he crosses his arms over his head, grabs hold of his sweater and peels it from his upper body.

The charcoal garment hits my area rug with a quiet whoosh.

"Like this?" He leans forward, his slacks still fastened around his trim hips, driving me insane with the blend of raw masculinity and proper gentleman.

"No!" I gasp around the urgent desire constricting my chest. "All of you. Naked. Nothing between us."

"Nothing?" He pops open the button at the top and sighs. The pressure on his rock-hard cock must be torture. "Not even a condom?"

I shake my head. "Loved having you inside me, natural, at Triple X. After. Nothing's changed for me. Only like that with you. I swear."

"Me too, Sarah."

I can't engage my logic long enough to continue the

discussion. Instead, I enjoy the brief show he gives me as he discards the remainder of his clothes. His cock dips, heavy with the weight of the blood pumping strong between his legs.

I lick my lips.

His thick erection bobs as if it's straining to press inside my eager mouth.

"Not tonight." He strokes himself long and slow for several circuits, as though the pressure is too much to bear. "It's important to me…"

"What is, Rick?"

"We should come together. With me inside you. Connected. Seal our promise. To support each other. Our commitment to whatever this is between us."

"Like blood brothers—" I stop myself when I realize he's not laughing.

"Sorry, dumb idea."

"No." I hook my stockinged calf behind his spine and urge him toward me. "It's nice. Romantic. Hot."

We both cry out when our lightly perspiring skin fuses.

Another lengthy kiss flares my arousal to white-hot levels. I whisper between tiny bites, "Need you. Hurry."

Rick's fingers are less steady. His trembling digits take several tries to unhook my bra. The satin straps and black lace climb my arms, adding to my confinement.

"Still okay?" He strokes my folded elbows, checking my comfort.

"Yes. Perfect. Almost." I grimace. "Empty."

"Not for much longer." He swears. "I can't wait to bury myself in your heat. Your moisture. Can't stop myself."

He lowers his face to my breasts, devouring the full mounds, taking the tight peaks into his mouth. He sucks, less gently than his earlier teasing. While he feasts on the offering, enhanced by the position of my arms, he nudges my panties down my legs. I lift my ass, wiggling to facilitate every advance toward our joining.

"Leaving the thigh-highs on. Like elegant wrapping on the perfect present. Hate to ruin it."

The awe in his tone encourages my smile to widen. He samples the flavor of my happiness as he settles fully in the vee of my thighs. His cock rides the furrow of my soaked slit when we rock together in time to the thrust and retreat of our tongues.

Our stares lock and we shift simultaneously, the angle of our pelvises guarantees the tip of his hard-on is poised to penetrate the tense ring of muscle guarding the entrance to my pussy.

Instead of plunging inside, he introduces his shaft a millimeter at a time with tiny twitches of his hips. Each advance heightens my passion, making me crave the entire length of him impaling me. His exquisite torture lights every nerve ending along the tense walls of my channel, guiding him deeper inside.

The appeal of tantric sex becomes clear when he finally fits us together as tight as possible. His heartbeat echoes deep within my grasp. We stay still, basking in the ephemeral moment we're first bonded, knowing it can't possibly last, hoping it only blossoms into something better, despite how inconceivable that seems.

He kisses me again and again and again until I'm lost in a world of pure sensation. I lie still, enjoying the fruits of his mastery. My pussy sucks on his cock as my mouth does his tongue. When he finally moves, the slight motion has an impact a thousand times as potent as the rough thrusts he's bestowed in brief interludes through my window.

I cry out.

He swallows my surprise, my pleasure and the hint of despair tingeing my temporary relief. It's too good. Too strong to resist for long. The engorged tissue of my pussy undulates in rhythmic pulses around his shaft, hugging the veiny length and the blunt cap of his cock, which parts my strangling embrace.

Rick stays buried deep, hardly moving, grinding the root of his cock against my clit. We strain toward each other in an attempt to get closer when it'd be impossible to do so without climbing inside him.

My legs wrap around his hips, my heels digging in to his clenching buttocks.

He curses softly in my ear and pauses to kiss the space behind my jaw, below my ear.

"Yes!" I shout when he probes the spot programmed to induce my orgasm.

"Right there, huh?" He flickers his tongue over the pressure point, making me grit my teeth.

"Not if you still…" I can't catch my breath. "Want us to come together."

"Shhh." He hushes me, mitigating my fears. "No worries there, love. Whenever you're ready. I'm with you."

The strain in his urging proclaims his willpower. How long has he ridden the sharp edge of ecstasy?

"Kiss me." I beg. "One more time."

"The first of a lifetime. I swear." He meshes our mouths, maintaining his infuriating pattern of miniscule lunges until I can't possibly hang on a moment longer.

The world freezes around me as I tense, hovering on the verge of euphoria.

"Let go." He fucks deep inside me and binds us together. "Now."

My eyelids flutter open. The instant I observe the depth of emotion lurking in his gaze I surrender. My body shudders as wave after wave of pleasure washes over me.

"Sarah!" He joins me, spilling his cum over the entrance to my womb, on the fringes of possibility. The liquid heat enhances my ecstasy, more perfect than I could have imagined.

In all my experience, nothing has come close to this. Nothing has touched me as profoundly as our shared release. My amplified climax acts like a magnifier, growing Rick's enjoyment ten times over. Pulse after pulse of his semen floods my pussy, linking us in a never-ending cycle of mutual fulfillment.

I don't know how long I've drifted in a cloud of hope, bliss and contentment, but I'm afraid to move and break the spell. For once, there's no rush to strip off a condom, wrap up a session or proceed to the next client.

Tonight I can relish the anything-but-simple pleasures to be found in the embrace of the man I was destined for, his body and mine linked as we enter our dreamland together. I waste no thoughts on the reality tomorrow will bring.

WHY DO FOOLS FALL IN LOVE?

I sit on the stool through my window, watching the crowd ebb and flow. How can everything seem so much the same when I'm forever changed? I glance at the mirror above my table again and again, discerning no outward sign of my transformation.

The golden glow filling my heart and soul isn't actually radiating from every pore as it feels like it should. Still, I sense it.

Irrevocable.

Undeniable.

Rick and I spent the entire day learning about each other—playing, sharing and making love. Tonight we walked to the district together, hand in hand. He escorted me to my booth, ensuring my safety before proceeding to Triple X and his job guarding the women he never touches.

For a split second, I worried I couldn't do this. But the moment I stepped through my window, everything clicked into place.

I *can* do this. I *want* to do this.

Because *this* has nothing to do with Rick and the magic we created last night.

This is a service. A physical comfort. Not a gift. Not an exchange of spirits.

Two disparate things.

I grin at the man who approaches, hopping up to greet him

before he knocks. I'll sell him whatever he needs from me. Anything but love.

* * * * *

I check the clock on my table though it's been mere seconds since the previous glance.

Rick didn't mention stopping by on break, maybe I assumed too much. Like a hopeless schoolgirl, I can't stand to be apart from him for even a few hours. The lingering kisses he'd dropped on my swollen lips when he delivered me to my window made me hope he'd succumb to the same restless anticipation plaguing me.

I shift my gaze to the street once more. My stare is instantly captured by a familiar face, one that's been etched onto my being permanently. I clutch the seat of my stool to keep from rocketing through the glass into his embrace.

It takes the space of several more pounding heartbeats to realize my lover isn't alone.

I frown when I recognize two of his friends—Bendt and Niels—trailing a step or two behind, exchanging shrugs and jokes. Both of the men had received recommendations for my services from Rick and have become frequent customers.

Fun, flirty and dirty.

Just the way I like them best.

Will Rick hold that against me after all his promises? The bottom of my stomach drops out as I realize how much faith I've placed in him. How badly I ache for what he's offered.

I haul my window open and snarl, "Is this some kind of sick test? You want to loan me to your friends? Or am I supposed to turn them down?"

"Whoa." Bendt puts his hands up and backs off a couple steps. "Hang on, Star. We didn't mean to piss you off. Rick said it'd be okay. You've let me and Niels do you together before. We didn't think three would be any different, sorry."

"Wait." Rick snags Bendt's collar and holds him in place easily as he braves my glare.

I try for furious. I must fall short because Rick brushes his free thumb over my cheek.

"It's not what you're thinking. Not a trap," he whispers while his friends study the cracks in the cobblestone walkway. "I'm dying to see. Like I said last night, your pursuit of pleasure turns me on. Your body and your heart are two separate things. I know it. It's the same for me. Still… Will you show me the difference? Let me witness it to be sure. Confirm my beliefs. For all the times I'm not around and barbaric jealousy threatens to overrule my sanity. Give me something to remember. Please?"

I step aside and open my window wide. The three men enter without hesitation. Bendt drops a healthy roll of bills into my lockbox. Rick leads the group upstairs, all four of us impossible to cram into the street-level booth. I lock the window and slide the curtain across the glass. Before the world outside disappears completely, I catch Mari's wide eyes and exaggerated clapping from across the street in my peripheral vision.

I blow her a kiss, snap the material closed then take the stairs two at a time. My insides rattle with every step.

"You're really okay with this, sweetheart?" Niels pauses with his hand on the button of his jeans. "Bendt told us he planned to visit and it sounded like a good idea to me. We didn't think you'd mind us splitting a session since we've done it before."

I peek at Rick to make sure. Hedonistic joy fills his eyes.

No recrimination, no condescension.

"Whatever you fancy, Niels." My fingers tingle at the thought of the three of them together. They're attractive. Skilled. Two men I'm entirely comfortable with, in addition to the one I feel a part of. "You surprised me, that's all."

"Gotta say I was stunned too when Rick piped up about tagging along. Thought he was a solo performer. Though I suppose it wasn't that *shocking* after the Kinkmas pageant." Bendt waggles his eyebrows as he strips off his ribbed T-shirt. "Who wouldn't want an encore after that?"

"Damn. Was everyone in Amsterdam there?" I flick my gaze toward Rick, thrilled by the pride blazing in his eyes.

"If they weren't, they missed out big-time." Niels hops onto the mattress and slides toward the wall on his knees. I climb after him and Bendt mirrors his best friend on my other side. "I came so hard I saw an entire constellation with you at the center. Something about it seemed so…real."

"It was." Rick folds his arms over his chest, leans his tight ass on my bureau and crosses his ankles, still fully clothed.

"What the—" Bendt's cock wilts a little as he turns to Rick with wide eyes.

"Don't worry. I'm not gonna kick your sorry ass." I grin at the mischief glittering in Rick's stare. "I want to watch my girlfriend fuck your brains out. Show me the difference between this and us. I've been here myself, you know that, but I suspect even the very first time it wasn't quite the same."

"Your *girlfriend*?" Niels swivels his hips to avoid my seeking reach.

"You're one sick bastard, Rick." Bendt braces his hand to shove off the bed. "I'm not up for being in the middle of some crazy shit. No wonder she almost ripped your ugly face off. Sorry, Star."

Rick's palm lands on his friend's shoulder, preventing the smaller man from leaving. "It *is* insane, I know. We know. But I'm asking you as my friend. Do this. Show me."

Silence stretches long enough for all four of us to grow uncomfortable.

Then Niels and Bendt exchange a glance and a shrug. "Fine. But get your hand off me or my hard-on will never come back to life."

"If that's a problem, you're definitely not commanding the same attention I do." Rick leans down to kiss my cheek then returns to his post in the cramped space. This time he shoves his shirt up his abs and unfastens his pants.

I lick my lips, craving another taste of him.

"Over here, sweetheart." Niels reminds me of my duty. The first time I've lost focus on a customer's needs. I blush as I allow him to guide my hand to his shaft.

"You've always enjoyed Bendt watching you fuck me." I purr as I caress his respectable length. "I should charge you extra for a larger audience."

His full laughter booms through the loft. Until it morphs into a choke when I rotate my hand to cup his balls while I massage the base of his erection.

"Toss me a couple condoms, Rick." I can't reach the drawer with his gorgeous frame in my way. "Lube too, please. They like to take me together."

"Jesus." He removes the items from their drawers and sets them beside my hip without hesitation.

"Don't act like a saint, Ricky." Bendt groans when I prep his shaft. "You know where the goodies are. You've used them too."

"Sure have." Rick's grin has a feral tinge when he attempts to smile through his arousal. "And loved every minute."

"Yes." Niels grunts when I roll the latex over his cock, following behind with my mouth. "Not too much of that tonight. I want to fuck your pussy, Star."

Instead of teasing him or bringing him to the edge first, as I might with Rick, I indulge Niels' requests. I roll onto my back and smile, welcoming him between my thighs. He's warm and solid. The pressure of his body over mine makes me sigh.

Both of these friends are easy customers. No major life drama, no odd hang-ups compel their visits. They like to fuck without promises and have things as they like. I can accommodate their tastes without much effort since I've learned their preferences over time.

I wonder what Rick will think when I allow them to make me the filling in a decadent sandwich. I enjoy the men bracketing me as they slake their desires. I suspect he'll revel in observing our abandon. There's only one way to know for sure.

I reach out, my hand searching beside my hip where Brendt kneels. I encircle his sheathed cock with my hand. He hisses when my fingers clench in response to Niels guiding his erection inside me from his place between my spread knees.

He doesn't get far before he lodges within me.

Niels retreats, slathering his palm with a dollop of lube from the tube by his knee. He works two gelled fingers into my opening before situating himself inside me once more. A step Rick has never had to take. The pressure of Niels' shaft stretching the swollen walls of my pussy elicits a soft moan just before he begins rocking, shuttling his erection in and out of me.

"You're so hot, Star." He groans as he buries himself fully then withdraws until just the mushroomed head of his cock remains fitted to my core. The space between our bodies allows Rick and Brendt to watch my breasts jiggle in time to their friend's thrusts.

I can't help myself. My gaze shifts to Rick. He's fixated on the spectacle before him, his hand stroking his full length, squeezing the leaking head of his cock before gliding to the base again.

If it were him riding me, he'd drop low and close, brushing our chests together, scooping me into his arms and relishing the moment we joined as tight as possible. I close my eyes and gasp when the image ignites my senses.

"You like having him here." It's not a question. The tension in my pussy doesn't lie and Niels can't miss the graduating clench of my ringed muscles.

No sweet, sultry kisses prevent me from responding. "God yes."

He pumps faster inside me as Brendt inches closer, thrusting into my hold.

"Do you want me to suck you?" I ask, my question interrupted by the force of Niels' lunges.

"Not tonight, Star." He nudges Niels' hip until the man acknowledges his cue.

Strong arms band around me. The world turns as Niels rotates us both. I brace myself on his solid chest and ride, grinding my aching pussy on his shaft. I crave relief as much as they do now. I'm sure we can reach satisfaction together, mutual absolution of our similar urge.

Then maybe, if I'm lucky, Rick will tend to the needs of my soul.

I tuck my head onto Niels' shoulder, presenting my rump to Brendt.

"You're sure you don't care if I fuck your girlfriend in the ass?" Brendt strokes my flank while he debates.

"Does she enjoy it?" Rick's tone is gravelly. I peek at him in time to catch him strangle the base of his cock, making the shaft seem huge as it strains against his grip. I wish he'd let me taste him while his friends take their fill.

He shakes his head with a tiny movement the other two guys don't seem to notice.

"Hell yeah." Niels interrupts his friend. "Most of the time she comes with us. I swear it wouldn't matter what we asked of her. She loves making us lose control, having the power to grant our wishes. Don't you, baby?"

"Mmm." No sense in denying it.

"Do it." Rick nods at Brendt then reaches in his bunched underwear to cup his heavy balls. Curious, excited and controlled, he makes me delighted to be his.

I smile into his eyes as the blunt cap of Brendt's cock builds pressure on my anus.

"Let him in." Rick coaches me, eliminating any pain I might have incurred due to my distraction.

I relax.

Brendt curses as he sinks several inches inside my ass.

The three of us hiss when his cock penetrates deep enough to prod Niels' shaft through my tissues. The friends pack me full, increasing the friction on each other even as they stimulate me from every angle.

Brendt cups my shoulders in his palm, allowing him to drive deeper. Niels wraps his long fingers around my hips then lifts his pelvis, fucking me from below. The rhythm they set has me bracing myself on Niels' chest to rock back against the impact of their thrusts.

I lean on one elbow, checking to make sure Niels isn't uncomfortable. The only sign of distress on his face comes from his single-minded focus on drilling his cock inside me over and over, racing toward the pinnacle of his pleasure.

My free hand snakes between us to spread the lips of my pussy around his shaft. His bulging veins stroke my knuckles on every pass. I gather wetness trickling between us and use it to slick my finger, which circles my clit.

I have to hurry, they aren't going to last long. Damn but they feel good inside me. I want to come with them, share their experience. I need Rick to see that even my passion with customers can't compare to the affection between us.

"You like him watching, don't you?" Brent whispers near my ear, on the far side of my head as though it were possible to hide his taunting from Rick in our tight confines. "You're about to squeeze me in half."

I moan when a particularly hard thrust from Niels causes my fingertip to career off target. I concentrate on maintaining a soft swirl over the knot of my clit while the two men fill me with their eager energy.

"Give Rick what he's looking for," Neils chimes in, not bothering to pitch his request low. "Come on our cocks, Star. Let him see what a bad girl you are."

"No." The ferocity of Rick's bark startles me.

The guys lose their pace inside me for a moment.

"She's good. So good." He soothes my trepidation with a smile then jerks his cock faster. "Show me how sweet you are. Show me how you sacrifice yourself to the whims of your clients. Show me how you absorb their ecstasy and make it yours."

Every bit of his understanding raises my arousal, pushing me closer to the brink of orgasm. I grind my pussy on Niels' cock and clench around Brendt's intrusion. The edge of pain only enhances the sensations pummeling me.

"There you go, love." Rick groans when I begin to mewl, the foreign sound escaping my chest before I can stop it.

I press on my clit more insistently, rubbing the button with the extra pressure I need. My muscles strain, my back arches and my eyes fly open, wide. My gaze is glued to the victory in Rick's stare when I come apart.

I hardly notice Brendt and Niels pumping their condoms full, emptying their come in my pussy and ass simultaneously.

It must have been good for them. Neither one budges, aside from the heavy pants squishing me between their chests for several minutes.

I squirm, trying to catch sight of Rick. What will I find in his eyes now?

What if it's not acceptance?

I can hardly catch my breath. Unlike last night, it has more to do with Brendt's weight than the euphoria flooding my veins.

"You're crushing my girlfriend." Rick pushes Brendt to the side, freeing me.

"How can you date a woman who loves banging other men?" Brendt grimaces. "Shit. None of my business. Brain not really functioning right now."

Rick laughs. "It's okay. The two of you fuck her together. Don't tell me you can't feel each other's cocks rubbing through the thin barrier of her body."

I shudder at the idea.

"I can. It feels good." Brendt actually manages to blush a little.

Imagine that.

"So does that mean you're hot for Niels?" Rick rolls his eyes when both men glare at him. "I didn't think so. Look, there's a difference between slaking desire—doing whatever it takes to get off and…how I feel for her."

"I, uh, thought that shit was fake." Neils scrubs his face. "This is all there is, the thrill of a massive orgasm. The instant when you fear your heart will explode from the magnitude of your climax."

"I did too." Rick sighs. "You haven't met the right person yet."

"And you have?" Brendt caves when he notes the serious glint in Rick's eyes. "Lucky bastard."

"I wanna see."

We all turn to face Niels. My jaw hangs open. He can't be serious.

"We did you a favor."

I giggle hard enough to force his softening cock from my grasp.

"Not saying I didn't enjoy it. But still…" Niels persists. "Show *us* the difference."

I hold my arms out, open to Rick. I need him. The relief Brendt and Neils provided hasn't extinguished the ache low in my belly.

"You're don't mind sharing this with them?" His friends scramble from the bed as he lowers himself into my hold. "Our magic?"

"I'm kind of proud of it." I turn pliant in his arms, softening when he nuzzles my mouth, sipping from my lips. "I missed you."

"Me too." He aligns our bodies until there's not a modicum of space between us.

I trace the pulse hammering at the base of his neck. Everything about him feels right. Perfect.

"Damn that was hot." He pauses to gather my breasts in his hands before lowering his mouth to suckle first one then the other. "You took Brendt nice and easy in your ass even when they stretched you. Gorgeous."

"Want to try it?" I fold my legs until my knees are pressed close to my chest.

Rick hooks his elbows behind my angled calves, spreading my pussy wide. "Maybe later."

He angles his hips, guaranteeing the head of his cock notches in the entrance of my pussy the next time I squirm.

"I need you inside me." I strain my neck to capture his mouth, sliding my tongue inside.

"He fucks her bare?"

I twitch at the question from Brendt. I'd forgotten the two men existed.

"Can't stand for there to be anything between us." I can't tell if he's talking to me or his friends.

"Me either," I whisper.

I lift my ass, using my legs to lever me closer to the man I've come to adore. He allows me to slip my pussy over his cock like a warm, silky glove without ever looking away from me.

He stares so deep into my eyes I can see the flecks of black and gold highlighting his irises. I spear my fingers into his hair, tugging him lower. I devour his groan as he begins to move, shoving his cock as deep as possible into my clutching pussy.

Long, languid glides of his ass drive him into and out of me. He teases me by poking his bulbous tip at the very opening of my cunt. Neither of us can stand that torture for long.

He curses then slides to the hilt, slapping my opened ass with his balls. He nibbles my jaw up to my ear while he glides inside me, inspiring us both to wild abandon. I'm afraid my nails will leave bright red marks on his back, but I can't stop myself from raking his shoulders in an attempt to urge him nearer.

It would be impossible for him to meld us any tighter.

"Fuck yes." He shouts when the bite of pain mixes with our euphoria.

Not one to be outdone, he buries his face against my neck, nipping and sucking until I'm sure I'll bear a token of his possession for days to come. The idea of his mark, his claim, instigates an explosion that rattles my teeth with its force.

I scream as I come.

Rick barely makes it through the strongest of my

contractions, which hug him, before yanking his cock from my pussy. He kneels above me, his head thrown back. Impressive cords form in his thick neck as he roars.

Pearly cum jets from his straining erection, decorating me with strand after strand of opalescent fluid. My thighs, my mound, my tummy, my breasts and even my lip bear the proof of his ownership.

I stare into his smoky eyes while the echoing grunts of his friends fade into the distance like background music. Neither of us blink until someone speaks, shattering the perfectness of the moment.

"Shit. I think we owe you double for tonight, Star." Niels clutches his chest as he struggles to catch his breath.

"I'll call it even if you inform Tommy that Rick won't be coming back to work tonight." I murmur without looking away from the man still shuddering between my thighs.

"Deal." Bendt grins. "We'll cover his shift."

"Thank you," we whisper in unison then treat each other to a grin.

Our smiles interlock as we indulge in another long, gentle kiss. When we finally break apart, sometime later, Niels and Brendt have slipped out.

"I guess they got what they came for." I stroke Rick's disheveled hair into some semblance of order.

"So much less than I need," he growls.

"How so?" I've never hoped to be all someone requires so badly before.

"They don't take their time. It's like they don't have the urge to touch every inch of your soft skin like I do. They don't...relish the satisfaction. It's a simple release for them. A thrill, for sure. But not the kind that rocks your foundation." Rick promises, "I know the difference. I love sex. The thrill of a conquest. I adore women in general and the compliment a lady pays when she bends over for me. But nothing is as good as when I'm with you."

"It's like the difference between eating a TV dinner and a Thanksgiving banquet."

"Exactly, love."

This time we both understand it's not a pet name anymore.

It's the truth.

Pure.

Simple.

"I can do this, Sarah." Rick kisses me softly, rocks me against his chest, his sticky cum hot and slick between us. "We can make this work. If you're still interested…"

"I am." I bite my lip.

"Then why are you so tense?" Rick rubs my shoulders, erasing the rigidity there.

"It has to go both ways." I search my heart and soul for any hidden objections and find none. He's one hundred percent correct. Sex and love are distinct. When they accompany each other, nothing can compare. Still, it's possible to have one and not both. Maybe even necessary for some people.

Like Rick's parents.

Maybe like Rick himself. I have to accommodate his fears even if he never chooses to exercise his options. Otherwise, I'm afraid I may doom our relationship before it begins.

"Huh?" Rick is so fucked out he struggles to surface from the residual pleasure turning his bones and brains to mush.

"You don't have to give up other women." I wink at him. "I know you like a little variety from time to time. Mari's jealous you visit me so often instead of sharing your studliness with her once in a while."

His gorgeous eyes brighten as he considers my proposition. "You mean that? Please promise me you aren't just saying it to be fair. You really believe it's possible?"

"Of course. As long as you're safe." I shrug. "I'll do whatever it takes to have the best chance at making this a success. The forever-after kind. All I ask is that you're honest with me. No hiding your needs. No lying about our nature."

"Always. I haven't craved something this bad since I was fifteen and saw a candy- apple red Yamaha XJ650R SECA in the showroom."

"You're quite a window shopper. Something about goods behind glass turns your head every time." I trace his spreading smile.

"Yeah, and I'm pretty determined to have what I lust after too."

"So you rode that motorcycle around like a badass when you were younger, huh?"

"Damn straight." He tips my face up until I can't avoid staring into his unblinking eyes. "I still have it. Still love it as much as I did that first moment. More even because of all we've been through together."

"But I've seen you riding a Ducati to work when you're running late. Or even your bicycle on spring evenings."

"That doesn't mean I love the original any less. I'm a little big for it now." He pats his six-pack, making me squirm as I remember how it flexes while he fucks me. "It has a place of honor in my garage."

"Good to know." I wince as I debate whether to speak my mind.

"Don't start pretending now. You suck at it anyway." Rick kisses me so sweetly I can't restrain myself. His thumb brushes the tension at the corners of my mouth. "Tell me what's causing this."

"Brace yourself." I grin at the hitch in his breath. "I think I'm in love with you."

"You're not sure? I can do some more convincing…" He rolls over until he's propped on one elbow, peering down into my eyes. "I love you, Sarah. Without a hint of doubt. I'll do whatever it takes to prove it to you. Anything to keep you in my life. Like this."

"Maybe you should leave me a big tip." I laugh when he tickles me. Until the teasing gesture turns smoky with desire—never far from the surface when we touch.

"Nope." He nips my neck then whispers in my ear. "You can't buy love, remember?"

"Yes." I plant my palms on his chest and shove, budging him a fraction of an inch so I can stare straight into his eyes when I promise, "But I can give it freely."

"And I'm sure now that I can accept." He leans in to rest his forehead on mine. "If you'll take mine in return."

"I do."

It isn't until the full rays of daylight pierce my window that we cross through my window.

Together.

Free For All

Jayne Rylon

My hair flutters around my face. It makes me wish I could close my eyes to savor the breeze generated by the downhill run on my bicycle. Each lovely arched bridge that spans one of the canals crisscrossing the heart of Amsterdam in a network of black ribbons is an exercise in work and reward. I strain uphill and savor the moments of coasting the exertion affords. For so long now I've concentrated on industry that I'd almost forgotten how magical it can be to squander a Sunday afternoon on pure, unadulterated pleasure. I'm ready to glide for a few hours.

I hum to myself as I recall my decadent indulgence of late. If a woman could overdose on bliss, I'd have dropped dead weeks ago with an enormous grin etched onto my face. I sigh as I watch the flex and play of Rick's muscles, evident despite the tailored clothing covering them. In front of me, he pumps the pedals of his flame-painted bike as though they hardly resist. His ass looks amazing in his slim-cut jeans, and I thank the universe again for the innate style of European men. Even a man's man like Rick never appears sloppy, only casually sexy.

As if he can read my thoughts, and lately I think he must, he glances over his broad shoulder and grins. "Keeping up, Sarah?"

I shiver violently. The thrill of my real name on his lips threatens to have me crashing into the public urinal on the corner of the street. The gray plastic modules usually make me giggle—

especially when tourists gawk, imagining a man holding his cock right there on the street as if it's scandalous to succumb to the call of nature. However, I don't find the idea of getting up close and personal with the fixture amusing in the least.

Rick's lyrical chuckle carries to me on the wind. It might as well be a caress lavished from his hand. He's perfected the use of those two syllables to drive me mad, often shoving me into orgasm as he groans them in a reverent chant in sync with the crash of his hips into the cradle of my thighs.

I crank up the speed, loving the tightening of sinew. After all the amazing home-cooked meals I've shared with Rick, toning is probably a good thing. Not that he doesn't help me burn off calories in much more sinful ways. I wobble, pressing my legs together as best I can to soothe an entirely different caliber of ache. I won't lie. The pressure from the seat on my swollen pussy isn't bad.

I pull alongside Rick.

He scans my flush and the ghost of my hard nipples, which poke against my cashmere sweater through the lacy bra beneath. His cheeks are stained red and I'm sure it's from more than the rush of air against his handsome face.

"Better watch where you're going, mister."

"I know exactly where this road leads, Sar-ah." So in tune with me, he can decipher every nuance in my expression—the reactions of my body—even when I attempt to blank them out to throw him off. It frightened me at first, his ability to know me. Now I've come to adore such intimacy, more intense than anything we shared in our early days through my window.

It has comforted me to wrap his understanding around me like a fuzzy blanket through the cold winter months of our bizarre courtship. With spring on our doorstep, I wonder what new buds will sprout while I pray the universe won't shout, "April Fool's!" then inform me the happiest period of my life has been some cosmic prank.

Despite the constant reassurance of this increasing bond, I'm afraid to believe it's true. Genuine. Eternal. Because I don't think I could survive losing Rick once I've claimed him as mine. Like severing a limb or tearing out my heart, it would cripple me. Destroy me. Utterly. I can't do that. Not after my painstaking attempt to remain solo. What other choice did I have after choking on a gluttony of loss as a teenager?

I refuse to dwell on the past today. Instead I look forward, zooming toward happiness and the bright green of a new season of my life.

"First one to Centraal Station wins." I stand up, harnessing increased leverage to rocket me onward through the dappled light splattering on the cobblestones we roll over with a cathartic rumble.

"What's the prize?" His laughing shout draws glances from couples strolling hand in hand down Paleisstraat toward Dam Square, likely aiming for breakfast from one of the sinful *pattiseries* lining the narrow alley. Scrumptious.

I don't bother to answer. He knows. We've played all sorts of games. I would swear we've left no sexual stone unturned except he surprises me every morning with the dawning of his creativity and our limitless desire for each other.

I spot the tram half a block away and zip across its path with a wave to the driver. Rick follows, gaining ground. Heat rises up my thighs. I lean into the handlebars as though that will improve the aerodynamics of my traditionally clunky bike. I blame the drag caused by the outrageous faux flowers woven around the pink frame and my pretty wicker basket attached to the front when Rick encroaches in my peripheral vision.

Up ahead, the hulking stone mountain of the train station comes into view, complete with the tangle of transportation pipelines pouring people into the beast from every possible approach like a faucet stuck on full blast. Trams, roadways, sidewalks, bike lanes and canals all converge here, in the very core of the city.

Just when I'm sure Rick will flash past me for the win, I hear him call my name, this time without a hint of playfulness. "Sarah! Look out!"

The shrill alarm of his bell peals without any effect. A rogue tourist on a rented, candy-apple red Mac bike bobs and weaves the wrong way through our lane. Visitors are more dangerous than the tram. The only thing in the city with the right of way over bicycles at least follows some rules.

Sure enough—in hideous slow motion—the newcomer

topples. He wipes out, splaying the carnage of his pride across the narrow roadway.

Without sufficient distance to brake, I yank my legs up to my chest and squeeze through the gap between his tennis shoes, which point straight up into the air, and the side of a building. Nightmare visions of a thirty-bike pile-up *à la* the Tour de France zip through my mind as I come to a stop past the tangle of man and metal, out of the trajectory of the steady stream of cyclists approaching. When I glance over my shoulder, Rick swerves to a graceful stop, hopping off his bike.

"Are you all right?" He hauls the heavy fellow to his feet as though he weighs nothing. I make a mental note to worship those sleek muscles later. One good turn deserves another after all.

As the guy tries to settle his shortish, dark, sprinkled-with-a-touch-of-silver hair, Rick dusts off the unfortunate man's back and ass. His locks persist in their adorable spiky disarray, despite his attempts to snuff all the flair from them.

"Yeah, thanks. I'm good." The tourist flinches from Rick's helpful hand when it nears the seat of his pants.

His American accent comprises a less accurate indication of his origin than that silly evasive maneuver. Puritan beginnings make visitors from across the Atlantic as easy to spot as if they had stars and stripes tattooed on their foreheads.

When I catch Rick's gaze, he rolls his eyes.

I can't suppress a chuckle.

The man glances toward me and smiles. Wide.

Rick perks up. He speaks low to the visitor, too hushed for me to eavesdrop.

The guy's eyes bulge along with his pants. Road rash forgotten, he tries to disguise his crude junk adjustment behind surreptitious flicks of his fingers over the khaki of his cargo shorts, which have long since been tugged into some semblance of order. Or at least as close as the baggy, disheveled fabric can get anyway.

From the inside pocket of his light blazer, Rick withdraws a business card. He slips it to the crash victim before clapping him on the shoulder. "Have a great vacation, Alex."

"T-thanks." The tourist doesn't take his glittering eyes off me long enough to blink.

Rick walks his bike beside me. "Blow him a kiss and I guarantee you'll find him outside your window tomorrow night."

"So what are you now? My pimp?" The twinge in my chest is quick yet fierce.

"Since when are labels our thing? I'm proud of you." Rick nuzzles my temple. "Besides, I have a feeling you'd be good for him. You could change his life forever. The poor bastard. He's clueless. And…well, I'd be lying if I said I don't get off on how desperately other guys covet what I have."

"Really?" A skim of my thigh against his crotch confirms the desire roughening his voice.

"Fuck, yes." He shifts far more stealthily than our new friend and clears his throat.

Before thinking, I open my mouth. "You know…"

"What?" He traces my cheekbone when I hesitate.

Why not go with it? I grin, slow and sure. "There are plenty of swingers' clubs around the city."

When Rick doesn't answer right away, my stomach sours. Have I found the thing that will turn him off? It's been looking as likely as a successful hunt for a unicorn or maybe a five-headed dragon, but I can't help myself. I worry I'll stumble over his limits one of these days. And then it will be too late to rescind the offensive offer. Maybe it already is. "Never mind."

"No."

My gaze flies to the flush livening his tanned skin.

"Don't do that, Sarah. When will you learn to trust me? I'm not about to bolt, for Christ's sake. Give me a second here, okay? You plant sexy ideas like that in my imagination and it's going to take me a few seconds to file them away for later. I don't relish the thought of coming in my pants in the middle of all these strangers."

"Finally something that doesn't flip your switch?" I raise an eyebrow, savoring the lightness I haven't ruined yet.

"Hussy." He yanks me to him in a bear hug and plants a warm, lingering kiss on my parted lips.

Someone passing by in a pedicab rickshaw whistles. I totally agree. The steam billowing from my ears might make a similar sound if I were a cartoon hooker instead of a real life sex worker.

"I take it back. Even erupting like a teenager could be hot

with you by my side. When we're together, that's all that matters. You're like some crazy sex drug." He squints then shakes his head. "A love drug."

We've both enjoyed plenty of romps in our lives. Release. Fun. Comfort. Companionship. No one knows better than I how many different facets can be cut into the act. None of those myriad experiences reflect with the intensity of our bond, which is easily bright enough to blind. It litters the landscape with rainbows every time we touch, no rain required.

"You know. We could turn around, go home and leave the canoeing for another day." I nibble on his lower lip, imagining a sleepy day off—sweet, slow sex followed by nature lulling us with the rocking of my houseboat. It rises and falls on tiny waves caused by vessels trundling down the Amstel, oblivious to the passion we share inside. Steamy windows create the only evidence of our lust for the captains with eagle eyes or tourists with telephoto lenses floating just outside our walls.

Rick moved in over a month ago, despite his initial kneejerk protest to the cohabitation proposal I'd blurted out during our romantic Valentine's Day trip to Schagen. That excursion had included an introduction to his divorced parents. It had taken a killer massage with a spectacular happy ending to melt the tension seeing them—together yet not—had infused in his shoulders.

Still, by then neither of us could remember the last time he'd stayed at his apartment during the days we generally dream through as creatures of the night. He conceded it seemed wasteful to renew his lease when I'd purchased our sanctuary, the profits from our Kinkmas pageant finally having convinced the previous owner to sell out.

I can't suppress a smile when I think of his patched motorcycle jacket hanging on the hook by the front door or his lucky beer stein in the cupboard. Not to mention the butterflies that assault me every time I notice the little red scuff my nail polish inflicted on the pretty butterscotch paint of the galley when he pinned my hands above my head and fucked me against the wall before we'd finished dinner one random evening.

He evaluates the gleam in my eye before groaning.

"Tempting. But no. You're going to love the wetlands. I can't believe you've never visited. We've been so busy lately. This will be a perfect getaway." He drops his persuasion to a whisper. "Just imagine the sounds of the birds, our oars dipping in the water and the rustle of reeds. Deep lungfuls of fresh, sweet air."

Damn, he does understand me. It takes all my fortitude not to swoon. "I'm sure you can find other ways to relax me."

His Adam's apple bobs beneath light strokes of my fingertips. A strangled moan doesn't keep him from shaking his head. "Nope. You're not going to ruin my surprise."

I glance at the pack strapped to the back of his bike. What could he have in there? "In that case, we'd better hurry. I think the ferry is about to dock."

"Do over!" he yells as he jets off in one fluid motion.

"No fair." It's hard to grumble through my laughter. "I already won."

"A technicality." He shakes his head, picking up speed. "Best two out of three. Ready, set…"

My knees jelly, cementing my loss. Good thing I'm sure his prize is guaranteed to be of the win-win variety.

"**W**HATEVER OUR SOULS ARE MADE OF,
HIS AND MINE ARE THE SAME."
~**E**MILY **B**RONTË"

After a mad dash to the landing, a brief trip across the river then a vigorous ride to the side of the road beneath a weathered sign that reads *Watergang*—seemingly in the middle of nowhere—I follow my boyfriend inside a tiny cafe. How odd to think of him like that. I've had plenty of lovers. Never a man I'd call a partner. Certainly not some kind of relationship another shade toward sentimental on the spectrum of attachment.

Girlfriend seems an appropriate tag for me. In this, I'm practically an infant.

"Rick!" An older gentleman perches on a slanted stool at the bar. The wood is so dark, details disappear in the shadows. Something about the dim, slightly musty establishment puts me instantly at ease. Close scrutiny is impossible in these conditions. The owner takes off his wire-rimmed glasses, sets aside his newspaper then combs his fingers through the sparse white tufts that allow his shiny crown to peep through like the sun on a partly cloudy afternoon.

"Come on. Just a few minutes, I promise." Rick captures my hand before I can reassure him we have all day. The rest of our lives, maybe. I hope.

Floor tiles, many cracked or dinged, click against the low

heel of my boots as we shrink the space between us and the man inspiring Rick to smile warmly. His loose-limbed swagger holds none of the dread that had bound him when we dined with his biological family, yet ten seconds is enough to tell me this man, this place is important to him too.

"So, is this the reason you've been absent lately?" Elderly people fascinate me with their frankness. It's as though they don't have time to waste on circuitous paths paved with politeness. The thick Dutch he poses his question in reminds me we've left the city behind. A few miles can make a big difference. I wonder how much Rick will admit to his less cosmopolitan mentor about me and my profession. Can he still be proud of me, even here?

"Do you blame me, Adelbert?"

"Not in the least." The older man squints at me then nods. "She's as beautiful as you claimed. Maybe more. This is your special window lady, yes?"

Several vertebrae in my neck crack when I whip my stare between them both.

"Absolutely. I'd like to introduce you to Sarah." Rick nudges me toward the gentleman with a supportive hand on the base of my spine.

Adelbert reaches for my fingers more deftly than I would have believed possible to press a kiss to my knuckles. "Enchanted, dear."

"I could say the same." I'm not sure what makes me lean in and hug him, but I've long since learned to trust my instincts. "Why do I suspect I have you to blame for teaching Rick to be so devilishly charming?"

If I'm not mistaken, a blush stains the older man's cheeks. Adorable.

"He's done his best with me. I think all those years of lectures are finally paying off." Rick's grin borders on stupid with affection. I can't help but fall a little more in love with him.

"I'm glad you listened to my advice, *zoon*." The smile Adelbert wings first at Rick then at me is bursting with kindness despite his very crooked front tooth. I'm surprised I don't melt into a puddle of goo on the uneven ceramic.

"Sarah hasn't spent much time beyond the city limits. Mind if

I show her around your big backyard?" Rick gestures to a map, shellacked to a board hanging on the wall, of the nearby nature preserve. The yellow haze of polyurethane enhances its rustic charm though it makes the name *Oostvaardersplassen* more difficult to read.

"Of course not. Take the canoe, *zoon*. Today's a great day. Calm, warming up quite a bit and I hear the herons returning lately."

"It might just go from good to perfect, thanks." Rick strokes my hair, brushing an errant curl off my cheek. He tucks it behind my ear. "Why don't you have a cup of tea while I get everything ready? Adelbert has this amazing loose-leaf oolong with cinnamon I'm sure you'd enjoy."

"That does sound delicious." When he nudges my chin, I tip my lips up to accept his chaste kiss.

"I'll be right back." Our fingers drag across each other until the very last possible instant. The loss of my connection with him makes me sigh. He walks backward a few steps, staring into my eyes. "I promise I'll be quick."

Right before his shoulders bump the door, he turns and disappears out the rear entrance.

"Would you care for anything with your tea?" Adelbert shifts on his stool.

"Please, there's no need for you to get up. I can manage if you'll tell me where everything is." I pat his thigh. He concedes with a grateful nod. For a few minutes I take direction until savory steam rolls off the steeping brew, enough for two cups.

"You're very much alike." Adelbert leans his elbow on the counter, dropping his chin into his palm. He doesn't need his spectacles to peer at me, a little too close for comfort. "Generous. Intuitive. Careful yet strong. But you arrive there from such different approaches. It's quite fascinating."

My chuckle holds a note of nervousness, apparent even to me.

"Sorry, sorry." He relaxes. "Hazel would swat me upside the head for overanalyzing. I can't help myself though. Did you know there are only about two hundred residents in Watergang? It's not very often we meet new people out here. Especially not one as important as you obviously are to our Rick."

"Hazel?" Something in his voice sounds like mine when I refer to Neuhaus truffles. I latch on to the easiest of his revelations.

"My wife." His gnarled finger points generally toward the cash register behind the bar. I pause to examine the black-and-white photograph, yellowed like the map and bent on the edges. A gorgeous woman with a devious twinkle in her eye sits sideways across Adelbert's lap. Her hand rests over his heart. "We never had children. She loved Rick as if he were her own."

"How long were you married?"

"Fifty-three years." He shook his head. "Not long enough. She passed away two winters ago. Cancer."

"I'm sorry for your loss."

He accepts the tea and my condolences with a nod.

"So, you really are the one I owe for teaching Rick true love is possible, if rare." I sip the steamy drink then whisper, "Thank you. If it weren't for his persistence, I might never have come to believe it myself."

"From the first time he wandered out here, looking for peace, a quiet place away from the complications of urban life—something simpler than the confusion he'd always known—I wondered if it would be possible to convince Rick not all chaos is bad. Love is a fantastic mixture of untamed emotion. Exhilarating and frightening at times. Never boring." Adelbert smiles. "I should have known once he met the right woman, there'd be no resisting."

"How can you be so sure?" I run my fingertip along the delicate handle of my teacup. "About the right aspect, I mean. I'm not exactly every man's aspiration. A one-night fantasy, maybe."

"Don't apologize for who you are." Stern undertones catch me off guard. Hints of the man he used to be shine through Adelbert's gentle complacency. "Life is an adventure and he's chosen you to explore it with him. When you truly love someone, it's hard to imagine you're good enough. That you're everything they want or need. I never lived up to what my wife deserved. Hazel assured me she felt the same despite how often I insisted it was untrue. I would laugh. She was the best thing to happen to me. But I could see the serious cast to her pretty brown eyes when she would become distraught. She sincerely believed every unfounded worry."

"It'd be impossible for a woman not to fall madly in love with you, Adelbert." I lean over to kiss his forehead then clasp his free hand in mine as we sit, sipping our drinks in silence for a while. I squeeze his fingers when I notice the tremor in them. My mind spins through several possibilities for distraction until one seems right. "I noticed your orchids in the window. I love to stroll through the flower market and pick up pretties for my enclosed porch. I'm not sure I've ever seen a blue variety before."

"Oh that! It was introduced earlier this year. No one knows if they're really a new species or if the gardeners devised a method to infuse the blossoms with dye. Cynics are saying they're using a technique like when you put cut carnations in a vase with food coloring and the petals pick up the shades. They don't believe it's possible to for the universe to create something that vibrant." He meets my stare. "I can't wait for the plant to lose those petals."

"Why?" I tip my head and peer directly into his eyes.

"Because when it comes out of dormancy and I see the blooms again, I'm positive they'll be bright blue. I might have joined the doubters in my younger years until my Hazel converted me to optimism. Thank you for reminding me of that." He shakes his head as though coming out of a daze before gifting me with a smile that lights up the room. "You must make a fortune through that window of yours."

"She's very popular in the district." Can I be imagining the way Rick's chest puffs up at that?

It's hard to see more than his silhouette with the sunlight limning his frame. Maybe the open door had something to do with the obliteration of the shadows. Either way, I'm glad to have him at my side once more. I snuggle into his embrace as he puts his arm around my shoulders.

"I don't doubt it. It took her less than ten minutes to have me spilling my guts." Adelbert releases my fingers then shoos us both with hands that seem less gnarled than before. "Enough chatting with an old fart. Go. Have fun. Enjoy the day and each other. *Zoon*, I hope you remember what your Aunt Hazel taught you."

"Yeah. I do." He refuses to meet my questioning gaze. "She also had impeccable timing though."

"True." Adelbert nods. "You'll know when it's right."

"Right for what?" I peek up but Rick avoids my glance.

"We'll be back for dinner if you'd like me to cook."

Dinner? It's not even lunch and I'm hardly Jane Goodall. I'm not sure I can survive an entire day in the wilderness.

Rick deflects my curiosity when he teases, "Sarah's pretty awful in the kitchen."

I smack his flat stomach with the back of my hand, drawing a laugh from the men on either side of me.

"Hey, we all have our faults. Adie is grumpy in the morning. I have too many to count. You're damn near flawless. Give me at least one thing to pick on you for. Deal with it."

I'll gladly take a little ribbing to put that amazingly imperfect smile on Adelbert's face once more. My new friend nods. "I'd enjoy your company very much. And that herbed chicken dish with the cheesy potato thing is pretty damn tasty. I'll prepare the ingredients."

"Deal." Rick rests his hand on Adelbert's shoulder for a moment before angling toward the exit.

"See you soon." I hug the old man before threading my hand through Rick's proffered elbow. I rest my head on his shoulder for a moment or two, wondering how many times I'll be pleasantly surprised by the man I love during my lifetime. Though he consistently raises the bar on himself, he has no trouble clearing the hurdles.

**"WE LOVED WITH A LOVE THAT WAS
MORE THAN LOVE."
~EDGAR ALLAN POE**

I gawk as we cross a modest yet lush backyard to the narrow rivulet that dead ends behind Adelbert's cafe. A canoe drifts at the far reach of a lead rope, tied to the wooden slats that disappear into the shallow, black water. "We're going in there?"

"Are you concerned about the size of my ditch?" Rick grins. "It gets bigger. Don't worry, baby."

I can't help but laugh as we pass several overgrown flowerbeds. "It's not the largest I've seen but far from the smallest. Plenty to get the job done, I suppose."

"Thanks. I think. Anyway, this is how everyone gets around here. There aren't any streets that lead to the main square of town. You could cut across the islands from house to house. This is faster." He gestures toward the old church steeple in the distance. "And it's a hell of a lot more fun than hopping in a car, or riding the tram, to a crowded market anyway."

"I trust you." I grasp his hand then allow him to lower me into the wobbly canoe.

"Good. Stay in the center." He hands me an oar. "And when you have to duck for a bridge, don't lean to the side unless you feel like swimming. It might be a little chilly for that today."

He squats to drop his backpack into the space between us

then slides onto his seat in the canoe as if it were as stable as one of the cement benches we've cuddled on in Vondelpark. I follow his lead, paddling equally on the opposite side of our pod. We slice through the glassy surface, working together. Water ripples around us, lulling me.

The quaint gathering of houses could be a Vermeer come to life or maybe Jacek Yerka's *The Spring Labryinth*, which I saw on special exhibition at the Stedelijk once. Exquisite fauna ranges from the natural sprawl of water lilies to the charming potted plants on the docks. Vines climb wooden bridges—vastly different in their design and coloring—which span from neighbor to neighbor, ensuring each manufactured island is anchored in the surreal landscape to another. Periodically we pass a windmill that still pumps water from the synthetic land, relegating it to its proper place in the dike.

I haven't felt such a strong affinity, a rightness, since the moment I stepped onto my houseboat during a real estate tour, or maybe since the night I slept with Rick for the first time outside my window on Christmas Eve.

He tucks his paddle over his lap then leans forward until his nose must meet his knees, impressing me with his limber flexibility. "Watch your head, Sarah. This one is extra low."

I follow his lead, unfolding once sunlight warms the back of my neck, proclaiming it's safe. We continue to wind through the maze of still water in silence.

A cat watches us pass from his perch on a crumbling stone wall like a sentinel guarding his kingdom from invaders. He stares with a level of haughty derision only a feline can muster. I'm so focused on the village, the assortment of ducks bobbing beside us, and the gorgeous old church rising from the fabricated land that I could never navigate the return to Adelbert's cafe on my own. Luckily I won't have to.

Rick doesn't turn around when we come to a larger channel. Instead, he raises his voice. "I'll need your help for a few minutes. Then you can go back to sightseeing and letting me do most of the work."

If he were closer, I'd spank him with my paddle for that irreverent tone. Not that it would do a lick of good against his solid derriere. Still, it could be fun. An idea for later…

"We're going to cross Kanaaldijk. This one heads straight into Amsterdam so traffic is steady. Mind any larger boats and their wake. It's warming up out here but I still wouldn't want you soaking, exposed to the breeze. After this, we'll be set."

"Aye, aye, captain."

He laughs but not for long. Together we dip our oars deeper and pull, propelling our craft across the much wider waterway, battling modest waves that feel enormous in the little boat. The exertion keeps me toasty. Or maybe that's a side effect of studying the interplay of Rick's fine muscles beneath his light jacket. Damn, he's gorgeous.

Without instruction I match my strokes to his so we glide steadily. My paddle mirrors his to ensure our trajectory remains a straight line. Without me, he'd be turning circles. Same goes double for me.

As we continue, cottages grow sparse then fade away altogether. Now it's just the two of us, floating through this strange, quiet paradise. The splash of disturbed frogs cannonballing into the marsh and the frequent call of a host of waterfowl herald our passage. I recognize the bitterns and cranes that occasionally visit my houseboat's deck.

I gasp in surprise when we round a bend and a lean cow munches on grass less than a foot away at the edge of her spongy roost on the bog island. For a quarter of an hour or more, we enjoy the natural songs without interruption. Until Rick breaks our comfortable hush. He points with his oar. "See that streak of white? Over there?"

I peek up in time to descry the flash made by dark feathers covering a very large wingspan. The stark edging is almost as bright as the sunlight it blocks an instant before the bird disappears behind a tree at the edge of our liquid highway. "What was that?"

"A white-tailed eagle." His awed murmur comes low and fast. "People used to think they were extinct. I remember Adelbert telling me stories about them as though they were already legendary. I might not have believed him when he swore they'd take your breath away until I spied one myself. Larger, more pure and inspiring than any secondhand retelling could capture. That was not so long ago. Just a few years, I guess. The first naturally occurring mated pair since their decline was spotted here in this preserve."

Somehow it feels right that I met Rick about that time myself. Virginal white might not be my color of choice, but I think what we have might be more rare than even his beloved aviators.

"I helped Adelbert build shelters for them, raise awareness, things like that." He shrugs though I haven't said anything. "Not much, really. Now there are several dozen. The population is stronger every year."

"I believe that. Between the two of you, I bet you're capable of nurturing anything to its full potential."

"Let's hope so."

I'm not sure I heard him correctly. Before I can ask, he guides the bow of our craft into the reeds. "And they say women make bad drivers."

"Very funny." He latches on to a metal hoop, which dangles from a post I hadn't noticed beneath the brambles. "We're here."

"Where is this?" I scan the area. No landmarks make it appear different than the hectares of wilderness we passed along our route.

"I'm not sure it's anywhere in particular. Except exactly where we're meant to be." He climbs from the canoe, reaches for the backpack, straps it on then extends his hand.

I twine my fingers with his warmer ones and allow him to usher me onto not-quite-dry land. "I must have been in the boat a little too long. Feels like we're still moving. Just like home."

"It's not your imagination." He steals a quick kiss despite my attempt to turn the peck into something that lingers. "The bog islands are basically floating. If you jump up and down, you can feel them bounce."

My hand clenches on his when he demonstrates.

"Okay. Enough of that." I frown. "I'm afraid you'll fall right through."

"Uh, maybe in spots." He tosses me the asymmetrical grin I adore. "Stick to the path and you'll be fine."

"I'm not straying a step from your side." I follow close on his heels as he heads deeper inland. "You know where we parked, right?"

He doesn't bother to acknowledge my nerves. He marches

onward until the sea of reeds and plants threatens to swallow us. A faint trail marks the passageway.

"I have to admit Adelbert put on a pretty good show, though once you know him a little better, you'll spot his tells as easily as I did."

"What's that supposed to mean?" I nearly run into Rick's strong back when he pauses in front of me.

"He went all out for us, didn't he?" The faraway rasp of his question spurs me beyond the bounds of my patience. I squeeze past him, careful not to trod on the wildflowers in the early stages of unfurling. "He must have guessed I planned to ask you—"

"Ask me—?" When I see what's caught Rick's attention, I freeze in my tracks. "What's all this?"

"I wanted today to be special." The wistful note in his answer has me spinning from the gorgeous layout in front of me to observe him instead. "I counted on Adelbert to help me. But this…"

"It's amazing." I brace my palms on Rick's chest as I peek over my shoulder, afraid the vision might have disappeared like a mirage on a sweltering day. This rustic oasis is a fairy tale come to life. "Thank you."

A fresh clearing hosts a square canvas tent. Rusty buckets brimming with river rocks and gnarled branches that didn't survive the winter make impromptu sculptures, anchoring the structure against the occasional gust of wind. Flaps tied wide open with fraying rope allow me to spy netting that cascades inside over a shape I can hardly discern. "Is that…?"

"An old flat-bottom boat." Rick chuckles. "Sure is. Looks like Adie improvised to keep the mattress inside it dry. Probably easier to drag out here that way too. That wily old bastard. I just asked him to pitch a tent for us and leave a solar heater in case it was chillier than expected this afternoon. Didn't envision five-star accommodations."

"You planned to seduce me?" I plant a fist on my hip and stand akimbo.

"Well, sort of."

"Why not definitely?" My pout doesn't last more than a moment. It morphs into a delighted smile when he scoops me into his arms and charges toward the gauzy material.

"See what you made me do." He burrows through the gossamer layers of our fortress until he can plop me onto the mattress. The time it takes him to strip off his backpack and set it aside is long enough to have him pinching the bridge of his nose. "I intended to be gentle. Take my time."

"The painfully slow approach is overrated." I lunge for his jacket and manage to peel it halfway down his arms before he balks.

"Not today." He shakes his head as he retreats.

I notice a slight chill for the first time without him sharing my personal space.

"We're going to do this right." He's adorable when his serious side kicks in. The concentration with which he unlaces his boots and sets them aside in a perfectly aligned pair makes me want to ruffle his hair, or fall to my knees at his feet, I can't decide which. Maybe both.

I settle into the horseshoe of pillows mounded at one end of our boat bed and drink in the sight of my lover wandering around the tent, hopping from braided rug to braided rug in his socked feet. It's odd to lie back and let someone else set the scene for our erotic interlude. He frees the material entranceway then lets it drape closed, making sure the panels overlap.

Cut off from everything surrounding us, my world narrows to him and me. Exactly how I prefer it.

I kick off my shoes then tunnel beneath the snuggly-soft quilts covering the plush mattress. Extra care was taken to fill the gaps between the hull and the padding, leaving no shin-busting edges exposed. I could hibernate here and still be comfortable four months later.

One by one, Rick activates half a dozen battery-powered lanterns. I catalog the grace of his movements as he roams from beacon to beacon. The glow he gives birth to draws intricate designs on the roof of our cozy paradise. I study the interplay of shadows and light while he fiddles with the heater. I'm not sure if his success with the gadget or the presentation of his fine ass in those jeans as he bends over is responsible for the blast of toasty warmth that seeps straight through my pores to the marrow of my bones.

I can't help myself. Without conscious thought, I cup my breasts to soothe the ache he's inspired with his careful preparations and the only possible outcome of his efforts. His shoulders rise and fall beneath the force of his deep inhalation and slow release. A laser-beam stare singes me when he finally faces forward, witnessing my involuntary writhing and the naughty activity of my fingers.

"You're so gorgeous, Sarah."

"I could say the same of you." My gaze cruises from his prominent jaw to his thick chest, narrow waist and the displacement of his jeans, which appear to strangle the erection distorting the fabric in the neighborhood of his crotch.

"All your clients must tell you that, but it's true."

"Only most." I'm vain enough to enjoy hearing it. I won't remind him the rest of the guys say something more along the lines of, "That was the best blowjob I've ever had."

"I wish I could make you understand. You're everything I was afraid to hope for." He sinks onto the foot of the mattress then crawls toward me like a lion on the prowl. Confident, deliberate, unstoppable.

When will he pounce? Soon, I hope.

"You're the same for me." I don't resist when he comes over me, pressing me flat to the bed as he advances. It's a delicacy to surrender control. Through my window I'm always the one with the power, no matter what privileges I grant a customer. It's always on my terms. This is like walking a tightrope strung between two skyscrapers with no net to break my fall if things should go to shit. With Rick, I'm never afraid of the heights he lifts me to.

"I need to be closer to you." He kisses me long and slow as he descends, allowing me to bear his full weight. His hand rubs the bare patch of skin between the top of my jeans and the hem of my sweater, which he's nudged a few centimeters higher.

I spread my legs, welcoming him into the cradle of my thighs.

"Yes." He nips my bottom lip then sucks the sting into oblivion. Time slips away as we devour each other in an unending exchange of pleasure.

Suddenly, too much fabric creates an intolerable barrier between us. Perspiration breaks out on my back, reminding me of the rising temperature.

Rick grunts when I press on his shoulder, as if he's reluctant to surrender his position.

"Roll over," I whisper between mini-kisses. "I promise I'll make it worth your while."

He complies, his heavy-lidded eyes only adding to the swelter of our retreat. His sexy sprawl takes up most of the bed. I slip from beneath the unneeded covers and blanket him instead.

Strong arms band easily around my waist. The thick length of his cock creates the perfect hump to rub my pussy on while I taste him one more time. Only now, I don't stop with a nibble on his parted mouth or a swirl of my tongue over his. Instead, I skim along his jaw to his chin then lower down his neck.

His moan vibrates my lips. I pause to torture him. When he shivers beneath me, I smile against the curve of his shoulder.

"Screw slow and gentle." He tugs at his shirt. I refuse to budge and allow him room to disrobe.

"No, you had it right the first time." I toy with the skin just above his collar for a moment before flicking open the top button of his shirt. "Let me unwrap my present."

"*Verdomme.*" He chokes a little when I lap at the sexy dip in the base of his throat.

"Feels more like heaven to me." I thread the next button through its hole with trembling fingers. I can hardly believe I'm lucky enough to have this man all to myself. For now. A flash of him in the swingers' club we discussed earlier zips through my mind. Would it fill me with pride to watch him thrill someone else? Or would jealousy overcome my appreciation for his dissolute talents?

"Yes." He buries his fingers in my hair, massaging my scalp. All thoughts but here and now fade from my mind with the sure press of his hands.

I graze my teeth across the freshly exposed landscape of his firm pecs while I torture him with the unfastening of another few inches of his shirt. I worship the series of small hills that stand witness to the eons he spends training at the gym. I study him as though he's a statue come to life. Only the finest artist could have devised a form so spectacular. It's hard to pinpoint when my ideal for all things masculine became embodied by him. Any flaws I used to notice have long since faded into comfortable familiarity.

"Don't stop." He caresses my check. "Unless you'll let me return the favor."

"I'm not finished playing yet." I nip his belly, savoring his grunt and the involuntary thrust of his hips. The motion presses his abdomen to my face. "You can take a turn in a while."

"I hope my heart doesn't blow a gasket before then." He flings his arm over his eyes as though he can't bear to watch without wresting the lead from me.

"You'd never leave me hanging like that." I draw a heart around his belly button with the tip of my manicured index finger.

"You're making it hard." He groans.

"That's sort of the point." I cup him through his jeans, squeezing the length of his denim-clad cock while I lick a line just above his waistband.

"Sarah." His moan doesn't sound like a plea. He won't tell me what to do. The freedom to explore and touch as I see fit is a luxury I'm not often able to indulge. Satisfying other people's urges, fulfilling their wishes, is what I love to do. But here, with him, sex isn't a job. It's what I need.

I peel the flaps of his shirt to each side, revealing the full expanse of his chest. The sight has me grinding on his thigh in a slow circle destined to expand the wet spot forming on my lacy panties.

His nipples draw tight, tempting me beyond reason. I flick the flat of my tongue across one before consuming the other with a strong draw of my lips.

Rick's palm slaps on the mattress. His jaw clenches and his neck cords.

I straddle his narrow waist to shove the shirt from his shoulders. He lifts to facilitate the process, allowing me to slide the fabric down his ripped arms and off his wrists before flinging it to the far recesses of our shelter. The incline of his torso grants me better access. I suck on him, shifting from side to side, leaving my fingers to pinch and play when my lips migrate to his other nipple.

It's a pleasure most men deny themselves though I'm not sure why. All I know is that Rick has no such inhibitions. Hedonism never had a better mascot than him. Or maybe me. No, both of us together. I smile as I separate our bodies only long enough to strip my sweater off.

"Is that new?" He eyes my sheer black bra, littered with sequins and a sprinkle of pave diamonds. "I would remember if I had seen it before. You probably don't want me to rip it off you, right?"

"You're learning." I shimmy for him, loving the transfixed stare he latches on to the jiggling of my breasts. Best not to tempt him too much. I really do adore this addition to my lingerie hoard. "I think you deserve a reward."

I reach behind my back to unhook the garment, worth every exorbitant penny. Rick's tongue practically lolls from his mouth as he watches the show. I have to raise an eyebrow to keep him in place when he starts to sit up. I let the straps fall from my shoulders then peel the band from my torso. I keep one of my forearms pressed to my breasts to pin the garment in place.

He swallows hard.

I smile then let my hand drop, taking the delicate fabric with it. I barely have to lean forward before Rick lunges up, returning the attention I paid him. He cups my ribs in his broad hands as he situates my torso in the optimal position for his assault. I clutch his hair, pinning his face tight to my chest as he demonstrates impressive flair of his own.

"Mmph." Despite years of practice, even I can't decipher what he intended to say with his mouth full of my breasts. He ruins my concentration.

We laugh together. I separate us a fraction of an inch. His breath buffets my nipple, making it harder, if such a thing is possible. "I said, 'Please tell me that bra has matching panties.'"

"You wouldn't prefer me bare?"

"Shit, are you?" His hands travel down my back to my ass, anchoring me as he grinds us together.

"Why don't you find out?" I brace myself on one palm behind me even as he shifts, turning the tables. He looms over me, stealing one last taste of my lips before kissing a trail down the center of my belly. "Wait!"

He pauses when I squeak.

"There. Right there. Do that again." I nudge his head until his lips hover over the spot he'd inadvertently electrified. Just above my hipbone, toward my center an inch or two.

The rumble generated by his hum of approval threatens to send me into instantaneous orgasm. I try to relax, hoping to diminish the intensity. He refuses to allow me to hide behind the tools of my trade.

"No. Let me give you pleasure. Don't ever deny us that." He nuzzles my stomach, making me purr with the scrape of his slight scruff. "Please, Sarah."

I shudder, surrendering to the moment, when he tries again. Even if he tips me into bliss by accident, I can claw my way there again and again when he treats me like this—a treasure, a rare and priceless find.

As if he knows exactly how much I can stand, he shifts. His hands work the button of my jeans then slide the zipper low. He buries his face in the gap left behind, licking the edge of the black lace barely shielding my smooth, waxed mound from view.

I can't wait to model the rest for him. Squirming, I help him peel my skinny jeans from my hips, down my thighs then lift my legs for him to slip them off my feet. I hear the dull *thwap* of fabric landing in a pool somewhere outside our sphere of blended lust and love.

He massages my feet then my calves, paying homage to every square inch of me as though he's never before seen the flesh he so recently revealed. When he gets to my thighs, his thumbs pressing a trough through the knotted muscle there, he can't avoid peering at the pretty wrapping over the core of my body.

The tiny lace panel in front leads to an intricate web of satin strings. They give the impression of the traditional panty shape while leaving maximum skin bared. Each intersection of the wispy strands is embellished with a sparkling stone.

He traces one of the geometric displays.

"Are those real?" He tilts his head, appraising the garment like a true panty connoisseur.

"The diamonds?" I wink. "Yep. Actually, there's nothing fake on this body."

"Hard to believe nature can be this perfect." He leans in to lick one of the glittering rocks then the skin beside it. "Or this beautiful."

"They're custom made. I hoped to impress you."

"You always do."

He dusts kisses over the fabric, licking the spot directly above my clit.

"Rick!" I shift, restless, but he knows what I need.

"I want to eat you with these on." He carefully nudges the lace to the side, revealing my pussy to his hungry stare. With one finger, he traces my slit.

I whimper and buck.

"They're stunning when you dance." He bares his teeth in a grin that reminds me of the big bad wolf. I always thought Red went for the wrong guy.

The fire shining from the center of the diamonds has nothing on the inferno he stokes inside me when he dips his finger into the entrance of my pussy. He inserts the digit as he closes the gap between us. A stream of cool air escapes his lips and swirls over my clit a moment before he contrasts it with the wet heat of his lips.

He drives me insane as he works his hand and mouth in perfect counterpoint. He manipulates me from both inside and out until a telltale tightening ripples low in my pelvis. If he doesn't stop, I'll come.

I try to warn him. The only sound that emerges from my mouth is a low, throaty cry.

"Don't fight me." He pauses long enough to command my release. "Come, Sarah."

My body obeys him. My spine arches, lifting my shoulders from the mattress as I shatter. A quick burst of pleasure bleeds some of the tension from me. It only makes me regret I couldn't hang on longer and enjoy the act very few of my customers are likely to request.

"So sweet." Rick kisses my thighs as he carefully removes my expensive trappings.

My sigh escapes before I can stop it.

"What was that for?" He returns, kissing me softly. I can taste myself on his lips. Blended, we're my favorite flavor. I don't speak before he registers the longing in my eyes. "You want more of that?"

Is it greedy to admit it? Not with Rick. "Yes."

He shoves to his feet and strips off his jeans in one sure movement. He kicks the pants aside, toes off his socks and lies next to me, his head angled toward my feet. "I could taste you all day."

I yelp when he plants open-mouthed kisses on my sensitive flesh before diving back in as though he relishes the soft, moist flesh of my pussy on his face. It only takes a few seconds before slight discomfort caused by overstimulation morphs into fresh pleasure.

I set my sights on something else I crave. I tap his hip three times before he responds.

He lifts his head long enough to ask, "You want my cock, baby?"

My cheeks heat as I realize it's true. Not because I have to please him, though I hope I can, but because I need to fill myself with him in every way. His taste, his scent, his heat. "Give it to me. Please."

"Here you go." He nudges me until we lie on our sides. My head rests on his thigh. He holds my legs wide open as he returns his focus to laving every fold of my pussy with his tongue.

I open my mouth and draw him inside. We both groan when he feeds me his cock inch by inch. As hard as he is, I feel him lengthening while I suck, employing every play in my best game-day book.

He nudges the back of my throat, encouraging me to swallow. I massage the head of his cock with the rings of my throat muscles. He doesn't pressure me, allowing me to go at the pace that's best for both of us. Completely relaxed, I take him as deep as possible. The burst of pre-come that adds a hint of salt to his flavor initiates an answering clench of my pussy around his embedded fingers. He angles them until they press against my G-spot and incite another orgasm.

Only years of practice keep me from biting him.

I'm still recovering when he shifts, rolling me to my back then spinning so we're eye to eye.

"I love you, Sarah." He licks the corner of my mouth, and then kisses me deep.

"Love. You. Too." I can hardly breathe through the overwhelming emotions assaulting me. Needing to show him, I reach between us and guide his cock to my saturated entrance.

He pushes through the circle of my fingers, lodging the swollen head of his shaft in my pussy. No words are necessary. We stare, unblinking, into each other's eyes as we merge as seamlessly as two humans possibly can. For a long while, we rest together, content to stay locked tight and lavish gentle touches on any part of our partner we can reach. I savor the sleek muscles of his shoulders, which bunch as they flex beneath my palms.

We exchange endless kisses, punctuated with tiny arcs of our hips that fuse us in an unbreakable bond. I run my hand down his back to his ass, holding him close to me. The bite of my nails proclaims my intent to hang on for dear life.

"Possessive much?" He smiles against my mouth. "I like that. Why don't you ride me, Sarah?"

He waits, knowing I usually prefer him to take me. Too many men come to my window looking to pay a lady to do all the work. Those are clients I refuse a second time. I enjoy men, and occasionally women, I can help. Men who require more than a living, breathing blowup doll for whatever their personal demons drive them toward.

Rick's offer feels like something else entirely—permission not insistence. My slight nod is enough to have him rolling, taking me with him. He brackets my hips with his hands, seating me fully on top of him. Gravity impales me on his shaft, burying him impossibly deep within my body.

I rise up then settle myself again several times, slicking the base of his cock with my ample arousal. Each circuit allows me to rub my clit against his hard abdomen. Once we're gliding together, I lean forward, seeking to maximize our skin-to-skin contact.

I gasp when my nipples brush over his lightly furred chest.

"I missed you too." He whispers into the sheet of my hair then rubs his nose against my temple. We move in sinuous harmony. His feet plant on the mattress so he can fuck up into me as I arch down. There are no frantic lunges or gymnastic bobbing here. Instead we rock against each other in a slow press and release destined to blow both our minds.

The blunt head of his cock bores inside me, reaching all the most effective places with minimal effort. We make out while I concentrate on caressing his shaft with my pussy, encompassing his whole body with mine and stimulating as much of his being as possible. At least half of that goal is achieved with our soul-piercing stare as we indulge in our duet of rapture.

"I can't imagine my life without this anymore," I murmur against his open mouth.

"Me either," he echoes. "Let me see you come again."

"Not alone." Experiencing ecstasy with him is more pleasurable than anything else.

"Just once." He grits his teeth. "That's all I can give."

"More than generous." I hope he understands I'm referring to something bigger than sex. The ideas refuse to coalesce when my brain is hazed with lust.

"Show me. Squeeze me. Fuck me."

I can't help but do as he asks. The raw passion in his command spurs me to action. I swing my pelvis in an instinctive motion I could never explain effectively. Believe me, I've tried with other women in the district. The movement isn't some trick designed to blow a man's mind. It occurs naturally as I pursue maximum contact between his body and the engorged flesh of my pussy.

"Yes." He bites my lip and cups the back of my head with one hand while the other palms my ass. "Sexy. Amazing."

I increase the amplitude of my strokes, surfing the break of ecstasy as it grows and grows to legendary proportions.

"Fly, Sarah."

A cry reverberates through the afternoon air. I'm not sure if it belongs to me or one of the rare eagles circling high above us.

A powerful blast of pleasure knocks me over. Rick picks up my slack, hammering into me from below while I unravel. He extends my climax until I'm begging for mercy.

I collapse in a boneless heap when he withdraws his cock and extracts himself from below me. I don't have to mourn the loss for long. Next thing I know, I'm on my side with him at my back, spooning me. He reaches between our legs to reinsert his thick erection into my still-spasming channel.

"Ah, that's right." He groans when my aftershocks travel along his length. "Now with me."

"I can't." I hope my wide eyes convey the insanity of his suggestion. With my world shaken apart I'm happy to receive his release then snuggle the rest of the day away in a passion-induced coma. "Fill me, Rick. Come in me."

He only smiles, slow and wide.

The first pump of his hips proves he intends to make the most of the leverage he's gained from our new position. He angles his hips then powers into me once more, nailing the spot guaranteed to make me see the stars I named my window persona after.

"Maybe just once more." I whimper. Every time I think it can't possibly get better, he proves me wrong.

He laughs.

"A whole lifetime of this, baby." He brushes my hair aside then focuses on my neck. The strong sucking kisses will leave a bright purple mark that I will wear proudly. "I won't settle for less."

His fingers pinch my nipples then walk south to the apex of my thighs. He ferrets out my clit and rubs in small circles timed to the crescendoing beat of his fucking. Miraculously, my body responds. The ridge of his cock head is strangled by the dense ring of muscle at the entrance of my pussy. Every time they lock together, a shiver of pure passion runs through me.

"Starting now," he roars.

"No." I can't help but correct him. "Started the first time. Saw you."

"Yes. Fuck. Yes." Rick cups my breast in his hand, not so much to stimulate nerves already far beyond caring but to hold on tight, to join us through the typhoon of bliss that rocks our boat bed nearly as savagely as it does my soul.

The first warm blast of his release inside me incites my orgasm. I service many men. Only Rick is granted this intimate privilege. The fierce squeeze of my pussy ejects him from within me. We both cry out at the loss. The resulting streaks of his come on my belly make me glad for the proof of his ownership. He reaches down and guides himself into the warmth of my body while his cock still pumps.

Each pulse sears my tissue with welcome heat that overflows

my pussy. He remains buried, the evidence of our coupling sealing us. Huge bellows of his lungs glue me against his chest. My fingers grip his forearm where it bands across the underside of my breasts.

Still he never lets go and neither do I.

We stay still and quiet so long I feel the need to whisper, "Are you awake?"

"Yep. I used to have a bad habit of conking out after a solid fuck." He smiles as he cups my cheek in his palm and tilts my face toward him for another kiss, this time infinitely tender. "That never happens with you."

"Maybe I'm not tiring you out thoroughly?" I roll to face him then slide my hand down his chest, over the ridges and planes of his taut abdomen.

"That's definitely not it." He traps my fingers, laces his through mine and rests the interlocked digits over his heart. I snuggle into the warmth still radiating off him in waves. "No matter how easy it'd be to close my eyes, I'd rather watch you."

"Spending time like this..." I burrow deeper into his embrace, nestling my face in the crook of his shoulder and neck before whispering in his ear, "Is the best thing in the world."

"I don't believe you." His quick denial has me retreating to stare into his eyes directly.

I brace my palms on his chest and prepare to insist before his grin registers on me.

"I've seen you devour those fancy mango pastries from Huize van Wely. Pretty sure those are your favorite things."

"Maybe I need another taste of you to be sure." I lick my lips then shift my pelvis against his mostly flaccid cock. All for show. I'm as sated as he appears.

Rick groans. "Don't distract me. I'm trying to be nice, not naughty."

He chuckles when I freeze. "Are you saying…?"

"Yeah. I might be. Let me grab the backpack." He flings out an arm without putting too much distance between us.

The unmistakable black-and-gold box he extracts from his bag wrings a moan from me.

Though I'd have been satisfied with gooey caramel sandwiched between the cinnamon wafers of a cheap stroopwaffle from the market near our houseboat or a slice of Gouda from our favorite *fromagerie* on Marnixstraat, I can't deny the sight of the gourmet confection has my mouth watering.

I do my best not to sit up and beg like a dog snuffling around beneath the Christmas spread for scraps.

"Here." He stacks several pillows into a cushy wedge then helps me recline, half sitting. "I sort of forgot utensils. I'll feed it to you."

I'm sure that after indulging such decadence I'll volunteer to chair the Death to Forks campaign. I open my mouth when he scoops up a portion of bright yellow goo along with some fancy chocolate garnish on a crumble of the tasty cookie crust. Unwilling to let a single molecule go to waste, I lick his fingers clean.

Again and again he indulges my sweet tooth, taking only tiny samples of the confection direct from my lips. When he transfers the last bite to my mouth, I sigh.

"I bought another one, the champagne kind." I don't like the line that crinkles his brow. "Maybe we should save it for later."

"What are you planning to celebrate?" As if this connection isn't enough.

"I—" He clears his throat then takes a deep breath. I start to worry around the time he shakes his head as though arguing with himself. "Nothing. Well, just us I suppose."

Instead of pressuring him, I've found it's best to let Rick

broach weighty topics in his own time. I don't harp on him if I can avoid it. Not after observing his parents snap at each other over everything from which restaurant was best for our dinner out to who loves him the most. I can understand why they divorced, but not how they can obviously still harbor feelings for each other. That constant tension would be enough to kill any attraction.

What will distract him enough to still the fingertips drumming on his thigh?

"I think us is pretty spectacular. Plenty of reason to toast." I nip his lower lip. "So what is it about us and making love in boats, hmm?"

He rests his forehead on mine and smiles. Score one for great sex as a diversion. "I'm not sure, but I think that's a trend we should continue."

"What do you mean? You want to head home? I thought we were having dinner with Adelbert? Or are you ready for round two right here?" As much as I adore carnal explorations, I would be lying if I denied I had hoped for some time, just the two of us, confiding in each other and lazing the afternoon away.

"Shh…" He curtails my rambling with a kiss. "Relax, Sarah. I'm not rushing us out or anything. It's just… I sort of had a plan coming into today. And then you changed my glide path without realizing it. You got me wondering, and now I think we should take a sharp left turn. But I like the road we're on and I'm not sure I want to veer off this course."

Before I can ask about what, he continues. "You know what you said outside of Centraal, about the swingers' clubs? Do you think fate is trying to tell us something since one of them is a big-ass boat?"

"Ohhhh. Yeah. I've heard rumors about the ritzy one on the out-of-service ferry. Isn't it called the *Love Boat*? One problem, I think couples have to be approved members. The waiting list is supposedly longer than one of Mari's bar tabs." Our friend, the prostitute who works the window across from mine, has a love of all things alcoholic. "We could put in an application if you'd like to try it."

"Or I could cash in a favor from the owner, seeing as he's Tommy's best friend and I've worked shifts for him on occasion." Rick wiggles his eyebrows.

"Why am I not surprised?" I swallow hard as my breathing turns shallow. I rub against him like a cat in heat, soothing the dull ache in my nipples.

"You sure you like the idea?" His fingers slip between my thighs, probing my moist entrance, still slick with the residue of his claim.

"In theory. Fantasizing about it with you is turning me on." Understatement of the century.

"I noticed." He brings his hand to his mouth and licks the juice from it with more relish than I reserved for the last crumb of my tartlet. "But the reality?"

"Are you sure that's what you want? I'm afraid of jeopardizing what we have for a night of fun."

"If it didn't scare me away to watch my friends fuck you or to know that you're servicing customers all night, every night, why would this be any different? I love watching you revel in your freedom."

"Okay." I squeeze my eyes shut. Time to get painfully honest. "What if I'm afraid of seeing you enjoy yours?"

"Then I won't—"

"No!" I try to sit up but he keeps me by his side.

"It's all right, Sarah."

"It's not." I shake my head. Every nightmare I've kept bottled inside for weeks pours out. "We already discussed this. There's no double standard. I have to accept this part of you. I want to support you. Hell, it kind of makes me hot but... I'm afraid. The stakes have never been so high before."

"I'll do whatever it takes to keep you, Sarah. Anything to be the man you need."

"Is that why you haven't visited any women in the district? I know we're new and fresh, but I thought by now some of that would wear off. That you'd—" I swallow the hypocritical lump in my throat. "I assumed you'd want to play with someone else on occasion. But even Mari says you haven't..."

He takes my hand and cups it in his, tracing the base of my ring finger. "Maybe it's me. I thought about it. Tried to a few times. But I just couldn't get into it enough to go through with it. What you do... We both know it isn't about the sex for you. For me, it would be. I can't do that without you. It's not appealing if you aren't sharing it with me."

I breathe deep, bands melting from around my chest.

His eyes close before he opens them, deliberately staring into mine. "I still want to do it. Fuck. I'm so sorry."

"Rick…"

He grunts.

I crawl beside him then coax him to lie with his head in my lap. He stares up at me while I brush his hair off his forehead. "Never apologize for who you really are. I love all of you. And if this is what you need, you know I'm there. I would never turn you away. Never stop supporting you."

"I don't deserve you." He kisses each of my knuckles.

"Adelbert told me every person in love feels the same way." I sigh. "I know I do."

"What?" He would sit up if I took my hand from the base of his neck.

"How can you doubt that for a second, Rick? You accept me for who I am. Given things, that's something I considered impossible. So how can I do any less for you?"

"I guess you can't." The smile that tips up the corner of his mouth is infectious. I beam right back. "I *am* pretty open-minded and all-around awesome."

I pinch his cheek. He retaliates by tickling me until our heavy discussion evaporates beneath a barrage of laugher. Several minutes filled with rolling around in our makeshift bed don't add any measure of professionalism or maturity to our bond.

"Truce." He hugs me tight to him to keep me from moving. Wrapped together in the aftermath of great sex and relaxed from the relief granted by our discussion, a nap would seem highly likely. Neither of us succumbs to sleep, instead reveling in our closeness for several hours of random conversation and shared silence.

Finally, I break the spell. "So, we're going?"

He doesn't answer immediately. I don't let him pretend not to hear me. "Rick?"

"Sure. Sometime." He nods.

"Tomorrow." I slap my palm over his open mouth when he would object. "No reason to put it off. Let's do this. Together.

And see where it leads."

Rick is quiet, gnawing his lip for long seconds. When he nods, it seems as though a huge burden has been lifted from his shoulders. "Okay."

"Is that what you brought me here to ask? About going to the club?" I hadn't mentioned the possibility until we were already on our way. Still, it wouldn't be the first time we shared a brainwave.

"Not exactly." He rubs my back with gentle strokes.

"Then what—"

"We'd better head in before it gets dark and Adelbert wastes away." He sits up without meeting my gaze then packs our garbage, and something I can't quite make out through the growing dusk, into his pack.

"Rick?"

"It's nothing, Sarah." The warmth of his smile reassures me when he tugs me to my feet and wraps me in his arms. "No, okay, it's something. When the time is right, I promise, you'll be the first to know."

"All right." I nod when I can't discern a hint of disturbance in his eyes.

"Come on, Adelbert must be getting hungry."

I have no choice but to follow when he strides into the twilight.

"WHEN LOVE IS NOT MADNESS, IT IS NOT LOVE." ~PEDRO CALDERON DE LA BARCA

Wind whips tendrils of my hair from the French braid I'd locked it in. Loose strands sting my face as I ride behind Rick. Tonight we streak through the twilight on his beloved Ducati instead of peddling on our bicycles. I must admit I prefer to cling to his heat and let the modern machinery do the work. I bury my face between his shoulder blades, counting on the broad span of his shoulders to protect me from the world around us.

How different it is to rely on someone after years of fierce independence. Somehow it doesn't seem as debilitating as I'd once considered such neediness. Knowing he would be equally lost without me balances our power. I grant myself permission to cling tighter to my man.

He revs the engine as though he's as eager to arrive at our destination as I am. We lean into the speed together.

He downshifts. I peek over his shoulder. Ahead, absolute blackness denotes the space where the river cuts through the unassuming countryside sprinkled with the glow of distant residential areas. A few more curves reveal a beacon, drawing us closer like moths to a flame. White lights drape from the decks of a mammoth ferry boat. I squint at the sudden brightness.

The bursts grow bigger in the night, reminding me of fallen stars. What other cosmic signs do I require to supplement my hopefulness? None.

Rick glides into a vacant space near a covered walkway. Silence in the wake of the roar of the engine is deafening. I peel myself from his back and wait for him to join me on the boardwalk leading to the docked vessel. He does, his stare locking on my flushed cheeks a moment before studying my studded leather jacket and skintight pants. It took both of us to pour me into them earlier. The effort was well worth it.

"You know, we don't have to—"

"Yes. We do." I nibble on his lower lip. "Let me give you what you need."

"I need you."

"You have me." I rest my head on his shoulder.

"Will I after tonight?" The graze of his fingerless leather touring glove on my cheek grants me visions of all sorts of naughty role-playing possibilities. I file them away for another time.

"Yes."

"How can you be sure?" I swear I can hear his heart pounding beneath my cheek. "This isn't worth the risk. Let's go home, Sarah."

"We're going inside." I wrap my fingers around his belt buckle where it peeks from between the unzipped flaps of his jacket. Without another pointless argument, I pivot and angle toward the entrance. He seems like he might object again but the door swinging open interrupts his futile attempt to change my mind.

"Rick. Good to see you." An enormous bouncer with a bald head greets us. The thick chains between his septum and bridge nose piercings fascinate me. He slaps a meaty hand on Rick's shoulder. The impact rattles our bones where we're still joined together. "Thanks for covering last time. My youngest daughter had the flu and Jillian was out of town visiting her sister."

"No problem." Rick beams. "How is the munchkin? Still have you wrapped around her little finger?"

"A man in a house full of girls is doomed." His growl doesn't match his adorable grin. "They run wild and there's nothing I can do."

I'm sorry for my irrepressible giggle when his attention swings toward me, breaking the moment.

"Ludger, this is my girlfriend. Sarah."

"Nice to meet you, but I thought your name was Star." He's gentle when he envelops my fingers in a delicate shake.

"You know him?" Rick cocks his head at me before catching himself. "Sorry, what happens through your window…"

"He's not one of my clients." I would remember. A man his size would hardly fit in my tiny Red Light loft.

"Whoa." Ludger stacks his hands in front of his chest and wiggles his thumbs. "Awkward turtle!"

"What the hell is that?" Rick tilts his head, asking exactly what I'm wondering.

"I dunno. My kids do it. Seemed appropriate for implying… I mean, I didn't know she worked the district. You know that's not my thing."

Rick grimaces. "It'd be okay if you had. If not, how do you know her?"

"Who do you think covered for you while you were busy onstage in Tommy's Kinkmas pageant?" Ludger laughs, a boom that might scare me if he weren't so damn huggable. "I suppose it wasn't an act after all, though. No wonder the show was so hot. I had to stop at least half a dozen assholes from storming the stage for an up-close-and-personal look."

"Was everyone in the EU there?" Rick's cheeks glow a little.

"You should be proud of what you can do together." Ludger smiles, revealing a silver skull and crossbones on his front tooth. "Jillian's the best thing that ever happened to me. If you find someone who can love you for who you really are, you're set for life."

I stare up at Rick, waiting for his friend's advice to sink in.

"Shit. You're right. Okay, Sarah. Let's do this." He holds out his hand to me.

I squeeze his fingers with one of my hands then kiss the palm of my other and reach up on tiptoes to pat Ludger's cheek. "Thank you."

"Not sure what that was for, but you're very welcome." He nods. "I heard you're a first-timer. I'll let Rick show you around. Think you should know the basic rules though. We have an undress code. Through this door is a changing room. Lingerie only on the other side. Besides that, it's nothing you wouldn't guess. Respect the wishes of the people around you. No cameras or cell phones either. What happens here, stays here. And most important, have fun."

"I don't think that's going to be a problem." I smile at the two guys then head toward the pink door Ludger had gestured toward. Rick aims for a similar blue portal on the other side of the lobby. "See you in a minute."

"Miss you," he calls softly.

"Oh please." Ludger mimes sticking his finger down his throat.

All hint of nerves obliterated, I grin as I rush into the undressing room. The plush, inviting space hardly registers as I whip off my top and jacket and jam them in the nearest locker. My pants take a few seconds more to wriggle out of. A quick flick of my fingers through my unbraided hair, and I'm ready to inspect myself in the enormous mirror.

Lavender lace-top thigh-highs encase my legs. A matching bra with an attached sheer baby doll allows the slender panel of my panties to show through. The thong highlighting the taut globes of my ass dispels the illusion of innocence created by the ensemble. Cute yet naughty.

Satisfied, I nod at my reflection then follow the rope lights in the floor, which lead to the main club.

Rick is waiting in front of the door. A pair of boxer briefs hug his hips and the bulge that grows when he sees me emerge. Form-fitting underwear never looked so appealing. His deep inhalation does amazing things for his physique. The tattoo encircling his biceps adds a hint of badass. I wipe my mouth to ensure no drool has escaped.

"So…what now?" I clear my throat when my question sounds like a mouse squeak.

"First stop is usually the bar. The top level of the club isn't much different from a regular hangout. Drinking, dancing and meeting new people are on the agenda." He puts his arm around my shoulder and leads me toward a long, polished wood bar.

"Except everyone's nearly naked." I admire the crowd comprised mostly of thirty-somethings in decent shape though the crowd runs the gamut. Nothing I haven't seen before. Still, open acceptance is refreshing.

"Yeah, there is that." He kisses my shoulder. "I hardly noticed with you here. Where do you hide these outfits?"

"I'll put on a fashion show for you sometime," I promise.

I smile when Rick wraps his hands around my waist then boosts me onto a stool at the bar. A gorgeous woman with killer black hair, funky owl jewelry and a no-nonsense attitude directs an assessing scan in my direction. "What can I get you?"

I study the twinkle in her striking blue eyes and the assortment of tattoos visible on her forearms, wondering what the story is behind the red book with *Literate 4 Life* encapsulated in scrollwork beneath it. Instant attraction has me grinning. "How about a shot of Patron silver?"

"Now you're talking." She sloshes a measure of alcohol into a shot glass then adds a second. "Here. Have two."

"Thanks. I might need those." I feel naked more from being out of my window than because of my scrappy clothing. The authority of my position is stripped away. Here I'm just like every other woman.

"You wouldn't believe the things I've seen working here." She rolls her eyes. Without asking, she pours a draft for Rick and adds it to the spot in front of us.

"I might." I smile—a little shy. That never happens to me. What is it with this place, this woman, tonight? Off balance, I reach for Rick's thigh to steady myself. "I'm sort of a sex worker."

"Sort of, huh?" Her grin turns wry. "Then you understand. Some people are real freaks."

"And you love every one of them." Rick leans in close. "Don't be fooled by her tough-girl act, Kelli is a marshmallow inside."

"I have a major sweet tooth." I don't take my eyes off her as I respond to him.

"Thanks, honey. But I'm happily married. And we don't play the swinging game. I have a hell of a lot of appreciation for women like you. One man is more than enough for me." She tosses me a wink, sets down my drinks and wanders off toward the slew of customers vying for her attention. At the last second she says over her shoulder, "I approve of you for our Rick. I was worried he'd fallen for some bimbo again. This one's cool, dude."

"Thanks, Kel. I already figured that out on my own. I don't always have my head up my ass."

"Could have fooled me." Her smile takes all the sting from her rebuke.

Rick flashes his middle finger at her.

I smack his hand. "Hey. Be nice to Kelli."

"Oh yeah, you can keep her." The bartender laughs as she's swallowed up by the thirsty crowd.

We chat while Rick drinks his beer. When I finish the last sip of my first shot, he asks, "Are you buying time because you're checking out the lay of the land or because you're nervous?"

I whip my roaming stare to him. "Can't fool you, huh?"

"Which is it?" He takes another slug then motions to my full serving of Patron. "Down that then tell me."

I lick my hand, loving the dilation of his pupils in response. Then I tap some salt onto my skin and tease him by doing a very thorough job of sucking it off before slamming the shot. My liquor-laden exhalation is strong enough to make fire-breathing dragons envious. "I was hunting for the right couple."

"Don't try so hard." The flex of his throat mesmerizes me as he swallows the last of his microbrew. "Whatever happens, happens. If that's nothing, it's okay. Dance with me?"

"Really?" I hop from the stool before he's moved a muscle. "I didn't know you were into that."

"I'm a fan of showing you off." He smiles. "Work me like a pole."

"I can do that." I link our fingers then sashay toward the crowd of people gyrating to the music. At least it's playing at a reasonable level. They don't risk stifling conversation between potential matches. I sway to the beat, sinking gradually into the groove.

In less than five minutes, Rick has turned away three couples without consulting me. My answer would have been the same. Flashy and overeager, they aren't our type.

I spin around him, presenting my ass before dropping down. I skim the bulge in his shorts as I crawl back up his leg. From the corner of my eye I catch a glimpse of a man and woman sitting on the sidelines. I could swear one of them pointed subtly in our direction as they noticed my dirty dancing.

Rick follows when I edge closer to their perch on a vinyl couch. The woman glances away when I spin in her direction. Her husband stares openly, without guile or any hint of sophistication. I shimmy my breasts at him and smile before facing Rick again. "What are your criteria?"

"You gravitate to the ones who need you most, don't you?" He yanks me toward him, letting me straddle his thigh. His steely cock grinds against my hip. "It's sexy when you show your big heart. And his wife is adorable. I'd love to make a good girl go bad."

I drag one finger up his torso as we sway together. When it reaches his collarbone, he dips, catching it in his mouth. He gazes in the direction of the couple as he sucks on the tip. My nipples turn rock-hard in an instant.

"Let's ask them to play." Our gazes collide. He nods, dislodging my hand.

He doesn't pretend to be coy. Without pretense, he approaches the couple, towing me a step behind. They look like they might bolt when we stand before them. I survey the woman, petite and neat. Her basic black corset is classic yet understated, especially given the venue.

"How's it going?" Rick addresses the man. He's fairly average in height and build. It's the gentle caress he bestows on the woman's hand that impresses me. Their wedding rings glint in the roving lights of the dance floor.

"P-pretty good." The guy has to try twice to speak. His wife studies their joined fingers.

"I'm Rick. This is Sarah." He gestures to me. "Tonight is her first time on the *Love Boat*."

I repress a snort at the ridiculous name.

"Nice to meet you. I'm Nikolaas and my wife's name is Lysanne. We've never been here before either. A friend of ours recommended us for a visitor's pass." The man offers his explanation as though anyone in the room would assume they were veterans.

"In that case, would you like to join us for a tour of the areas downstairs?" Rick's easygoing, inviting nature makes me hornier than his adept dancing. Generous and kind, he's making a potentially nerve-racking experience effortless both for the young couple and for us. I've never loved him more.

"What do you think, Lys?" Nikolaas turns to her with a soft smile, putting the ball in her court. I like them more by the moment.

"I—" She scrunches her eyes shut then shakes her head. "I know I'm the one who talked you into this, but I'm not ready, Niko. I'm so sorry."

Rick holds up his hands, palms out. "No apologies necessary for us. Enjoy the rest of your night."

I try not to let my disappointment show. No use in increasing the burden on Lysanne. I hear Nikolaas reassure her as we drift apart. "It's okay. That's why we came. To find out—"

Knowing they're struggling with the same issues as us only increases the budding chemistry I could swear arced between us. Sometimes attraction just isn't enough.

"There are other fish, baby." Rick kisses my cheek as he leads me toward a staircase near the stern of the ship. "How about a little more personal tour?"

"Sure." I clasp his hand as he escorts me down the ornate flights. The gold-painted balustrade winds lower, leading the way. As soon as we reach the bottom, I can tell the difference from upstairs. The color palette changes to from calming blues and light yellows to dark red and bold earthy tones. Sensual murals cover the majority of the space, depicting the world's largest orgy. It's beautiful and skillfully painted. I wish I could study the brushstrokes.

"The lower deck is divided into several distinct public areas as well as private rooms." He cups my elbow and guides me through a door. "This one is for couples looking to explore BDSM."

I'm impressed with the quality and range of the equipment. Several people are gathered around a woman strapped to a table. Two men occupy stocks in the far corner while someone administers a stern spanking. Nothing here catches my eye at the moment. It'd be hard to top our Kinkmas experience and I think I'd prefer something a little less showy.

"Not tonight." I smile up at Rick. He nods and moves on.

The archway we cross marks another drastic change in décor.

This room is deep blue. Swirls of steam billow out of a raised area in the center of the space. The mural morphs into a riot of fornicating mermaids and sailors that could put the Sirens to shame.

The splash of water catches me off guard. "How?"

"They had a custom hot tub built for this space. It's big enough to swim in if you really wanted. Some parts are shallow, so you can lie mostly submerged without worrying about drowning while you're fooling around. But the best feature is the underwater seats with strategic jets that anyone else can control." A woman shrieks when someone jabs a button on the control panel beside their place. Her cry quickly morphs into a moan. A man plucks his partner from the bubbles, bending her over the side of the tub. Water sloshes over the edge when he thrusts inside her and fucks vigorously. "Sometimes they have contests. First one to come is fair game for the others."

While the idea is intriguing, I glance down at my lingerie.

"We can swing back after you've seen the rest. That way you're not slogging around all wet."

"Too late," I mumble.

He hears if his laughter is any indication.

"What's that way?" I point toward the forest-green room peeking through on the other side of the spa, now overflowing with moans.

"Some people call this the gangbang room. But really it's more like an open forum." My eyes widen at the size of the enormous leopard-print mattress filling the center of the space. Couples and groups of lovers in every combination of men, women and multiples are strewn across its surface. A woman in one corner is surrounded by several men. They take turns fucking her while others delight in the stroke of her hands or the warmth of her mouth. "Only on certain days do they allow single men to visit and women who are interested can sign up for the gangbang. The rest of the time…"

He gestures to the free-for-all before us.

There's something undeniably fascinating about the tangle of participants flowing from one group to another, freely sharing and seeking their next touch from whoever is available and willing. The magnetic pull of their abandon nearly has me shedding my underwear to join in. If only it were a little more personal. I'd had something else in mind for tonight's experimentation. "Oh my."

Rick chokes. "You sound like Hazel. I like this room too. It's almost my favorite."

My eyes are glued to the action, which inspires me to wade into the hedonistic throng.

"Want to see the last one?" He starts to move on but I'm welded to the floor. Rapture fills the room with positive energy I can't help but admire. "Sarah?"

"Hmm. Yes." I remember tonight is supposed to be for him. In reality, I'm curious about his favorite pleasures. "Show me."

"The last room is a sensual massage parlor." He rubs his chest with his free hand as though he can't bear the pressure building there. If he's even half as turned-on as I am, that's no surprise.

"Really?" I blink. Silk pillows, colorful canopies and an array of crystal bottles brimming with oil make the space look as though it were stolen straight from the most sybaritic harem of a powerful sultan. Despite the packed crowds in the other rooms, this one is quiet. Mostly empty. A few couples occupy an area shielded from the rest behind sheer curtains. The shadow of their sinuous movements is alluring.

Three men and three women wearing a slew of bells around their wrists, ankles and necks—but little else—mill around the outskirts of the area. When they notice us, they approach, gesturing toward the luxurious space.

"Will you allow us to pamper you?" One of the women addresses Rick while two of the men encroach on my personal space.

"Go ahead, baby." He nudges me toward the enticing spread of cushions.

"That's not why we came." I gesture with my chin toward the three women now ringing him. "I want to watch them please you. Tonight is yours."

"Every night is ours." He grins. "But I'm not about to turn down a fantastic rubdown."

"Me either." I should have realized he'd share my love of the service. Stimulating contact on every part of my body never fails to relax me and prime me for customers. I oftentimes indulge before a long shift, knowing the demands my clients will make of my body.

"We offer couples' massages." One of the men supplies a new option. "Tonight we're featuring Tantric or Nuru, erotic or not."

Rick looks to me. I shrug. "Your call."

"Is Nuru massage the kind where you slather on the seaweed slime then slip and slide all over each other?" His straightforward description, and the glance he flings at the inflatable mattresses on a PVC sheet in one corner, has me giggling again.

"Something like that, yes." The woman is a good sport. She isn't offended by his generalizations.

"Let's go with Tantric." He takes my hand, pulling me with him onto the super-luxurious cushions.

"Lie on your stomachs with your heads near each other." One of the men provides dulcet instructions that lull me. Moans from the green room barely reach us here. Chanting, the peal of chimes and rich Asian music half convince me I've travelled around the globe.

A vivid mural of Shiva overlooks our total surrender to the touch of near strangers.

Rick and I clasp hands. We turn our faces inward so we can share the moment. Eyes wide open, I watch as one of the three women surrounding my boyfriend drizzle oil along his back. The other two descend, coating their hands and every inch of his bronzed skin with the slick substance. One of them looks to me as her fingers hover over the waistband of his briefs.

Some of my fear abates when the jealousy I brace myself to ward off never rears its ugly head. I'm thankful they are able to draw a sigh of pleasure from him. I nod. The last scrap of his clothes is dragged slowly down and off his body. The women spread out, rubbing his arms, back, ass and legs with precise glides of their skilled hands. I appreciate their technique for a few moments before sure fingers unhook my bra.

Another pair of hands cups my shoulders and lifts my torso so the first man can strip my baby doll from my frame. The third man wastes no time divesting me of my panties. He rolls my stockings down my legs.

"No matter what you wear, you're more gorgeous without anything hiding you," Rick whispers, his face inches from mine. I wish he were close enough to kiss while I revel in the firm press of thumbs along my spine and the light strokes over my ass, which migrate toward my feet.

He shivers when one of the women attending him discovers the sensitive spot at the base of his neck. The adjustment he makes to his hips is a clear sign to us all that he's aroused. He would remove his hand from mine to adjust the lay of his hard-on but one of the women anticipates the necessity.

She strokes around the curve of his hip. I can tell when she cups his erection by the strangled groan that escapes from his parted lips.

"I bet that feels good, Rick." I squirm beneath the ministrations of my own attendants. "Her hand is soft and slippery."

"You may roll over at any time." One of the women murmurs the suggestion.

"Do you want her to touch your cock more?" I can't remember why I thought I'd surrender power by letting another woman service him. She's my tool and his pleasure is my goal. The bond we share isn't diminished by including others in the circle of our passion. Instead it burns brighter, refulgent in the space we share.

"I think I've created a monster." A muscle in his jaw ticks. "I'm not going to last very long if you keep teasing me like that."

One of the men above me chuckles. "We can administer a little payback if you like."

"Please do." Rick smirks then lifts his head so he can observe.

Strong hands wander from their massage of my ass, along my inner thigh. A thick finger rubs at the entrance of my pussy. I moan and spread my legs just enough to give him room to maneuver.

"That's right, baby." Rick dusts his thumb over my knuckles. "Turn onto your back."

"I will if you will." He practically dares me.

We move simultaneously. The careful motions of the

attendants are easier to focus on from this perspective. They stroke us with light touches, gesture and chant with a calm surety that convinces me there's more at work here than a simple caress of skin on skin.

It's more difficult to see what the women are doing to Rick, but his grunts, sighs and moans are telling. We snuggle closer until we're able to exchange lingering kisses. A little awkward at first, given our positions, heads together but facing opposite directions, we quickly adapt since it allows us to sip from each other while the six attendants set our bodies on fire.

My eyes roll when someone presses the knots from the arches of my feet then drains the tension from my ankles. Another man completes a thorough exploration of my breasts while the third rubs slickness over my mound and belly.

Rick groans and tenses. "They're stroking my cock, Sarah. And massaging my balls. It feels so good."

"Are you going to come for them?" I pant at the idea of his semen—released by the hands of a nameless, faceless woman—mingling with the oil on his flat belly, beading and rolling off of his greased skin.

"No. For you." He stares straight into my eyes.

I'm sure now. I can do this. I can be what he needs, with him, in this place.

"Let's go back to the green room," I whisper. "I want to see you fuck someone else. I have to watch."

There's something about the idea that catches me. When we're lost in the moment together, I don't get to admire every nuance of his animalism. Seductive and powerful, I want to observe the power of his passion, knowing he's mine and that we're electing to explore this together.

"It's the same for me, Sarah." He's practically panting now, his face flushed. "I love to see other men, and women, worship you."

The masseuses retreat when we sit up by tacit agreement. They fade into the background, perfectly in harmony with our needs.

Over Rick's shoulder, I catch a glimpse of the couple from upstairs, idling off to the side.

"I'm sorry," Lysanne apologizes. "Is it okay that we

observed? I hope we didn't break any rules. We just... We wondered what it would be like."

I face Rick and smile. He nods. "That's perfectly fine. Did you like what you saw?"

I didn't think it would be possible for her to blush to deepen but she proves me wrong. "Y-yes."

"Our offer still stands. You're welcome to join us." Neither of us move, as if afraid to spook the pair of newcomers, more innocent than Rick and I have ever been in our lives.

Nikolaas lowers his head and whispers to his wife. She peeks between him and us several times before nodding. Niko presses a gentle kiss to her lips before leading her toward us. He pauses at the edge of the cushions then unhooks each tiny clasp on her corset one by one.

I snuggle behind Rick, both of us sitting, my spread pussy pressed to his lower back. I snake my hand around his side then cup his thick erection in my palm. I stroke him so slowly it has to tease more than satisfy. "She's quite pretty. I bet she'll be soft and sweet when you push inside her."

I whisper, for his ears only. His cock jerks in my grasp, making him slip from my now-greased fingers.

Once completely nude, Lysanne turns to Nikolaas. Though shy with us, she is far from a stranger to his body. She strips his underwear from him with one quick movement that sets his cock bobbing. Not as large as Rick, he's upholding his average tendencies.

Together, they crawl toward us. They stop short by several feet. I slide from behind Rick, kneeling to the side so that I'm in front of Nikolaas and there's nothing between Rick and Lysanne. From here I can detect her trembling. Without thought, I cross the space between us and wrap her in a hug. Our breasts press together, transferring some of the oil, making my skin glisten her pebbled nipples.

"You're doing great." I tug on her fingers until she approaches my man.

She waits for direction. I glance at Nikolaas, who is stroking his cock idly. No signs of hesitation mar his flushed cheeks.

I take a monstrous breath then guide Lysanne's hand to Rick's abdomen. He shudders at the initial contact, his steely shaft jabbing upward when his hips flex.

"Did I hurt you?" She would retreat if I let her, but I don't. I trap her hand against his steaming flesh.

"Not at all." He groans. "Unless you count teasing me like this."

I grin. "Turnabout is fair play."

He beams up at me. "I knew I loved you for a reason."

We advance on Lysanne together. Rick lowers her gently to the mattress while I nudge her to her back. She doesn't resist us for a moment. Together we cover her supine form. Rick wastes no time. He's suckling her breasts before I can check in with her. No need to worry. She cries out then buries her fingers in his hair, impressing me with her ability to release the weight of her inhibitions and float on the rising tide of pleasure.

I prop her head in my lap then motion for Nikolaas to join us. The instant he adds his mouth to the other side of Lysanne's body, her cries escalate. I love the wonder in her gaze when she looks at me. Wide-eyed and eager, she reaches up and back to hold my hand.

I cast a glance around the room, finding what I need within arm's reach. Beside the row of oil bottles, a glass bowl holds dozens of condoms. I grab two and press one into each of the men's hands.

Rick doesn't hesitate. He rips open the foil packet and sheathes himself as Nikolaas kisses a trail down his wife's abdomen. While Rick prepares himself, Nikolaas readies Lysanne. He laps at her pussy, slicking her unnecessarily if the gloss of arousal between her thighs is any indication.

I pinch my nipples, teasing myself as I watch Rick nudge Niko aside then notch the bulging head of his cock at Lysanne's sopping entrance. He stares at me and I smile. I take a secret thrill from knowing this woman will never forget him and how well he is about to fuck her. An experienced lover like Rick will blow her mind. She'll have him once, a special treat, while I can dine on caviar every night.

It seems only fair to give her a taste of heaven.

I nod almost imperceptibly at Rick.

He drops low and twitches his hips forward, inserting his cock into Lysanne's pussy. She must be tight since his penetration is slow and labored. Nikolaas slides his hand between Rick and Lysanne to rub her clit, speeding up Rick's progress. Still he must stretch her to the bounds of comfort. She whimpers when he buries inside her completely.

Full. On fire. Needy. I know what that feels like.

I press on Rick's shoulder. He doesn't question my intent. Instead he rises up, still knitted completely but now sitting on his haunches between Lysanne's thighs. Niko glances up at me, waiting for instruction. I dust his hand away from his wife's pussy then shift so I'm kneeling over her face. I tip forward and lick the spot where Rick and she are joined.

"Oh God!" she shouts when I flick my tongue over her engorged clit then alongside Rick's shaft. He groans when the heat of my muscle compounds the silky fist of her pussy gripping him.

As though he can't stay still a moment longer, Rick withdraws a few inches then slides inside our acquaintance once more. He develops a pattern I complement with open-mouthed kisses on Lysanne's clit. It isn't long before she's writhing beneath us, begging—for more or for mercy, I can't quite tell which.

My empty pussy aches. Watching Rick pleasure Lysanne has me trembling with need. I peer up from behind my lashes at the man sharing this moment with me.

"Sarah." Rick brushes my hair off my shoulders and into his grip. He uses it to tug my face in his direction. He bends to kiss me, long and slow enough to have groans raining on us before he separates us. "This isn't your window. You don't have to give all the time."

I blink.

"Show us what you want." He gestures with his chin. "Take."

I peek over my shoulder at Nikolaas. His cock is nearly purple where I catch glimpses above and below his shuttling fist. "Tell him to fuck me."

Lysanne moans below me. Her fingers reach up and spread my pussy. The cooler air on my moist flesh is a divine relief from my scorching desire. When the shock wears off, I hear the rip of a condom packet. A few seconds later, Niko is poised between my legs.

"Do it," Rick growls at the other man, surprising me with the tenacity of his command.

Niko's hands are rougher than I would have guessed on my hips. His tight grip thrills me. He reveals some authority of his own when he directs me. "Drop lower. I want Lysanne to eat you while I fuck you. I want you to come on my cock. You're amazing. You deserve pleasure. As much as we can give you."

Lysanne's lips cover me, mimicking my actions on her. Something in the skilled roll of her tongue over my clit makes me positive this is not her first girl-on-girl rodeo. Go, Lysanne. Niko complements his wife's delivery of rapture. He rides me with more gusto than skill. The uneven lunges of his modest cock inside me are more than enough to dazzle me when paired with Rick's litany of groans.

Something about this taboo thrill guarantees Rick and I will seek out this experience again. The intimacy of my familiar lover blends with the new and untried aspects of a stranger. I am safe to explore and free to indulge whatever carnal craving arises.

I look up and find Rick watching me. He fucks Lysanne like a madman now, drilling her with his sheathed erection. Still he never looks away from the site where Niko's cock tunnels inside me. As if he can sense my attention, his gaze flicks to mine. He roars as our stares lock.

In this moment, time suspends. I freeze and so does Rick. And in this singular instant I know, without a doubt, that this insanity we share is love. Perfect. Infinite. Indestructible.

I rely on Niko's banded grip on my hips to support me. I hold up my hands without breaking the motion of my mouth. With my fingers curved, thumbs touching on the bottom, I depict my love in the shape of a heart.

Rick smiles then mimics my gesture, showing me his matching symbol.

I gauge Lysanne's escalating cries then suck on her clit, applying pulsing pressure she can't resist. She screams and comes, the first domino in a linked expression of ecstasy.

"Yeah. Fuck." Her husband grunts as he fills the condom covering his cock, buried deep inside me. "Come on his big cock, Lys."

It's not until I glance up again that Rick joins them. He buries his fingers in my hair, curses then explodes while fucking Lysanne hard and deep. I massage his balls as they empty with steady pulses.

I hold the base of the condom covering him in place when he withdraws his cock.

He tumbles to the cushions beside us, tugging me off Lysanne, gathering me to his chest.

Niko holds out his hand to mirror the gesture with his wife. She shakes her head. It takes her several gulps of air to speak. "We didn't make Sarah climax."

"Thank you." Her generosity is heartwarming. "I'm fine. Honestly. Giving you pleasure, watching Rick take his, that's all I need to be satisfied."

After all, I'm used to servicing customers. Sure, I share pleasure with some of them but certainly not all. It doesn't make me love what I do any less.

"That's not fair." I like Lysanne's stubborn streak.

Rick adjusts his hold so that he can reach my pussy. He rubs over the slick flesh of my mound. "She's right. We owe you better for taking care of us. Fuck, I'm sorry. I got carried away."

"Niko, I think you should…" Lysanne blushes as she realizes what she's about to say. Still, I'm impressed with how far she's broadened her horizons in one night. She straightens her spine then rephrases. "I want to watch you eat her p-pussy."

Rick holds me tighter. "I'd like that too if you're game."

Niko looks to me then his wife, then back to me. He drops to his knees and slinks toward me. With one last glance at Lysanne, he whispers, "Are you sure?"

"Yes." She buries her fingers in his hair and jerks. His lips surge forward across the tiny gap between us. I gasp when he flicks his tongue over my clit.

"Lick her whole slit," Rick directs Niko. Good thing as I have no voice left. Three pairs of eyes study my every reaction.

Lysanne lies next to me, her head on my chest to observe her husband at work. When I whimper, Rick joins her, except he fastens his lips around the nipple closest to him. Niko raises his head to survey the erotic landscape. "Lys. Do what he's doing. I want to see you suck her tit."

She doesn't hesitate. She latches on with more pressure than I would have anticipated. I'm sure this will not be their last encounter at the club. The exchange is bringing out sides of them both I guess they've kept hidden from each other far too long.

With two mouths at my chest and one on my pussy, I don't stand a chance at resistance. Six hands travel over any part of my body they can reach. One sinks between my thighs. Niko inserts two fingers in my tightening channel. My head falls back, exposing my neck. Rick pauses his assault on my chest to nibble a path up the column to my ear.

"How does it feel to be the one receiving?" he whispers in between nips on my lobe. "Indulge in their attention. Take your pleasure, Sarah. Be selfish for once."

I am shocked when a growl bursts from my throat. I push Rick's head until his lips are aligned with my breast again. I command, "Suck it."

"That's my girl." He obeys.

I cut my stare to the man feasting on my pussy, making wet sounds as he flails his tongue over me in sloppy slurps. "Slower. Neater. Right there."

He takes direction well. Lysanne whimpers as she observes her husband tailor his actions to my tastes. I wonder how forceful she'll be in teaching him to pleasure her later. The thought inspires a rush of pleasure. I spread my legs wider and grind myself on his face.

"Add another finger."

Niko slips a third digit inside me. He spreads them, stretching my contracting muscles. My playmates collude to enhance my enjoyment. Soon all I can do is writhe and relish the rapture slamming through me.

My muscles begin to quiver. My thighs clamp on Niko's shoulders and my hands grasp at Rick's and Lysanne's backs. That's all the warning I can give them before my orgasm hits. It shakes me with the force of an earthquake, leveling my foundation and tearing apart the final vestiges of my doubt.

They pamper me while I soar then float in a sea of bliss and relief. Before my head has cleared, I hear rustling in the background. Rick's voice is warm and soft when he says, "Yes. The sauna is down the hall on the left. There are private rooms next door if you'd like some time alone before you head home.

Thank you for joining us. I wish you all the best."

Lysanne murmurs a response but I don't catch it, content to wallow in the security of Rick's embrace.

When the silence lingers, I try to move but can't seem to coordinate my limbs.

"Relax, Sarah." He rolls to his back, draping me over his chest then pets my flank. "There's no rush. We have all night."

"No. Forever," I mumble.

"That too." He smiles, his lips curving against my temple.

For long minutes, maybe as much as half an hour, we linger in the hazy aftermath of passion. My thoughts gradually return to something coherent. They replace the low-level buzz that feels a lot like a happy *mmmm, mmmm, mmmm* over and over.

"Still awake?" This time it's Rick who asks me.

"Wouldn't miss a second of this," I reassure him, my throat scratchy from shouting my pleasure.

"Me either." His fingers travel a circuit down my spine, over my ass then up my side. Each time he skims over my ribs, I smile.

"Ticklish?"

"A little." I chew on my lip.

"Spit it out, Sarah." He diverts from his path to trace the spot I worried.

"My clients may pay me for sex, but love is really a free-for-all." I sigh. "They could have anything they wanted with a true partner."

"If they're lucky enough to find the person they can make it work with."

When I flex my knuckles, he massages my fingers.

"Right." I take a deep breath. "Am I enabling them? Keeping them from looking for the mate who is their perfect complement? Am I harming the people I want to help?"

"I don't see it that way." He smiles down at me. "Sometimes you're teaching them what they need to move on."

"I guess that's true." I nod, rubbing my cheek on his chest.

"What's this really about, baby?" He's quiet when he coaxes me to respond.

"I've been thinking… Maybe I should quit." I scrunch my eyes closed. "With the house paid off and your job plus my savings, we'll be okay."

"Financially? Sure. More than all right. But what would you do?" He sits up, bundling me into his lap until he can stare directly into my eyes, which are less than three inches away. "This has never been about money for you. You love your job."

"I love you more." I shake my head. "And as much as it's true that I like to care for my clients, I also know I could be someone's crutch. I know because I hid through my window myself. I might have stayed there the rest of my life if I hadn't met you. You forced me to come out."

"Why is that, Sarah?" He must hold his breath as his chest stops moving.

"I used to think people who visited my window were the only ones who would accept me for who I am and what I want." It's time I told him the whole truth. "I've always had this drive. This need to touch and be touched. To connect with other people. It's so much more than sex…"

"I know that."

I can see his faith right there in front of me. He understands. It's a miracle. One I'm not willing to sacrifice by leaving him in the dark. "My family couldn't accept me."

His arms tighten around my waist and shoulders when I feel like I might shatter. Still he doesn't interrupt, as if he knows once I begin sharing, I won't be able to stop. He's asked me for this so often he must have thought I'd never be able to admit my secrets. Tonight I'm afraid if I don't, I'll lose him.

And that I can't live with.

"I tried to explain what happened the first time. When I shared myself with a client. Though to be honest, he didn't have to pay me. I could tell what he needed and I gave it to him. Freely. Not because I loved him or because he coerced me. Because I knew I could help ease his loneliness." I ungrit my teeth to allow a huge breath to feed my narration. "I still remember the rush. How it filled me with joy when I opened myself to a man who needed me the first time. I was seventeen. And I knew right away what I wanted to do for a living."

"You have a gift." Rick stares at me, awe flooding his gaze. "I could tell the moment I spoke to you. Maybe even from the way you moved in the window before I had the guts to knock. As one of those men who needed you, I could tell you understood. So many of the women in the district don't. They do it for cash. Or power. But you… You were always special."

"Thanks. My family didn't believe that. They were very religious. They told me to atone, to pray for God to forgive my mistake. It probably didn't help that the man I serviced was our minister. I'm sure they thought we were both going straight to hell and dragging them into the flames with us by association."

Rick drops his forehead forward. It meets mine, lending me his strength.

"It wasn't some kind of slip-up. I didn't believe it could be wrong to experience what I had. To help someone else while bringing us both pleasure seemed more like healing that hurting."

"So why would you even suggest quitting now?" Rick rubs my back. "I love you, Sarah. All of you. Unconditionally. You don't have to sacrifice this for me."

"I guess I just didn't realize before tonight that there were other ways to achieve the same goal." I burrow closer to his warmth. "This was a whole new level. Being a part of us and a part of them. Two couples who can take each other somewhere almost spiritual."

"You can have both, baby." His breath puffs against my neck. "I'll support you no matter what you decide, but I don't think you should give up your dreams. I'll never abandon you or force you to choose between me and your work like your family did. Please believe me."

A concern that's been nagging at my heart for weeks bursts free of the place I'd locked it up. "You haven't visited any of the other windows since Christmas. We talked about it. You didn't trust me like you're asking me to trust you. Why?"

"I already have everything I want in you, Sarah. I thought about it. Hell, I even tried with Mari once." He clears his throat before smiling soft and slow. "It just didn't work. I appreciate the freedom you granted me, but I've come to realize that's not what I required at all. It was fear that made me insist on it before. I'm sure now. Positive. You're everything. Sharing like tonight—I'll want to do this again. A lot."

"I could get on board with that." I squirm when I think of the possibilities.

"Without you, the world is all oatmeal."

"What does that mean?" I tilt my head.

"Bland, something that would give me sustenance yet never be appetizing. I'm more of a bacon and eggs kind of guy." He licks his lips.

"What if you get bored with me?" I hate the tremble in my voice.

"How can I when you're willing to evolve? Everything we do together is another adventure. I want you by my side. Forever. Exactly as you are."

"I hope for that too." No, more like I obsess about it. I wish life offered guarantees.

"Then maybe this is the perfect time after all." He rises, depositing me on the mountain of pillows. The flickering candlelight gleams off his sculpted chest as he crosses to the row of pretty cut-crystal bottles containing the massage oil the masseuses had applied to us earlier. "I sort of chickened out before. Twice really. Yesterday in the tent. Then tonight I planned to have those guys pamper you before giving you this."

"What?" I push up on straight-locked elbows to peer at the small bottle he hands me.

Something tinkles against the side of the container when my hands shake. "Rick, there's a ring in there."

"Sure is." He takes a deep breath. "Don't worry, that's not really oil, it's colored water. I wouldn't risk hurting Hazel's diamond even though the crew promised it'd be fine. Well, your diamond now. If you'll accept it."

He drops to one knee on the royal purple silk covering the

plush lounging mat. I scramble upright only to have my knees fold again, leaving me with my ass on my heels. "What are you doing?"

"What does it look like, Sarah?" He scrubs one hand through his hair. "I had a whole speech prepared. I practiced it on Adelbert. Damn that was awkward. And useless since it all flew out of my brain. Shit, I'm not good at things like this."

I gawk while he rambles.

"Are you serious?" Finally I interrupt though he hasn't asked me a question yet.

"Absolutely. Sarah, I love you. I always will. Please do me the honor of sharing this crazy life, wherever it takes us. Marry me?"

I stare, my jaw hanging open.

"For Christ's sake. Say something. Yes? No? Go to hell? Anything. Is it that hard to imagine being my wife?"

"Your—"

"Oh shit." He starts to rise. I slap my hand on his thigh and dig in until he resigns himself to staying put.

"Sorry. Sorry." My brain is whirling faster than the spokes on our bikes when we race downhill. "You said you never wanted to get married. Your parents…"

"Are not us."

I toss away the stop from the bottle and dip my index finger into the water until I can fish out the gorgeous antique ring.

"There will come a day when we're separated, no matter how much we do to avoid it. I'm committed to making sure that happens as far in the future as possible. Like a hundred years from now. And even then I pray you know it would never be my choice to leave your side. I love you, Sarah."

A single tear trickles down my cheek. I can't answer him.

"You still have doubts?" I hate the frown creasing his handsome face.

"No. It's not that." I shake my head. I refuse to lie to us both. "I mean, I guess it's hard to believe you're real. That no one will take this away from me."

"I'll keep proving it to you, Sarah." He sighs as he climbs to his feet, tugging me with him. "Every day until you're confident."

I should reassure him. I mumble against his hand when he places his fingers over my lips.

"You don't have to say anything else. It's okay. I'm a patient man when I have a goal in sight." He steals a fierce kiss. "You were meant to be mine. As much as I am yours. Someday I won't have to tell you. You'll know it as deeply as I do."

I hear his reassurance loud and clear. It's the last shove I need.

"Rick?" I take a huge, shuddering breath and prepare to leap. "Yes."

"Yes, what?" He squints at me.

"Yes, I'll marry you." I fling myself into his open arms. "I promise I'll be the best wife you can imagine. If you'll have me, I'll give you everything. All I am. I already have."

"Thank God." He lays the kiss of a lifetime on my lips before he bundles me in his arms and races from the room. His fingers clutch my ribs and knees as he bounds up the stairs to the main level, which has almost completely cleared out as groups have wandered to the play areas or gone home for the night.

I still haven't caught my breath by the time I spy Ludger sitting at the bar, shooting the shit with Kelli and someone with a riot of unnaturally red curly hair. The world bobs around me.

"She said yes!" Rick shouts to the bodyguard and his other friend before spinning us in circles.

"This calls for shots," a familiar voice shouts. I try to place it. It can't be. My weaving vision almost makes it look like my best friend Mari is chilling out with Rick's pals. "I get to be the Maid of Dishonor, right?"

"Mari?"

"Who the hell else?" She might have had one or two drinks already gauging by the level of sarcasm spilling from her. "I mean if it weren't for me, you never would have wooed Rick's bottomless stomach."

"How?"

"I thought you might like to celebrate if things went well." Rick sets me on the floor. He scrubs fresh tears from my face. "Or at least you'd have a ride home if you kicked me to the curb."

"You thought Mari would be my designated driver?"

"I guess you could have taken a cab together." He smothers a chuckle when Mari levels a death-ray glare at him. "Yeah, should have thought that one through. But I was practicing my positive thinking."

"Works every time." Mari nods sagely, if a little out of control.

Kelli plunks a mostly empty bottle of Patron on the bar. "A toast. To Rick and Sarah, may you always be hot and your love be hotter."

We pass the bottle around, each of us taking a swig. The burn spreads through my chest, warming every corner of my soul.

"Perfect." Kelli gestures with her chin. "Now put some fucking clothes on, would you? Nobody wants to see you wearing just those sappy grins."

Rick and I face each other and laugh. The universe consists solely of him. Naked or not, I hadn't noticed. My soul is bared to him permanently.

"TRUE LOVE STORIES NEVER HAVE ENDINGS."
~RICHARD BACH

Rick and I stroll through streets teeming with music, clusters of friends heading out for the evening and clouds of sweet-smelling smoke that waft from inside Amsterdam's infamous coffeehouses. No more than a kilometer away, someone is mopping the floor of the Anne Frank museum. They'll clean behind the attic bookcase for the drove of visitors who will flood the once-secret space again tomorrow.

Live and let live. It should be the official motto of our home city, though the silly t-shirts and postcards with the triple X's make for more commercial souvenirs. I glance at a shop window and the corkscrew in the shape of a little red man with the X's running in a line down his stomach like buttons on a gingerbread man. I squint at the oddity. Huh. They should market it as a cockscrew, really, based on the clever placement of the opening device.

I thank the universe again for landing me in the one city I truly belong. How much luckier can a woman get?

Rick grips my hand a little too tight. I don't mind the bite of his ring digging into my pinky and middle finger. I love knowing I'm his. And he's mine. I study the sparkle of rainbows falling like glitter from my engagement ring. They dance across the damp ground as the first illuminated windows of the red-light district pop into view.

"Are you okay?" Rick slows his pace. Could he be as hesitant as me to say good-bye? Even for a few short hours.

"Yes." I snuggle against his side when he holds out his arm, tucking me close to the furnace of his body. The weight of his muscles around my shoulders leeches any of my uncertainty. When he holds me, nothing can do me harm. "Just going to miss you."

"I'll be right up the street. Want me to bring over some lunch? I'll probably take a half hour break around two or maybe three, before the second show starts."

"Is it natural to need someone as desperately as I need you?" I'm starting to think Rick might be my drug of choice. I'm hopelessly addicted. But is he something damaging like heroin or lifesaving like a diabetic's insulin? It can only be the later.

"I'm not sure, Sarah." He pauses, twisting his fingers in my hair and canting my head so that he can stare directly into my eyes. "But I'm so glad I'm not alone in this. Otherwise, they'd lock me up as some creeper for stalking a lady of the night."

I can't help but laugh. How right he is. "In that case, I'm grateful you have no restraining orders on me. Maybe I'll bring you lunch. How does chicken satay from De Haven van Texel sound?"

"Amazing," he whispers against my lips.

We jump like guilty teenagers when a rap on the glass behind us cuts through our dreamy stare, which might have lingered for a minute or ten. I never can be sure when the world narrows to just the two of us.

"Mari!" We both grin as we wave to our friend without breaking apart. The faux redhead occupies the window across the street from mine. We've stalled right outside her space.

She blows Rick a kiss then points to her watch.

"Ah, shit. I'm gonna be late again."

"Say hello to Tommy for me. He'll understand." I turn toward my studio. Rick doesn't leave my side. He always waits for me to open or lock up at the end of the night, ensuring everything is as it should be before he leaves me to my business.

"No kidding." Rick rolls his eyes. "That bastard keeps asking for details as though we're onstage at his club every night. Have sex in public once and people think you're an open book. You know he won't leave me alone about doing an encore at the club?"

"If you decide you'd like to give it a go, you only have to ask."

"And you wonder if I'll get bored with you? Crazy woman." His pupils dilate and he steps closer as I fiddle with the lock on my window. "Hell, I might need to come by during break for a quickie after thinking about that for a few hours. Like the good old days."

"My heart is ever at your service." I climb the first two stairs then turn around to execute a tiny bow before kissing his cheek now that we're eye to eye.

"Shakespeare? Did you think I wouldn't know because I'm more brawn than brains?" He steals one last taste before backing up a pace then two.

Maybe we can work on our insecurities together. We have a lifetime after all.

"Believe it or not, I kind of like the bard."

"I'm not surprised. He's my favorite too." I wink. "Have a good day at work, Flavius."

Rick's laugh rumbles through the street, causing several heads to turn. "At least you didn't call me the fool."

"Well, you do intend to marry the whore."

Thunderclouds gather in his gorgeous eyes.

I shrug and wiggle my brows.

"Okay, okay, truce." He holds his hands up, palms out. "Have fun. Be safe. See you for lunch."

"I wouldn't miss it for the world." I stare straight into his eyes until he can't mistake my intention. "I'm starving already. And no snacking I do between now and then will put a dent in my hunger."

"I love you, Sarah."

"Love you too, Rick. Always."

THANKS FOR READING!

Did you enjoy this book? If so, please leave a review and tell your friends. Word of mouth and online reviews are immensely helpful to authors and greatly appreciated.

To keep up with all the latest news about Jayne's books, appearances, merchandise, release info, exclusive excerpts and more, sign up for her newsletter at

www.jaynerylon.com/newsletter

More than 25 prizes are given out to subscribers in each monthly edition.

Eli London stared at the drop of sweat gathering on the shoulder of one of his mechanics, Alanso. He flexed his fingers around the torque wrench he'd retrieved for the man, refusing to let go and trace the path perspiration took over deceptively wiry muscles.

Inked artwork brightened as the bead dampened several tattoos. First a tribal scribble, then a portrait of Al's long-lost mom, and finally the top of an intricate cross that disappeared beneath the bunched fabric clinging around his waist. Torn and oil-stained coveralls hugged a high, tight ass.

All Eli could think of these days was that damned ass, which Alanso now shoved out in his direction while the bastard tuned some rich kid's engine. With hardly any effort at all, Eli could smack it. Or bite it. Or screw it.

Son of a bitch.

Nothing good could come of this obsession. Damn his cousin Joe for putting crazy thoughts in his brain. The guy was a member of a construction crew that liked to work hard and play harder together. Their polyamorous bedroom gymnastics had become obvious when Eli and Alanso had walked in on a scene he couldn't forget. But just because that bastard had been lucky enough to find a whole team of buddies his wife adored—no, loved—didn't mean such a wild arrangement could work for everybody in the world.

Eli had no right to wish for the same. Yet lately, each time he looked at the half dozen guys and girl he considered his grease monkey family, he found himself sporting a hard-on stiff enough to jack up a tank with. Thankfully, the oblivious gang hadn't identified the source of his recent frustration. Though they certainly had borne the brunt of his bad temper, adding guilt to the unslakable arousal stripping his gears, leaving him spinning his wheels.

Stuck and stranded. Alone with his dirty little secret.

Except for Alanso.

Why had that mechanic been the one to witness Joe and his crew's alternative loving along with Eli? Probably because they went most everywhere together. Eli shoved the memory of his right-hand man's right hand from his mind. Or at least he tried. The guy had tortured Eli with greedy pumps of his trembling fist while the crew's foreman, Mike, demonstrated just how hot it could be to take on one of his own. By screwing Joe while the mechanics had stared, in awe of the power exchange.

Eli knew that if he slammed Alanso against the 426 inch engine block of that 1970 Dodge Challenger R/T coupe, the man would spread and welcome him.

Boss, friend…brother.

And that's where the fantasy turned to battery acid, burning Eli's insides with the bitter taste of responsibility and logic.

How could he want a guy he considered family? How could he violate that trust?

He couldn't afford to lose Alanso.

Not from his business, definitely not from his life.

So he could never seize what he craved. Frustration bubbled

over.

"What's taking so long, Diaz?" Eli knocked thick, bunched biceps with the tool he carried. "We're trying to make a profit here, you know?"

Alanso couldn't seem to wipe his glare away as easily as he rid his brow of the moisture dotting it. He snatched the wrench from Eli and returned to his task without taking the bait. If Eli couldn't screw, the least the guy could do was give him the courtesy of engaging in a decent fight. His teeth ground together.

"You hear me, huevón? This isn't some charity case. Hot Rods is a business. Don't spend all day on a five-hundred-dollar job." Eli thumped the hood, knowing how the impact would reverberate.

Alanso's shoulders tensed. The clench of muscles along his spine altered the shape of his tattoos. Still, he said nothing about the low blow—or how he'd repaid the Londons a million times over for their hand-up through a solid decade of friendship and loyalty—and continued about his job. One he was damn fine at performing. No one could make an engine purr like Alanso.

"You want half-assed, go hire a motorman from the chain in town." He didn't bother to acknowledge Eli with a look.

Still, as Alanso's boss and best friend, Eli knew that tone well enough. It'd be accompanied by Al's tattooed middle finger sticking up along that wrench, he'd bet.

The defiance made Eli long to grab the other man's chin and force him to gaze up. Maybe then Alanso would see the desperation making Eli more unhinged than Mustang Sally during a particularly bad bout of PMS. God help them all.

He'd never wanted something he couldn't have so badly before. Except maybe to heal his mom during those horrid weeks she'd spent dying.

Terror and a soul-deep pain that never entirely faded turned him into something no better than a cornered animal. Eli lashed out. "Good idea. Maybe they'd spend less time checking me out and do their goddamned work."

A clang surprised him. He didn't quite realize what had happened until a spark flew from the metal tool where it connected with the concrete floor of the garage. Alanso had winged the thing an inch or less from Eli's thankfully steel-toed boot when he spun around.

He wouldn't have missed by accident.

"Para el carajo! Maybe I should've done more than look. You're obviously too hardheaded to man up and come for me. So the deal's off the table. I've wasted too much time on a dude who's in denial. You're right about that." Alanso sneered. "I'm tired of waiting for you to grow some cojones."

"Keep your voice down." Eli checked over his shoulder. Kaige and Carver didn't so much as glance in their direction, but the stillness of their bodies made it clear they caught at least wisps of the conversation. Years of tough living had taught the men to tread lightly in conflict. At least until swinging a punch became necessary. Then it was likely to become a free-for-all.

"Joder! Now you want to shut me up. Come mierda." Alanso scrubbed a hand over his bald head, leaving a streak of oil that tempted Eli to buff it away, maybe with his five o'clock shadow. "Wouldn't want the rest of the Hot Rods hearing about the good life and how we're not living it, right? They might revolt."

"Hey, I've never kept anyone against their will. You all chose to stay here. With me. The door's open." Eli waved toward the enormous rolling metal sheets that protected the garage bays at night or when the weather turned cold. Through them, the pumps of the service station his dad had started were visible.

A flash of something miserable twisted Alanso's usually smiling lips into a grimace. The gesture had Eli thinking of something other than what it would feel like to get a blowjob from the man. That was a first after weeks of studying that mouth.

He reached out, but it was too late. Alanso dodged, taking a step back and then another.

"You know what, Cobra." He grabbed his crotch hard enough to make Eli wince. "You can suck it. Or, then again… No, you can't. That checkered flag has dropped, amigo."

Reflex, instinct, dread—something—inspired Eli to lunge for the man who turned away. Warm, moist skin met his palm.

"Get your effing hands off me." When the engine guru pivoted, the unusual chill in his brown eyes froze Eli in his tracks. "You had your chance. You blew it. For us both. I'm out of here."

"You're quitting?" Eli gaped as the bottom fell out of his stomach. "Wait—"

"Hell no. I told you I'm over that bus-stop phase." Alanso sliced his hand through the air between them. His knuckles skimmed Eli's chest. They left a slash of fire across his heart. "I've got places to go and people to do. There are things I gotta learn about myself. And for the first time since we were fifteen, you're not going to be a part of that with me. Your loss."

"I-I'm sorry." Eli couldn't find a way to say what for. For violating their friendship, for wanting to destroy what they had or for acting like an ass by postponing the inevitable—he couldn't make up his mind. "Don't go."

They'd drawn a crowd. Even Roman inched closer now. The tough yet quiet guy stared openly at their spectacle. Charged air had somehow tipped off Sally too. She emerged from the painting booth, crossing the bays at an alarming rate. If she got tangled up in this, Eli would never forgive himself. Of all their gang, he knew better than to trample on her emotions. Her heart would rip in two if she had any idea of the rift opening at his feet right now.

Just like his chest was hewn.

"I'm not leaving leaving, Cobra." Alanso lowered his voice. "This is my home. I hope some things haven't changed. Let me know if I'm no longer welcome and I'll pack my stuff. But I can't do this anymore. Not for another damn minute. I have to know what it's like. To be honest about who I am and what I want. Before I lose any more respect for either of us."

"Fine then." Eli leaned forward before he could stop himself. The awful sensations sliding through his guts had to stop. Fast. Before the rest of the garage got caught in their crossfire. He shoved Alanso hard enough the man stumbled across the threshold before catching his balance. It felt like forcing a baby bird from the nest. He only hoped Al spread his wings fast enough. "Get the hell out. Do what you gotta do."

Alanso mouthed a plea out of sight of the guys now wiping hands on coveralls and milling near in a semi-circle. "Come with me."

Eli slammed his fist on the big red button on the doorframe beside him. With an ominous rattle, the metal door began to lower between them, severing all communication as completely as if the aluminum were a drawbridge over a monster-filled moat.

ABOUT THE AUTHOR

Jayne Rylon is a New York Times and USA Today bestselling author. She received the 2011 Romantic Times Reviewers' Choice Award for Best Indie Erotic Romance. Her stories used to begin as daydreams in seemingly endless business meetings, but now she is a full time author, who employs the skills she learned from her straight-laced corporate existence in the business of writing. She lives in Ohio with two cats and her husband, the infamous Mr. Rylon. When she can escape her purple office, she loves to travel the world, avoid speeding tickets in her beloved Sky, and–of course–read.

Jayne loves to chat with fans.
You can find her at the following places when she's procrastinating:

Twitter: @JayneRylon
Facebook: http://www.facebook.com/jayne.rylon
Website: www.jaynerylon.com
Newsletter: www.jaynerylon.com/newsletter
Email: contact@jaynerylon.com

OTHER BOOKS BY JAYNE RYLON

Available Now

COMPASS BROTHERS
Northern Exposure
Southern Comfort
Eastern Ambitions
Western Ties

COMPASS GIRLS
Winter's Thaw
Hope Springs
Summer Fling

HOT RODS
King Cobra
Mustang Sally
Super Nova
Rebel On The Run

MEN IN BLUE
Night is Darkest
Razor's Edge
Mistress's Master
Spread Your Wings

PICK YOUR PLEASURES
Pick Your Pleasure
Pick Your Pleasure 2

PLAY DOCTOR
Dream Machine
Healing Touch

POWERTOOLS
Kate's Crew
Morgan's Surprise
Kayla's Gift
Devon's Pair
Nailed To The Wall
Hammer It Home

RACING FOR LOVE
Driven
Shifting Gears

RED LIGHT (STAR)
Through My Window
Star
Can't Buy Love
Free For All

SINGLE TITLES
Nice and Naughty
Picture Perfect
Phoenix Incantation
Where There's Smoke

AUDIOBOOKS
Nice and Naughty
Dream Machine
Night is Darkest
Report For Booty
Powertools
Kate's Crew
Morgan's Surprise
Kayla's Gift
Devon's Pair

Coming Soon

<u>COMPASS GIRLS</u>
Falling Softly

<u>HOT RODS</u>
Swinger Style
Barracuda's Heart
Touch of Amber
Long Time Coming

<u>MEN IN BLUE</u>
Spread Your Wings
Wounded Hearts
Bound For You

<u>PICK YOUR PLEASURES</u>
Pick Your Pleasure 3

<u>PLAY DOCTOR</u>
Developing Desire

<u>SINGLE TITLE</u>
Four-ever Theirs

Hot Ride
by Opal Carew
For more information visit www.opalcarew.com

Halley glanced toward a big, powerful looking motorcycle parked close to the brick wall. It was black and intimidating, adorned with a blazing red and orange flame. It had shiny chrome wheels and a big, black leather seat.

"It's nice," she said as they walked toward it.

"Nice?" He chuckled. "Maybe big. Dangerous. Powerful." He grinned. "But nice?"

Oh, God, he was big and dangerous and powerful. Everything she dreamed of when she thought about her wildest fantasies coming true. And here he was, smiling down at her. She already missed his strong arms around her.

She gazed into his midnight blue eyes. "I like big, dangerous and powerful." She stepped closer and flattened her hand on his hard, muscular chest. The feel of rock-solid, sculpted muscles under the thin fabric of his T-shirt set her heart thumping. "Like you."

She dropped her shoes and purse, and slid her hands over his shoulders then stroked his raspy cheek. His eyes simmered with heat as she tipped up her face, then drew him toward her. His mouth brushed hers lightly, and she flicked her tongue against his lips and slid timidly inside. He growled and deepened the kiss, wrapping his arms around her and pulling her tighter to his hard body, then gliding his tongue deep into her mouth.

She melted against him, heat simmering through her. But then he drew back.

"This isn't a good idea."

She blinked at his words. He was rejecting her?

"Don't you find me attractive?"

"It's not that."

Feeling bolder than she ever had, and determined not to let this opportunity slip away, she grasped his hand and drew it to her chest, then placed it over her aching breast. Her nipple hardened, pushing into his palm.

His dark eyes glowed like a blazing fire, glittering with sparks.

In a sudden movement, she felt herself pushed back against the building. Her breath caught as his big, solid body crushed her tight to the cold brick wall.

Oh, God, had she made a mistake? He was so big and intimidating, and right now, he looked determined and... almost feral. He pivoted his hips forward and she could feel a hard bulge against her stomach, proof that he was aroused by her. Anxiety spiked through her, and a little fear, but right alongside those feelings was a wild surge of excitement.

He grabbed her wrists and pushed them over her head, then held them tight, his striking midnight eyes locked on hers. She could feel the erratic pounding of her blood pumping through her veins.

She had never felt so alive.

God, she wanted him to take her. Right here. Right now.